Madame Bliss

Madame Bliss

The
Erotic Adventures of a Lady

CHARLOTTE LOVEJOY

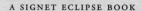

A SIGNET ECLIPSE BOOK

SIGNET ECLIPSE
Published by New American Library, a division of
Penguin Group (USA) Inc., 375 Hudson Street,
New York, New York 10014, USA
Penguin Group (Canada), 90 Eglinton Avenue East, Suite 700, Toronto,
Ontario M4P 2Y3, Canada (a division of Pearson Penguin Canada Inc.)
Penguin Books Ltd., 80 Strand, London WC2R 0RL, England
Penguin Ireland, 25 St. Stephen's Green, Dublin 2,
Ireland (a division of Penguin Books Ltd.)
Penguin Group (Australia), 250 Camberwell Road, Camberwell, Victoria 3124,
Australia (a division of Pearson Australia Group Pty. Ltd.)
Penguin Books India Pvt. Ltd., 11 Community Centre, Panchsheel Park,
New Delhi - 110 017, India
Penguin Group (NZ), 67 Apollo Drive, Rosedale, North Shore 0632,
New Zealand (a division of Pearson New Zealand Ltd.)
Penguin Books (South Africa) (Pty.) Ltd., 24 Sturdee Avenue,
Rosebank, Johannesburg 2196, South Africa

Penguin Books Ltd., Registered Offices:
80 Strand, London WC2R 0RL, England

First published by Signet Eclipse, an imprint of New American Library,
a division of Penguin Group (USA) Inc.

First Printing, March 2009
10 9 8 7 6 5 4 3 2 1

SIGNET ECLIPSE and logo are trademarks of Penguin Group (USA) Inc.

LIBRARY OF CONGRESS CATALOGING-IN-PUBLICATION DATA:
Lovejoy, Charlotte.
Madame Bliss: the erotic adventures of a lady/Charlotte Lovejoy.
p.   cm.
ISBN 978-0-451-22597-9
1. England—Fiction.   I. Title.
PS3612.O8347M33 2009
813'.6—dc22   2008045013

Set in Adobe Garamond
Designed by Ginger Legato

Printed in the United States of America

For Twin Girl, who always gets the joke

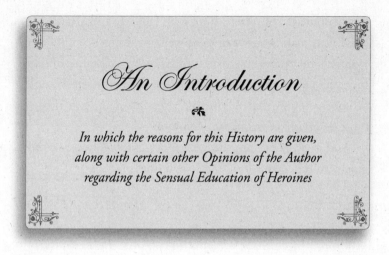

An Introduction

*In which the reasons for this History are given,
along with certain other Opinions of the Author
regarding the Sensual Education of Heroines*

Innocence in women is a vastly overrated quality, and an unnecessary one at that. Men will always try to keep the female sex in this ignorant state, the better to preserve their advantage over those whom Nature has already contrived to be more gentle and tender, more ornament than effect.

Yet I ask you, my readers, to look into your own hearts, and answer true this question: what is innocence but a lack of the knowledge? How can any woman truly choose the path of righteousness, if she has never been tempted by sin, or faltered, and returned wiser to the ways of goodness? And further: why is it better for women to remain so inexperienced and unformed, and never taste the delights, the pleasures, the joys that only love can bring?

Being as the world can be a priggish place, there will be those who will judge the heroine of these pages no true heroine at all, but a low and undeserving creature, a harlot, a hussy, a concubine, a courtesan. But to be fair, Miss MARIANNA WREN is many other things as well, a shining example of a woman who can rise up and triumph over misfortune, and be merry along the way. In short, she exemplifies the sweet tangle of contradiction that lies within every woman, and thus is most deserving of being the Heroine.

And as all good (and bad) heroines deserve, her story begins with innocence lost, and love found....

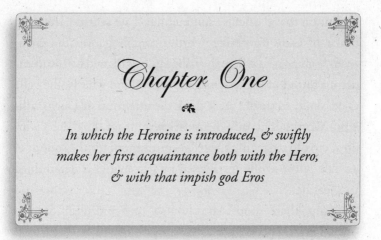

Chapter One

❧

*In which the Heroine is introduced, & swiftly
makes her first acquaintance both with the Hero,
& with that impish god Eros*

The summer sun still hung low and lazy in the Devonshire sky, the shadows cast by the oak trees long across the meadows and the dew nodding heavy on the tall grasses. Yet it was not like any other morning, for in those same tall grasses lay a squalling, woeful female infant.

This sorry newborn babe knew nothing of men, for even the father who sired her had refused to give her his name. Of a mother's love, she knew little more, for her mother, poor woman, could contrive no better course for her child than to cast her away at three days' age, and abandon her against a hummock at a lonely country crossroads. The tender infant had no sustenance, no comfort beyond a tattered blanket to shelter her from the elements, and if she'd not been intended for greater things, she surely would have perished from thirst or hunger or mongrel dogs, with none to mourn her tiny corpse.

But on that particular summer day, Fate sent the traveling coach of Lady Catherine Worthy rumbling over the cross-roads, and near to where the babe lay. Frightened by the thunderous sound of the coach's great ironbound wheels, the babe cried aloud so shrill that it drew the attention of Lady Catherine Worthy. The lady thrust her head from the coach's window, crossly mistaking the babe's pitiful wail for the squeak of an axle purposefully misaligned by wheelwrights determined to cheat her.

"Stop, there, stop!" she shouted to her driver. "Stop at once, I say!"

The great coach lumbered to a halt, yet still the sound persisted, shrill and vexing. Her Ladyship leaned farther from the window, the lace-trimmed lappets on her cap flapping on either side of her face, and waved her hand imperiously at the footman who rode on the box behind.

"You there!" she called. "Someone has tossed away a pup by the road. I see it myself, there in those weeds. Go back and fetch it now, haste, haste! There is nothing I loathe more than some low villain discarding a pup like rubbish."

The footman trotted back and plucked not a dog, but the babe, from the grass. Bewildered, he looked back to the coach, holding the wriggling (and quite damp) infant at arm's length away from his splendid silver-laced livery coat.

"It's not a pup, m'lady," he shouted. "It's a baby."

"A baby, you say?" Disappointment filled the lady's voice. "Not a pup?"

"No, m'lady," the footman said, squinting warily down at

the wretched child in his arms. "Do you still wish me to bring it, m'lady?"

"A baby." Her ladyship sighed mightily. "I do not suppose we can leave it here, else wild pigs shall eat it, and there's another soul lost from Heaven. Is it a boy baby or a girl?"

With a single indelicate finger, the footman lifted the baby's swaddling blanket to peer inside: the first ever to ogle this poor infant so, but far from the last. "A girl, m'lady."

"A girl." Her ladyship sighed again. "Very well. Our Christian duty demands that we offer assistance to those who cannot provide for themselves. We shall keep her, and order her baptized this Sabbath."

Thus through the charity of her ladyship, the foundling girl came to live among the serving staff at Worthy Hall. She was duly baptized, and named Mary, for Our Lord's Mother, and because that was the name her ladyship called all serving girls. As a surname, she was given Wren, because her ladyship deemed that a proper bird for an orphan to emulate: small, humble, industrious, and plain.

Alas for Lady Catherine's careful plans! As Mary Wren grew, it became clear that there was very little of the humble wren in her. Her temper was not given to humility, but to spirit, and though she was too often corrected with the rod by her betters, she still spoke freely whenever she perceived injustice or unfairness.

Yet the unfairness often fell towards Mary herself. While she toiled hard at every task presented to her as the lowest scullery maid, working from before dawn until long past sunset, her labors were never judged sufficient by Cook or Mrs. Able, the housekeeper. No matter how hard Mary worked, she never could seem to please, and she despaired over how sorry a character they would give for her if ever she dared to leave for another place, at another house.

Least wrenlike of all was Mary's appearance. By the sixteenth anniversary of her coming to the Hall, she had grown into the rarest beauty, and much more a swan than a wren. Her complexion was clear and bloomed like a damask rose, her hair dark and curling, her teeth even and her eyes the brightest sapphire. Further, she'd grown into a lushly ripe young woman, her breasts full and high and her waist small, and despite her modest servant's dress and cap, she was remarked by men of every station wherever she went.

Pray recall that at the tender age of sixteen, Mary was still innocent, a virgin in every possible way. She did not seek the constant attention she received, nor did it please her. Instead it made her feel uncertain and confused, even shamed, so much so that her cheeks were constantly ablaze with her misery.

To no surprise, the footmen, grooms, and other men on our staff soon discovered this, teasing Mary whenever they could. They'd torment her even in the servants' pew at church each Sunday, contriving ways to pinch the roundest part of her bottom each time she knelt at prayers, or snatch aside her kerchief from her bosom to reveal more of her softly rounded breasts to their prying eyes.

Thus one summer morning, when Mary heard the other

women in the kitchen giggling and whispering about a rare handsome young gentleman who was among the party of visitors new arrived at the Hall, she didn't join their gossip, but concentrated instead upon shelling the beans for the servants' nooning.

"They say Lady Nestor won't stay a night away from home without Mr. Lyon at her side," said Betty, a chambermaid, as she sipped her dish of watered tea with a true lady's daintiness. "Her ladyship claims she would perish without his counsel and his succor, he's that pious a young gentleman."

"Oh, aye, succor," scoffed Susannah, the cook's maid, as she sliced onions into neat white rings. "I've seen that Johnny Lyon, the handsome rascal, just as I've seen how her ladyship fawns and dotes upon him, though she's old enough to be his mother. The only succoring between those two comes with her mouth tugging upon his pious prick."

"Not before the lass, Susannah," Betty cautioned, even as she laughed raucously. "Don't sully Mary's maidenly ears."

Maidenly or not, Mary's ears had already heard their fill of Mr. John Lyon. Another orphan like herself, he'd been taken up by Lady Nestor, Lady Catherine's oldest friend. But while Lady Catherine had made Mary a servant, Lady Nestor had decided her orphan showed uncommon promise, and had paid for Mr. Lyon's education as if he'd been a gentleman born. She'd determined him for the clergy, but her servants as well as the ones at Worthy Hall judged him far too handsome to be wasted in a pulpit.

This was all Mary knew of Mr. Lyon, nor did she care

to learn more. She'd heard enough. She bowed her head and pretended not to listen, a ruse the other two women at once saw through.

"*Those* maidenly ears?" Susannah jabbed her knife in the air to signify the maid. "Why, Mary's no better than the rest o' us. You'll see. Some pretty lad will catch her fancy and tickle her between her legs, and she'll be on her back with her petticoats in the air faster'n you can speak the words."

"I will not!" Mary said warmly, her head still lowered over the bowl of beans. "I've vowed to Lady Catherine with my hand upon the Holy Scripture that I'll stay a maid until I wed, and not be tempted to sin."

"Vows so foolish as that are made to be broken, Mary," Betty said, not unkindly. "You shouldn't swear to oaths that can't be kept, even if her ladyship asks it of you."

"I've a notion to test her," Susannah said. "Mr. Lyon's coffee is almost ready, Mary. You take it up to him in the drawing room."

Betty gasped. "Mary can't go above stairs," she said indignantly. "She's kitchen staff."

"This once she can," Susannah said, determined to have her so-called test. "Mr. Lyon wants his coffee, and has been ringing and ringing for it, and Mary here's the only one in the kitchen who could take it up. Unless you be too timid to do it, Mary?"

"I'm not frighted by this Mr. Lyon." Mary set her bowl on the table with a thud, and untied her apron. "He's only a mortal man of flesh and blood, and no more."

"Oh, aye, he's *flesh* enough," Betty said, chuckling. "Charming, luscious manly flesh, in all his glory. But I warrant even a maid like you will soon see that for yourself. Go now. Take the tray, and mind you keep clear of her ladyship."

"And mind you come back directly to tell us everything. *Everything*." Susannah thrust her tongue from her mouth and touched it to her lips, suggestive enough to make Betty burst with fresh merriment.

Like the cawing of two crows, their laughter followed Mary as she climbed up the back stairs with Mr. Lyon's tray in her hands. She was much vexed by their amusement, coming as it did at her expense, and she thought of a score of clever retorts she should have made to end their teasing. She'd not been tempted by any man or boy heretofore. Why should she weaken now?

But by the time she reached the front hall, her temper had cooled. Test or no, she didn't belong here, and she hurried across the black-and-white marble floor towards the drawing room as swiftly as she could. Her plain linsey-woolsey gown seemed woefully out of place amongst the upstairs splendor, and even the painted faces of long-ago Worthys hanging on the walls seemed to sneer their disapproval down from their gilded frames.

She'd face consequences enough if Lady Catherine came upon her, but the ones she feared more were from Mr. Punch, the butler, and the housekeeper, Mrs. Able, both more exalted in her world than the mistress. If either one discovered Mary so far from the kitchens, she'd be thrashed for certain, and likely be burdened with extra tasks for punishment as well. With such a threat to spur her on, she was close to running by

the time she scratched on the drawing room door, and woefully out of breath, too.

"Enter," came the deep masculine voice inside. With the
tray balanced clumsily against her side, Mary turned the knob,
and pushed the door open with her hip. But because the day
was warm, or perhaps only because she was so anxious, the
door stuck tight in its jamb. Fearful at being faulted by Mr.
Lyon for this delay, she swung the full force of her hip against
the recalcitrant door, and turned the knob again.

Of course the door chose that instant to give way, and
Mary flew headfirst into the room, staggering and bumbling
like a wayward sot as she struggled not to drop the tray with
the coffeepot, dish, and sweet biscuits. She lurched forward
across the oaken floorboards, her gaze intent upon the tray,
her horrified face reflecting back to her in the distorted curve
of the polished silver pot. Like a windblown sailor dancing
along the foretop spars, she finally found her footing, steady-
ing herself and the tray with a happy small sigh of relief and
accomplishment.

But oh, what peril still awaited her next, more wrenching
and hazardous than a thousand falls and stumbles combined!

"Are you unharmed, miss?" he asked, his voice rich with
his concern. "Not injured, I trust?"

Mary looked up from the coffeepot, and tumbled again,
this time into the endless green pools that were the gentleman's eyes. Struck dumb, she could only nod in wordless
agreement to his query, and marvel all the more at his face
and person.

He was neither so beautifully perfect as to be an Adonis,

nor of such a warrior's sturdy physique as to qualify as another Hercules. Yet the young gentleman who stood before her possessed more charm and masculine grace than any other of his sex that she ever had known. Perhaps twenty years in age, he was tall and well made, his shoulders broad and his belly flat, and Mary could not help but marvel at how well muscled his legs and chest appeared to be, such as is the case in gentlemen much given to riding. He was dressed with sober elegance, in a dark gray superfine suit of clothes that only served to accentuate the sea green of his eyes, and he wore his own hair instead of a London gentleman's fashionable wig, his gilded curls tied with a black silk ribbon and becoming nonchalance at his nape.

"You are certain you're unharmed?" he asked with the sincerest concern. "Quite well?"

Once again Mary nodded. Mr. Lyon—for so, of course, it was he—smiled, a single dimple lighting his cheek, and the poor smitten girl felt herself sway beneath its charming beacon. He sensed her weakness and seized the tray from her to place it on the table behind him. Then with great gentleness, he took her arm and guided her to a nearby settee, conveniently placed beside a tall arched window.

"There," he said, joining her. "Now breathe deeply, and collect yourself."

Mary closed her eyes and leaned towards the open window, breathing deeply as he'd instructed her. When at last she felt more restored, she opened her eyes, only to realize those same breezes had mischievously disordered the kerchief around her neck, and her breasts, scarce contained by the

sturdy barriers of her stays and her bodice, now lay impu-
dently bare before him. Beside her, Mr. Lyon's eyes were wide
at such an unconscionably brazen sight, his lips pressed together so tightly Mary feared he'd forgotten to breathe as
well.

"Oh—oh, sir, please, forgive me," she stammered as she
fumbled to restore her scattered modesty. "I'd no wish to be so
bold, especially before a gentleman of the church!"

"Not yet, my dear, not yet," he said, raising his gaze with
effort back to her face. "To serve Our Lord is my greatest
hope, true, but I've still much more study before I make my
final choice."

"Indeed, sir," she said. "I've heard her ladyship has complete confidence in your gifts."

"Her ladyship is most kind," he said, touching his forehead with humble respect. "I can only hope to approach the
regard she has for me."

She smiled shyly. "I'm sure she's every reason to admire
your abilities, sir."

"Her ladyship is most generous in her praise." He shrugged
with that self-deprecatory charm that is so rare in handsome
men. "But here, perhaps you can help me."

Mary nodded eagerly, too ready, alas, to oblige him in all
things.

"I need an audience, you see," he began. "Someone who'll
listen, and criticize my work where it's lacking so I might improve it."

"Oh, sir," she said sadly, "I'm but the lowest scullery maid,
sir, and unschooled in literary matters as that."

"Nonsense," he declared. "Even a hermit in a cave has taste of one sort or another. You'll do better than any Cambridge don. I'm sure of it. What name does your cook call you by?"

"I'm Mary, sir," she said, flushing again beneath his attention. "Mary Wren, sir."

"And I am John Lyon, your servant, Miss Mary Wren." He grinned and winked, as if to show he understood how foolish and teasing a statement that was to make to one who was in fact a servant.

"Yes, Mr. Lyon." She laughed with delight, for she'd never been called "Miss Wren" in all her life. How pleasing it sounded to her ears, and how especially sweet for being in his voice!

He laughed with her. "How vastly agreeable you are, Miss Mary Wren. How could I ask for a finer audience?"

To Mary's sorrow, he rose from the settee, but ventured away only long enough to gather up a sheaf of papers from the desk, and soon returned to sit beside her. The settee was small, and as he shifted to better arrange himself on the cushions, the narrowness compelled his knee to press against hers. She said nothing, not wishing to appear rude, nor was there space for her to move away even if she chose to.

"I've written about the temptation of Eve by the serpent," Mr. Lyon said, fanning the pages in his hand. He paused, and looked over the papers at Mary. "You do know of Eve, and her mate, Adam?"

"Oh, yes, sir," she said promptly. She liked how his knee pressed against hers, and the strange feel of eager excitement that came with so simple a touch. "Adam and Eve lived in the

Garden of Eden, until the serpent beguiled Eve into biting the apple of sin, and God cast them out into the darkness."

"Very good, Miss Wren!" He seemed surprised yet pleased by her recitation, as every man does when discovering a woman who understands the nicety of sin. "A fine, concise telling."

She smiled and basked in the glow of his approval. "Lady Catherine made certain I learned my letters, sir, so I could read Scripture."

"Then you're scholar enough to counsel me, Miss Wren." He looked back at the papers, turning them towards the light through the window behind them. The sun was slipping below the trees, and to catch its fading rays, he needed to twist and turn his arm until it rested along the curving back of the settee, behind her shoulders.

"Now then," he began, his face contorted in an academic scowl. "My thesis is that Eve could not help being weak and succumbing to temptation, because that is woman's natural flaw."

"That she be weak, sir?" Mary exclaimed. "You would blame mankind's fall from eternal grace upon women's weakness?"

"Why, yes," he said evenly. "That is common knowledge, Miss Wren. Adam, being of stronger resolve, would have resisted the serpent's temptation. Now, if I may continue, then—"

"You may not, sir!" she cried, forgetting herself in her indignation. "Not until you admit that men can be every bit as weak as women!"

"Is that so?" He leaned closer to Mary so that his chest pressed into her arm and their faces were almost touching. "Would you care enough for your argument to risk a proof?"

"A proof, sir?" she asked, not understanding his question. Her ignorance was not quite complete, for she did understand that his nearness was making her heart quicken, how her skin warmed where his body brushed against hers, how she felt at once eager and languid, and ready for she knew not what. "And—and what is that, sir?"

"Oh, it's a simple enough test, sweet." His voice was low and coaxing to her, his words a feathery brush over her cheek. "You do your best as a woman to lead me into temptation, and I shall see if I can be the stronger as a man, and resist."

She frowned a bit, for his very male argument was still new to her, one she'd not yet heard from any man. Besides, by then she realized she was slipping back into the soft curve of the settee's arm, or perhaps it was Mr. Lyon himself who was easing her backwards with his insinuating presence.

"Don't frown, Mary," he said softly, almost troubled. "Where's the temptation to a man in that?"

"I didn't mean to frown, sir." She smiled up at him to show she meant well, and rested her palm on his cheek as further consolation. "Not to you, sir."

His smile in return was dazzling, like a rainbow after a storm. "Ah, Mary, you are so sweet, you make me believe not only in temptation, but in love."

"Love, sir?" she asked, startled to hear such a word uttered by him so soon in their acquaintance. "You are in love, sir?"

"With you, dear Mary," he whispered, his arm slipping around her waist to support her. "I was lost the moment you came through that door."

Before Mary could offer up her reply, he was kissing her, the first time ever she'd permitted any man to make her such a freedom. His lips moved over hers with a heated urgency she'd never known before, and as she gasped with surprise at the unfamiliar sensations, her lips parted as she sought more air. Of course he chose to misread her amazement, taking it for a welcome she didn't know enough to extend. Soon his tongue was sliding between her lips and against her own, as sure and fiery as Cupid's dart of love.

Of *love*: surely that must be what she felt! Mary's head seemed to spin so that she feared she'd swoon, and she clung to Mr. Lyon for support, her fingers clinging to his shoulders as if for her life.

With her hands to hold them steady, she felt his slip between them, and ease itself most cunningly beneath her kerchief and inside her bodice. Yet though her conscience cried out against such impunity, her heart had heard that magic word LOVE, the key that would unlock most any maiden's lock.

And Mary was no different. She let him push aside the straining cloth, and felt her new-ripened breasts spill out to meet his eager touch. She'd always wondered why men should be so fascinated by these baubles, which she believed were fashioned for the nourishment of babes and little else.

It didn't take long before she understood it all. She sighed as his clever fingers began their winning caresses, pulling and teasing her tender flesh until her nipples had tightened and grown stiff and proud. She arched against him, aching for more, even though she'd still no notion of what that *more* could be as she began to gasp and writhe beneath him with unmitigated delight.

"See how you tempt me, Mary," he said, his breathing harsh against her throat. "I wish to be strong, yet love makes me weak. Your love, Mary, you and— Ah, sweet, what's this?"

Again his eyes widened with surprise as he drew back from his attentions. She knew at once what had caught his eye, and with her ardor instantly dowsed, she struggled to cover her secret shame.

"No false modesty, Mary, please, not between lovers," he said, holding her wrist to keep her shielding hand away. "What a delicious secret you've kept hidden, sweet!"

"Can you fault me for so doing, sir?" Mary cried, finally pushing herself away from him to sit and put her clothing to rights. "Oh, please, sir, I am so shamed!"

He had discovered her birthmark, the spot that had showed upon one side of her left breast as long as she could recall it: a tiny, perfectly formed heart placed not far from the true one that beat within. In Mary's complete innocence, she'd always suspected that Nature's coquettish placement of this little heart must be a sign, a brand to show a wanton temperament, and a tendency for affections too freely given and received. This birthmark had always tormented her, and to this moment she'd taken great care never to reveal it to others. But now—now to her considerable sorrow—she'd carelessly let Mr. Lyon uncover her secret, and her humiliation with it.

"Why should you be so shy, when it's the most delicious birthmark I've ever seen?" he asked in perfect honesty. "To be so marked by Venus herself, in a place where only a true lover's eyes might discover it."

Mary looked at him sideways, uneasy, with her arms still crossed protectively across her breasts. "You do not find it ugly, sir, or distasteful?"

"Oh, my poor dear, not at all!" he exclaimed. "Was there ever another woman so rapturously blessed with such tribute from Venus? Was there ever another man so honored by this fascinating revelation?"

"You're certain, sir?" she asked, still unconvinced. "You are not speaking so from kindness or pity?"

"Of course not," he declared heartily. "Come, I'll give you proof of my lover's devotion. Show your dear secret heart to me again, and I shall kiss it as a solemn pledge of my admiration."

Surely, she told herself, she could ask for no more than that, and with trembling fingers, she once again revealed the coy little heart and her tremulous breast with it. With wor-shipful murmurs meant to calm her anxiety, he lowered his lips to the site, and offered the most dedicated and respectful tribute imaginable. From the birthmark, he swiftly shifted back to the nearest rosy nipple, suckling first with his lips and then flicking lightly with his tongue while with his hand he offered equal delight to her other breast.

Overwhelmed by sensation, she closed her eyes in modesty, and to better comprehend his sweet devotion. Clearly Mr. Lyon wasn't like the footmen and grooms who tormented her so. Clearly he didn't deserve the smirks and lewd jests that the older women in the kitchen cast his way. Clearly he was a gentleman, who cared for her sensibilities, to treat her with such tender regard.

She sighed sweetly, giving herself over to his attentions, and circled her arms around him. She'd never before held a gentleman (or any other man, for that matter) with this familiarity or freedom. She was amazed by the difference in his body from her own, the hard, lean muscles of his arms and shoulders, the manly strength she discovered beneath her hands, as if he were eager to follow her every bidding.

Daring further, she slipped her hands inside the skirts of his coat to his breeches, and discovered the round, firm cheeks of his buttocks, snugly covered by the soft wool of his breeches. She spread her fingers open, delighting in the neat way the splendid, taut curves filled her hand, and in response he groaned aloud, grimacing as he released her nipple from his lips.

"Oh, sir, have I injured you?" she whispered breathlessly, loath to let him go. "Have I hurt you in some way?"

"Not—not at all," he said, though his ragged breathing betrayed a distress similar to her own. "But here, let me guide you."

Swiftly he shifted apart from her, only long enough to draw her hand around to the front of his breeches.

"There," he said. "See the proof of what you have done to me."

She saw, and she touched, and she marveled. She had, of course, come across unbuttoned footmen who were either too lazy or too drunk to find the privy making their water behind the stables. Likewise she had glimpsed their male members in their hands or limply stuffed back into their breeches: shriveled, limp affairs, unlovely to any eyes but their possessors'.

But here indeed was proof that Mr. Lyon's staff must be wrought of much finer flesh and blood. Behind the buttoned fall of his breeches, its blunt head pushed proudly forward, its height and breadth barely contained, and fair ready to burst free of the buttons that struggled to contain it.

At such a sight, Mary blushed, more from wonder than from lingering modesty. At once Mr. Lyon caught her hand in his, and led it to his straining cock. She touched him gingerly, curiously, but enough to make him groan again. This time she did not draw back, but swept her hand along his hard length, marveling at the heat she could feel even through the cloth. He pushed hard against her palm, his hips rising to meet her caress.

Yet even more astonishing was that by stroking him in this fashion, she felt her own pleasure growing in perfect sympathy. Her heart was quickening, her bared breasts growing somehow heavier and more sensitive. Though the window beside them was open to the breezes, the most extraordinary sensation of heat was building low in her belly, as if her private parts were possessed by a fever that made her ripen with longing. She felt strangely swollen, even damp, with an almost unbearable desire to touch herself for surcease.

"You suffer, sir," she whispered, her eyes wide, her breathing ragged, her legs shifting restlessly together as she sought to ease her own distress. "Yet I do as well. I feel as if I burned with a fire's heat, sir, as if flames did lick me from within, as if—"

"*Mary.*" He stopped her words with kisses that were now demanding rather than tender, pressing her back farther into the arm of the settee. The wool of his coat grazed her nipples, another kind of sweet torment, and she arched upwards against his chest, seeking more of him than she'd words to explain. She felt the window's breezes on the bare skin above her heavy stockings as he threw aside her apron and petticoats and bared her thighs as he had bared her breasts. When he slipped his knees between her legs, opening her more widely to his advances, she welcomed him, shifting so as to give him better access to her charms.

The fever of urgency made them both clumsy, throwing both caution and clothing aside in their haste. Her kerchief and cap fell from the cushions to the floor, two buttons tore from his coat in his hurry to pull that garment from his body, and yet neither paid any heed. An hour before, and Mary would not have known him from Adam, yet now she could think of nothing more than the pleasure this handsome gentleman was bringing to her.

With teasing deliberation, she felt his fingers glide along her inner thigh and dally briefly in the curls of her mound before, at last, coming to settle on her cunny. She caught her breath as those artful fingers parted her, opened her, in a way that she'd never realized was possible.

The moisture she'd sensed welling within now eased the

way for his touch, taking him deep within on its slick and honey-sweet path. Lightly he stroked the tiny nubbin of flesh that held her pleasure, making Mary gasp and clutch at his hand: not to stop, not at all, but to continue on, *on,* like any good huntress with her quarry in reach. She arched against his hand as he pressed deeper into her cleft, and clung to his shoulders, her knees tangled around his brawny forearms; and if a moan of delight escaped her lips, why, then it was the glad hosanna of a happy acolyte to the one freeing her from the thrall of innocence.

But then there came another sound, another voice from the hall, a voice so fearful that Mary's eyes flew open with horror. She pushed Mr. Lyon aside and jumped to her feet, frantically arranging her bodice and cap.

"What the devil?" her dear gentleman demanded, his voice hoarse and rasping with his unfulfilled need.

"It's not the devil, sir, but the butler," she cried in a desperate whisper. "He's tipping the blinds against the sun in each room on this side of the house, same as every afternoon, and if he should find me here, so far from the kitchen, why, he will scold me, and thrash me, and—"

"Hush, sweet, hush," said Mr. Lyon, his green eyes flashing with outrage on her behalf as he rose, too. Even as he buttoned the fall on his breeches, he was more than equal to the challenge of Mr. Punch. "You'll not suffer at that rascal's hands, not on my account."

But Mary had no wish to send him against such a fearful foe, not when it seemed she had only begun her delicious acquaintance with Mr. Lyon.

"Please don't, sir, I beg you," she said breathlessly, tugging her bodice back in place over her breasts as she fished behind the settee for her kerchief. "Consider the scandal, sir, pray do. I won't have you risk your glorious future for my sake."

He scowled at being restrained, but at once saw the logic to her appeal.

"Then flee, if you must," he said with open regret. "But swear to me, my love, that you'll not forget me."

"Forget you, sir!" Mary cried with astonishment. "Never, sir, never."

"Then come to me this night, when the others are asleep," he urged, seizing her once again in his arms. "We can meet in the garden, or the orchard, or the loft over the stable."

She shook her head, her ear still primed and listening for Mr. Punch's footfall. "I cannot, sir, not to those places. I'm watched too closely by the others. What of your bedchamber above stairs?"

His expression turned dark. "My chamber is too near to Lady Nestor's rooms for that. She's a good woman, aye, with every care for my welfare, but watchful as a cat."

At the mention of his benefactress, Mary guiltily recalled her own savior, and her solemn oath to Lady Catherine now pressed like a stony weight upon her conscience. It had been as nothing for Mary to swear to preserve her maidenhead when there'd been no temptation to do otherwise. But Mr. Lyon was temptation indeed—as handsome and virile a temptation as any wavering virgin could want—and tears glazed Mary's eyes at the awfulness of her sacred (if rash) oath.

On this very settee, she had tempted a pious Christian

gentleman to sin with her. She'd wantonly spread her thighs for him to please her, and in turn she had touched and stroked his prick as if it were the most luscious plaything imaginable. Worst of all, she'd no regret save that they'd been interrupted at their sport by the coming appearance of Mr. Punch. Surely by now her mortal soul must be in peril of damnation!

"Oh, sir, I cannot," she whispered sorrowfully. "I cannot."

He struck his fist to his chest, over his heart. "Do you doubt me, Mary? Do you question my love for you?"

"No, no, sir, never that," she declared, raising his hand from his chest to her lips. "It's that I have sworn—oh, Heavens, there *is* Mr. Punch! I must go, sir, else be caught, and sent away!"

She leaned forward and kissed him quickly, a kiss stolen from him as others had so often been stolen from her.

"I will contrive to see you again, dear sir, and soon," she promised in a desperate whisper. "You have my pledge upon it."

Then before this splendid gentleman could say more nectar-sweet words to tempt her to linger, Mary turned and fled the room. Yet even as she ran, she was already plotting and planning towards the next moment she could slip away to meet her darling Mr. Lyon, her LOVE, and with every worn step upon the kitchen stair, she likewise took another step on her giddy journey towards her own irreparable ruin.

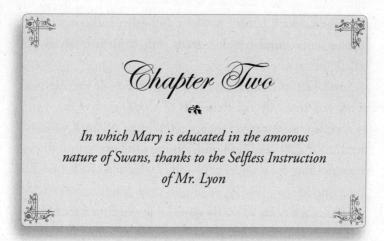

Chapter Two

In which Mary is educated in the amorous nature of Swans, thanks to the Selfless Instruction of Mr. Lyon

Over the following days, Mary resolved to resist the attractions of Mr. Lyon, both for her own sake and for his. In that brief time spent in his solitary company, she'd learned enough of the delights of the flesh to realize that her own personal flesh was very weak and susceptible where his splendidly lean and well-muscled flesh was concerned, and that it would be wiser for her to avoid his temptations altogether.

This was a noble goal, and one more readily achieved than might at first be guessed. Though Mary and Mr. Lyon both resided beneath the same broad slate roof of Worthy Hall, their paths seldom crossed each other's in the course of a day. As a scullery maid, Mary was expected to remain below stairs, and never to show herself to those who lived above. Likewise it was understood by all in the house that Mr. Lyon, as a gentleman (or reasonably close to one), was not to venture into the kitchen, pantry, scullery, and other such portions of the servants' domain below stairs, nor to their quarters beneath the attic, either.

And just as Mary's day, and often much of the night as well, was ruled by the demands of Cook, so was Mr. Lyon compelled to dance attendance on Lady Nestor's whim— fetching shawls, reading aloud, closing windows against drafts, even pouring tea on occasion—all of which left little time for pursuing Mary.

But as the poets so wisely state, Love will always find a way, and when Love is coupled (as it were) with Desire, then surely the pair is seldom denied. Separated though Mary and Mr. Lyon were by rank and by stairs, he still was able to demonstrate his devotion to her. When he passed the servants' pew at morning prayer on Sunday, he made sure to grant Mary a glance so heated and smoldering that it was a wonder the very church did not burst into flames. One morning from his bedchamber, he glimpsed her hauling a slopping pail of wash water from the kitchen through the courtyard, he hastily wrote the words "Remember Love" on a scrap of paper, folded it, and tossed it from his window to land on the cobbles at her feet. Most daring of all, he bribed one of the footmen as his confederate, and contrived to have a beribboned nosegay of primroses waiting on her pillow one night.

In return, Mary did nothing to encourage him. It would be a fine thing to say that her virtuous resolve had triumphed over the heady temptation that Mr. Lyon presented. A fine thing, yes, but untrue: for despite her best intentions, Mary thought constantly of Mr. Lyon, of his smile, his kiss, even (shamelessly) of his bounding prick.

She thought of him the instant Mrs. Able shook her awake in the dark hour before dawn, she thought of him as she peeled carrots and chopped turnips, and she thought of him each night as she lay wakeful and tossing with desire in her chastely narrow bedstead at night. Her greatest fear was not whether she could resist his seduction of her, but that he would be forced to leave Worthy Hall with Lady Nestor before the deed could be accomplished, and thus her days passed in a constant fever of longing and of dread.

But soon Fate pitied the condition of these two lovers, and contrived to ease their situation. One afternoon, the house-maid Rebecca was carrying the large tea tray upstairs to serve Lady Catherine and Lady Nestor. As she entered the drawing room with the tray in both hands, she could not see Lady Nestor's small black-and-tan spaniel come racing up to yip at her feet. The dog tangled in Rebecca's skirts, tripping her so that she landed face forward in a clattering shower of broken porcelain, hot tea, and yowling dog.

Through enormous good fortune, the spaniel escaped un-injured, though the sobbing Lady Nestor was so distressed by his narrow escape that she retreated to her bed for the rest of the afternoon. Rebecca, however, suffered both a bad sprain to her ankle and a break in her arm near the wrist, severe enough that Lady Catherine had no choice but to send her home to her mother's cottage for nursing.

But one person's misfortune can be another's joy. Again

with no choice left to her, Lady Catherine reluctantly raised Mary to the position of housemaid. She was handed a more presentable gown to wear, one without any mendings or patches, and more delicately soled shoes, so she'd not mar the floors or carpets in the drawing room. She was also given a beguiling new cap, one with a small frill around the face, and warned to keep her hair neat beneath it, with none of the straggling locks that often appeared in the kitchen. In fact, she was warned about many things, from not gawking at her betters to taking care to keep her hands and neck clean before Lady Catherine, or risk being instantly let go.

None of these warnings worried Mary. Now that she'd risen above stairs, she'd no intention of ever going back, and she'd do whatever she must to keep this glorious new position. If she worked dutifully enough, someday she might even become a lady's maid.

As her first solitary task, Mary was assigned the dusting of the books in the library of the late Lord William, Lady Catherine's brother. (Being younger unmarried siblings of the Marquis of Conover, Lady Catherine and Lord William had been given Worthy Hall, a dower house, in which to reside as long as they each lived: a cordial spinster-bachelor arrangement that had suited all parties for many years.) The library was preserved with much solemn ritual, as much as a memoriam to Lord William as a repository of books.

But to Mary, who'd never previously been permitted within this chamber's walls, Lord William's library was a wondrous place. The tall-backed wing chairs were covered in red leather, and placed before the empty grate as if to beckon readers to linger. Muted portraits of long-ago Thoroughbreds and favorite spotted hunting dogs alternated with gold-framed looking glasses. The windows were shuttered against the fading rays of the sun, and as a result the light in the room was pleasantly filtered, like the sun that sifts through the leaves to fall at last on the forest's floor. Tall cases filled with leather-bound books lined the walls, each crowned with a small white bust of some famous Worthy of the past.

It was at these scores of books that Mary stared with awe. She had been taught to read, of course, as part of Lady Catherine's beneficence, for her ladyship insisted all her servants be able to read Scripture. But beyond the Holy Book, Mary had read but one other (and that most decidedly unholy: a well-thumbed thrilling romance left behind in the house by a female guest and now circulating endlessly among the maidservants). To be confronted now by so many volumes, representing so much knowledge that she did not possess, was daunting indeed—though not perhaps so daunting as Mrs. Able's instructions.

"Her Ladyship wishes us to use the wing o' a goose for dusting His Lordship's books," the housekeeper declared. "Glide the wing along the tops o' the books and no deeper than it shall go with ease. Never rearrange nor remove any book from the case. Her Ladyship will see it directly, and you'll be turned out. Mind you keep at your work by yourself. If I learn of any of the menservants in here with you, why, then you'll be turned out for that, as well."

"Yes, ma'am." Solemnly Mary took the goose's wing. The wing was exactly that, lopped off from the bird and dried with the bones and feathers intact. Mary found it rather gruesome, using such a thing for cleaning books, but knew better than to say so to Mrs. Able.

"Tend to the books in this case first," the housekeeper said, already watching Mary closely for any signs of faltering. "I shall return in half an hour's time to inspect your progress."

Mary bobbed a quick respectful curtsy as the housekeeper left, and the latch clicked shut after her. Dusting was much less onerous than scrubbing a roasting pan after a leg of mutton, and armed with the goose's wing, Mary turned towards her task with determination—a determination that was, alas, sadly short-lived.

She'd barely begun when she caught sight of herself in the tall gilt-framed looking glass between the windows. She paused, startled by her own image, then smiled shyly. Of course she'd seen her face in a pocket glass, and reflected in the square panes of the kitchen windows. But she'd never before considered herself at length, from her shoes clear to her crown, and it felt oddly as if she were seeing a stranger rather than herself.

She tucked the goose wing into her pocket, the feather jutting out from her hip like a wing of her own, and tentatively twirled her new petticoats around her ankles, studying her movements in the glass. Awkward with inexperience, she tried to make a curtsy to her reflection, sweeping her skirts the way she'd seen the grand ladies do. The faded blue linen (for it was new only to her) made her eyes appear even brighter and her skin more like new cream. Yet even as she made this appraisal, she flushed to realize the depth of her vanity. Surely Lady

Catherine meant for her to be industrious here among all these books, not to preen and pose like a peacock!

Yet still she could not help from smoothing her palms along the bodice, admiring how much smaller her waist appeared in a fitted bodice like this than in her old straight-cut gown with only her apron's strings to give it shape. She couldn't wait for Mr. Lyon to see her in her new guise. She'd watched the other women in the servants' hall prepare to meet their sweethearts, and now she followed their course, daringly pulling the neckline of the bodice lower in front, and arranging her kerchief to make for a more alluring display. Her breasts were held high and round by the tight lacing, almost as if being offered on a plate, and she flushed again as she recalled how Mr. Lyon had admired—nay, worshipped!—them with fingers, his lips, his tongue.

Once again she recalled that afternoon with him. Her heart beat faster, and her lips parted as the memory of those amorous delights returned. Still before the glass, she dipped inside her bodice to cradle the luscious flesh of her breasts, imagining her hands belonged to Mr. Lyon instead.

She turned just enough to show in the glass her birthmark, the tiny raised heart, and regarded it with new interest. He'd considered it a sign of beauty, something to be admired, kissed, even worshipped, and not hidden with shame. Now she viewed it as something to be revealed with a flourish to a lover as a special boon, even an enticement, and the idea of displaying the heart-shaped mark gave her a little shiver of excitement.

Lightly she rubbed her palms over her nipples, just as Mr.

Lyon had done, teasing them between her thumb and forefinger until they became stiff and hard, exactly as they had for
him. She felt the same quickening in her blood, the same
gathering of heat low in her belly, and the more she caressed
her breasts, the more the same pleasure streaked to her cunny.
She felt the same delicious tension begin to flutter and grow,
and with a little whimper she tipped back her head and closed
her eyes to imagine Mr. Lyon all the more clearly.

Yet as lost as Mary was in her fantasizing, she still heard the
brass latch turn and the door begin to swing open. With a
gasp, she flew off to the far side of the fireplace, ducking behind one of the tall marble columns that supported the chim-
neypiece. Frantically she tugged her bodice back over her
breasts, praying that the housekeeper would not catch her.

Preserve her, if it was Mrs. Able, she'd be sent away this
very day, for caressing herself in such a wanton manner
that—

"Mary?"

Preserve her again, for there before her stood Mr. Lyon
himself, more handsome and manly than she could ever imagine. He smiled at her, as charming, as wicked, as knowing, as
any gentleman ever could be.

"Yes, sir, 'tis I." Her face burned hot with shame and guilt,
and in her confusion she stared down at the floorboards, her
hands knotted at her sides. "I was cleaning His Lordship's
books, sir."

How easily that lie had slipped from her lips, and for what
purpose? What if he'd already realized the truth, and had seen
her fondling her own breasts so freely before the mirror? Did

the flush in her cheeks betray her, or the disorder to her bodice? What if he'd guessed what she'd been about, pleasuring
herself whilst she thought of him?

"As you were, sweet," he said softly, such kindness for her
sorry predicament that grateful tears fair stung her eyes. "I'll
not disturb you while you're at your work. I've only come here
for a book of sermons that Lady Nestor requested."

"Yes, sir," she whispered miserably. She watched him reach
up to a higher shelf, noting how broad and strong his shoulders appeared in his well-tailored jacket, and how fine and
taut the curve of his buttocks in his pale gray breeches. "You've
come to fetch sermons for Lady Nestor—sermons! Oh, sir,
how wrongful of me to long for you, when her ladyship in-
tends you for the pulpit and a life of goodness and honor."

With a quizzical air, he looked back over his shoulder at
her. "Who has told you that?"

"Everyone, sir," she said, unable to contain her sorrow. No
wonder he preferred these dusty old books to her, but la! what
a waste it would be to condemn such a comely gentleman to
good works and a parsonage! "That it is Lady Nestor's fondest
desire that you read for the ministry so that she may grant you
the living that she controls."

He turned back to face her. "That is Her Ladyship's prefer-
ence, yes. But it is not mine."

"No, sir?" Her voice rose with hope, and she dared to ask
the other question that plagued her. "Forgive me for speaking
plain, sir, but there is likewise talk that Her Ladyship expects
you to be, ah, more to her. Is this true, sir? Is it?"

He smiled, more of a grimace of distaste. "You would ask

if I'm another of Her Ladyship's trained pups, licking and worrying at her like an old bone in return for my keep? Is that how plainly you speak?"

"Oh, sir, I didn't say that!"

"But that is what you meant," he said, and sighed wearily. "I know the tattle that's said of me, and of Her Ladyship. I know there are those who believe me to be in keeping to service her. But it is not so, Mary. You have my word."

"But have you told Her Ladyship as well?"

"I will tell her when the time is right for me to leave," he said. "I owe Her Ladyship so much for the opportunities she has granted to me that I'd never willingly wound her, but show her only the greatest kindness in all things."

"You are resolved?"

"I am," he said firmly. "My life—and my heart—must remain my own, and I intend to follow my own designs for both."

"Oh, sir." With that part of her conscience regarding him and Lady Nestor now safely at ease, Mary smiled with such relief that her eyes filled with tears.

"It's true," he continued. "Soon I mean to leave Her Ladyship's household, and make my own way in this world. To London, Mary. That's where I'll go. That's where my fortune and glory will lie. In London."

"London," breathed Mary in awe. To her who'd spent her whole life in Devonshire, London was as distant and fantastic as a fairy city. "Fancy!"

But when Mr. Lyon saw the telltale glisten, he misread the cause, or leastways chose to.

"Do you doubt me, then, Mary?" he exclaimed, his expression fiercely righteous as he struck his fist to his chest, over his heart. "Do you question my love for you, or my devotion?"

"My LOVE": are their any more certain keys to unlock a lady's heart (and her innocence) than those two words? Has ever a man discovered a faster way to yielding bliss with any maid than to promise eternal LOVE?

Mary gasped and pressed her hands to her cheeks, overwhelmed by the power of this magic incantation, still so new to her ears.

"How can you ever think such a thing, sir?" she cried. "How could I ever question your love, any more than you should question mine?"

"Dearest," he said, and nodded as solemnly as if he'd sworn the greatest oath imaginable. "That is how it should be between lovers. Only love can rule our hearts and our passions, and give us the joy we deserve. It is the power of love, and of lovers."

She clasped her hands together with happiness. "Of love, sir, oh, yes, of love!"

"Yes, love." He nodded, magically seeming both worldly-wise, yet sentimental. "I am sure of it. My studies have taught me that while the Church of England is most admirable at addressing the soul, it's woeful regarding the delights of the flesh."

"Oh, sir." Mary's rapture faltered at that. Her entire education as well as her religious training had been limited to what she'd been taught in the small parish church near Worthy Hall, and while talk of love made perfect sense to her, that of the soul did not. "Forgive me, sir, but that's wicked heathen talk."

"Is it, Mary?" he asked, cocking a single brow. "You're a clever lass. Surely you must have noted by now that little in this world of ours is all right, or all wrong, but a mixing of both."

"I do not know, sir," she said, troubled.

"Well, then, there is your answer," he said easily, with a graceful turn of his hand. "If it were so, you'd know it. Because you can't, it isn't."

She frowned, confused by this perplexing logic. "By your lights, sir, if right cannot be separated with ease from wrong, then wrong is right, and right is wrong?"

"Recall the last time we were alone together," he said. "Recall how you felt, what rare feelings of pleasure filled your body. Many would say that was wrong, that it was sinful, yet could anything that brought such joy be wrong?"

"I do not know, sir," she said slowly, trying to make sense of his most sensible argument. "But if heathen folk could—"

"Heathen folk understood," he said firmly. He turned and considered the books once again before drawing one from the shelf, and flipping through the pages as he brought it towards her. "The ancients, the Greeks and the Romans, were what you'd call heathen. They didn't worship in a proper church as we do, but they did understand the necessity of pleasure, no matter how fanciful. See here."

He came to stand beside Mary as any instructor might, and held the pages open so she could see. On one page were a great many words in a language she didn't understand, purest gibberish to her, but on the other was a picture that needed no words to explain.

A beautiful woman reclined on a grassy knoll, her golden hair braided and curled with regal extravagance. Beyond large pearls in her ears and more around her throat, she was naked, and in the act of being mounted and ravished by an enormous white swan.

As shocking as this might be, it was clear that the woman was in the throes of deepest passion, her head twisting to one side and her full lips parted with ecstasy, her knees thrown wide and raised up to give the monstrous bird better access for filling her yearning quim. The woman arched upwards, every muscle taut as she strained for release, while the bird curved his long neck to pluck delicately at one of her plump nipples.

"You like the picture?" Mr. Lyon asked, a question that really needed no asking, not from the way Mary could scarce look away from the picture, not from how he held it out to her like an irresistible offering.

"I—that's not possible, sir," she stammered, even as she blushed with shame at such a lewd picture, but with interest, too. "I've seen the fowl in the yard, the roosters servicing the hens and the gander with the goose, but never like—like—"

"Of course you wouldn't," he agreed. "It's no ordinary swan, but the ancient god Zeus, in the guise of a swan to make good his seduction of Leda, Queen of Sparta. Her husband the king deemed it a rape, but to see the lady in such rapturous transports—"

"I see, sir," Mary whispered. The heat she'd raised within

herself earlier had returned, even warmer than before, her palms damp and her heartbeat quickening. Who would have dreamed there'd be such a book, with such a picture, in the library of Worthy Hall? Surely Her Ladyship didn't know of it, else she'd have ordered it burned long ago, but Mary— Mary was glad Her Ladyship hadn't. "I *see*."

"I knew you would, Mary," he said, easing closer to her with the book still open in his hands. "I'll grant that it's an odd contrivance, a swan rogering a Spartan queen, but I knew you'd ... enjoy it."

He balanced the book over his forearm, gliding his other hand lightly over the page as if caressing the wanton queen for himself, feeling the pale silk of her flesh.

"Mark the queen's posture, Mary," he said, "how she has curled her legs over the swan's wings to take him deeper, how she's crossed her ankles to hold him there, where she can feel him the best. That's the way a man likes his lover to hold him, too, to show how eager she is for his prick. This picture's so cunningly done, I'll wager you can almost feel the queen's delight for yourself, can't you?"

"It's a fancy, sir." His sleeve brushed against her bare arm, and she shivered, even from so grazing a touch. "I can—I can see that."

She could see everything, and she could feel it, too, feel how her own body ached and yearned to find the same release that Queen Leda so desperately sought. It didn't matter how improbable the coupling in the illustration might be: it still made Mary long to experience the same degree of pleasure. Restlessly she pressed her thighs together, shifting her legs back and forth as if that false, empty caress could ever be any substitute for a genuine, passionate, flesh-and-blood lover, like the gentleman behind her.

"Yes, Mary, I knew you would," he said, leaning closer to whisper in her ear. "I knew you'd— Hah, sweetheart, what is this?"

To her mortification, he'd discovered the goose's wing for dusting, tucked into her pocket and forgotten. He held the wing in his hand and laughed softly, for the connection between the swan and the feathered wing was too droll to overlook.

"Oh, sir!" She skittered away from him, flustered beyond measure by such a hapless reminder of her lesser station. "The wing's for dusting the books, sir, leastways that's what Her Ladyship requires, sir, the tops of the books the depth of the wing and no more, else I'll be turned out, and—"

"Mary, Mary, my own sweet Mary," he said, following her with the book still open to the picture. "You don't truly wish to run from me, do you?"

At once she stopped, her breath quickening. The sunlight that slipped through the slatted shutters made for a bright stripe to burnish his golden hair. Below that, his eyes were hidden in the shadows, a mystery to her, while his mouth was curved in an unreadable half smile.

He tapped the wing lightly across his lips, as if thinking. "You wouldn't be frightened of me, would you?"

"No, sir." She raised her chin. She would be brave. She'd not back down. Yet to have him question her this way was oddly exciting, continuing what he'd begun when he'd first shown her the picture. She felt her blood thrum and course through her body, and the now-familiar heat gathering between her legs. He did that to her, for her, and why in truth should she ever be fearful of that?

"I'm not feared, not of you, sir, not now, and not before," she said. "I was—I was shamed that you found the wing in my pocket, proof that I'd not been doing my task."

"Shamed because you were idle?" he asked. "For no other reason than that?"

"No, sir," she said, even as her cheeks flooded with the memory of how she'd been touching herself when he'd surprised her. "No other reason than that."

"You are certain, Mary?"

She looked down, avoiding his scrutiny, and saw the thick bulge of his cock in his breeches, lit by another slash of sunlight. If he'd excited her, why, then she'd done the same to him, and what a pretty game it was between them!

Slowly she raised her gaze to his, and smiled, deliberately daring him to question her more.

"Yes, sir," she said. "I am as certain of this as I am of anything."

He took another step closer, into the sunlight, so his eyes glinted green with a mixture of arousal, and of amusement.

"Then show me, Mary," he said softly. "Show me the truth."

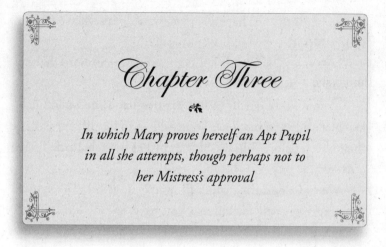

Chapter Three

❦

*In which Mary proves herself an Apt Pupil
in all she attempts, though perhaps not to
her Mistress's approval*

As Mary watched, Mr. Lyon tossed the book aside, and reached out to take her arm and pull her close. He turned her about so that her back was pressed to his chest and her buttocks nestled snugly against the front of his breeches, and his hard cock within. When she looked up, she realized he'd also situated them so they stood across from the looking glass, their combined image now filling the gold-framed glass, where earlier only her own had shown. He circled one arm around her waist, holding her there with him so she couldn't slip free.

But Mary had no wish to escape. He'd already stirred her blood with the picture and his lascivious observations about it, and now with his body pressed so intimately against hers, she could think of nothing else.

"Look at yourself in the glass, Mary," he whispered, his lips so close to her ear that each of his words teased the tender skin of her throat. "That's what you were doing when I found you, wasn't it?"

"Yes-s—s-s," she said, her confession scarce more than a shuddering sigh.

"I thought as much." With his free hand, he pulled her kerchief aside and eased her bodice down to free her breasts as they'd been before. Mounded high by her stays, her pale flesh quivered.

"Were you admiring yourself, sweet?" he asked. "Were you thinking what delicious breasts you have, so full and round? And that secret little heart of yours: was there ever a more positive sign of a passionate nature? All I have to do is bare your nipples and they harden for me. Look at them, Mary, as firm and red as little berries. Were you thinking of me, to make them stand like that?"

Not trusting her voice to reply, she only nodded, and tipped her head back farther, against his shoulder.

"You were, Mary," he said, lightly nipping at the tender spot beneath her ear. "You were, you wicked little cat."

He thrust his hips against the twin cheeks of her bottom, making her feel the hard length of his cock. Even through the layers of their clothes, his arousal was unmistakable. From instinct she moved against him, rubbing herself against his length in a wordless invitation that she still didn't understand entirely herself.

He groaned, pulling her closer. "It was the picture, too, wasn't it, Mary? That picture of the greedy queen, lying back with her legs open for more?"

At once the sinful image filled her head again, and as it

did, she gasped with fresh surprise. He'd taken the goose wing meant for dusting, and was slowing trailing the long feathers along the side of her throat.

Despite all the men who had admired her, she'd never thought of herself as beautiful before this. But now, because of Mr. Lyon, there was a rare wanton glow to her that even she couldn't deny. She looked ripe and beckoning as his tanned fingers drew the gray wing across her pearly flesh. Lying as she was against his shoulder with her breasts bared and full, her face flushed and her eyes heavy-lidded with longing, she could understand why the footmen loitered about her like bees around honeysuckle. What man wouldn't want to possess her when she was as enticing as this?

"Are you thinking of the swan, Mary?" he said, his voice a deep, rough growl. "Are you thinking how much Leda wanted Zeus, that she'd let herself be taken that way?"

How could she not think of it, when he did this to her? She squeezed her eyes shut, arching back against him as she offered herself to his caress. The pleasure was there again, making her feel swollen and wet and hot and so full of empty need that she could scarcely breathe. He drew the feathers along the side of her breast and beneath it, teasing her by tracing the feathers along the heavy curves before, finally, he drew them across the very tip of her nipple. She moaned aloud, the delicious torment too much to bear as she thrashed against him.

"Hush, Mary, hush, else you'll be heard." Swiftly he covered her mouth with his palm to muffle her cries, and she kissed it, tasting it for his scent, his flavor, taking impatient small nips with the edges of her teeth. He dropped the wing and caught a fistful of her skirts, pulling the linen to her waist and shoving it aside to bare her.

"Open your eyes, Mary," he ordered, his whisper hoarse. "I want you to see your face when I make you spend for the first time with me."

She looked, and saw: framed by the crumpled blue linen and her dark thread stockings, her thighs were creamy pale and quivering as his hand covered the neat patch of dark curls over her quim. He parted her knowingly, his fingers dipping between her swollen lips, opening her, gliding between the lips of her cunny to press and stroke the inflamed flesh within her. She sucked in her breath with a whimper, fretting, struggling both with him, and against him.

"Don't fight, Mary," he ordered. "Don't hold back. Let it come."

He pressed harder, deeper, and suddenly she couldn't have held back even if she wished it. The shuddering pleasure swept over her like a wave across the sand, carrying everything else away with it. She cried out against his hand as her knees buckled beneath her, and if he hadn't been supporting her, she would have slid to the floor, overwhelmed.

"There you are, sweet," he whispered, brushing aside a tumbled lock of her hair to kiss her nape. She could smell the honeyed fragrance of her pleasure lingering on his fingers, surely the most delectable fragrance in the world. "There you are."

She was exhausted, overcome, fuddled beyond measure by

what he'd just wrought upon her body. She turned to face him, curling her arms around his neck to shower him with the sweetest of kisses that he deserved. But there was nothing sweet about his kisses in return. His mouth on hers was rough, impatient, demanding more of her as he slid his hand once again beneath her petticoats to the still-inflamed flesh beneath.

With haste and urgency born of his own desire, he pushed her back against the nearest wall. His expression was fiercely determined now, without a hint of his usual graceful charm, and his handsome face was flushed and taut. He kissed her hard, as he would fair devour her, while his hands freely explored her person.

Briefly he ground against her, then drew back long enough to unbutton the fall of his breeches, and release his rampant prick. Mary's breathing was still ragged from her first spending and from anticipation of another, and her fingers trembled as she reached down to help him with the buttons of his breeches. Her shyness was gone, all modesty forgotten. She knew what would follow now—girls raised in the country among animals always did—and yet she neither struggled nor feared. Why should she? She'd found such delight in the first taste of pleasure and of love that he'd offered her that she was greedy now to plunge into the whole wondrous feast.

"Oh, sir, how I do love you!" she whispered fervently as he swept her skirts high aside. "How I—"

"Damnation," he exclaimed, abruptly drawing back. "Mark that! It's Her Ladyship's voice!"

Now Mary could hear the voices, too, for voices they were: his Lady Nestor, and her Lady Catherine, bearing down in the hallway towards them.

"Sweet faith, I'm ruined!" Mary shoved him away and frantically tried to put her clothes to rights.

"Here," he said, handing her the goose wing that had started so much mischief. "Pretend to be at your work. Haste, lass, haste!"

She hurried to the shelves she'd been told to dust earlier, while he retrieved the book with the picture of the wanton queen and shoved it back into its empty place in the case. Rapidly he raked his fingers through his gold-blond hair and tugged the front of his long waistcoat over the bulge in the front of his breeches, and altogether managed to compose himself just as the door behind him swung open, and the two ladies appeared.

"Here you are, sir." Lady Nestor sailed into the library with her skirts billowing about her, being of the opinion that if her panniers were sufficiently wide on either side of her hips, then the onlooker's eyes would be so distracted as not to notice her squat stature. "I'd begun to wonder if we should send out the hounds for you."

"Forgive me your distress, My Lady," he answered easily, bowing low over his leg. "But I was distracted—nay, even seduced!—by the excellent offerings of Lord William's library."

At that, Mary looked up sharply from her curtsy, startled he'd dare venture something so close to the truth. It couldn't be accidental. Surely he'd intended the second meaning for her secret amusement, no matter what the risk. He was counting on Lady Catherine's ignorance of at least one of her brother's books, just as he was counting on the two ladies not to guess exactly what kind of offering had been seducing him only minutes earlier. Oh, what a roguish gentleman, to play such a dangerous game. What a wicked, charming gentleman!

Yet here he stood with a book of sermons in one hand, smiling benignly at Lady Catherine, who smiled proudly in return.

"You are perfectly right, Mr. Lyon. You will find most excellent examples of piety within this room." Lady Catherine and Lady Nestor were ladies of a certain age, old friends but older rivals. Without husbands or children to inspire their jousting, they'd fallen to bickering over good works and religion—and now Mr. Lyon, as well. "I doubt you've found the like at Lady Nestor's house."

"Mr. Lyon has lacked for nothing at my house, my dear," answered Lady Nestor tartly. "Not a single morsel."

Lady Catherine's smile widened; she was pleased at having taken first blood. "To be sure, you have been most generous with what you had to give. But my late brother was so known for the depth of his theological collection that learned clergymen came clear from London to view his volumes."

"Please, please, my ladies, no strong words on my account." Mr. Lyon held up his hand up for peace—the same hand, thought Mary, that had stroked her so cunningly. He'd not looked once at her since the other women had entered, as was to be expected for a gentleman, nor had the two ladies taken note of her, either. Servants were meant to be as good as invisible to their betters.

But Mary understood. In a way, having to remain silent with her head bowed until she was noticed was a blessing. She doubted she could have managed more even if he'd wished it. Her knees still trembled beneath her weight, her heart continued to race, and there between her legs, she was acutely aware of the warm cream of her spending, as if Mr. Lyon himself were stirring her still.

"I've no doubt of this collection's fame for piety, My Lady," he continued, with an extra little nod for Lady Catherine's benefit. "There is much here on these pages to inspire even the most inexperienced."

Of course by way of inspiration, he must have meant the picture of Leda and her ravishing swan, and at that Mary gulped, an odd, throttled sound that was perilously close to a laugh.

Lady Catherine wheeled around to face her. "Whatever is the matter with you, girl? You're not ill, are you? I can't have you above stairs with us if you're poorly."

"Do you hope to catch this gentleman's eye with your foolishness, girl?" Suspicious, Lady Nestor glared at Mary, as fiercely possessive of Mr. Lyon as any hawk with her chick. "You won't be the first slatternly chit who's dared, you know. But you'll not succeed. No, no! Our Mr. Lyon won't be tempted by the likes of you—that is certain."

"I'm sure the lass means no ill will, My Lady," Mr. Lyon murmured, stepping forward to come to Mary's defense. "All the while I've been here, she's shown the greatest industry at her occupation."

"Thank you, sir." At last Mary looked up, levelly meeting his gaze. As perilous as this teasing game of his might be, she'd take his challenge. To speak so outrageously before the two older ladies was shocking, yet the risk excited her as it did him. She felt emboldened by Mr. Lyon's attention, by his love, and she wanted him to see that she wasn't the same shy scullery maid who'd nearly dropped the tea tray at his feet. "I find much joy in the completion of whatever I am given to do, sir."

His green eyes sparked with appreciation, though the rest of his face remained carefully unmoved. "Joy is certainly one of the greatest gifts shared to man."

"Begging pardon, sir," Mary said, twisting the goose's wing in her fingers to remind him, too, "but joy is a gift to women, too."

"Don't be impertinent, girl," Lady Nestor said tartly. "You presume on this gentleman's good nature and tolerance. He is a saint, a veritable saint, and will not be influenced by a common creature like you."

Lady Catherine sniffed with disdain. "I am sorry, friend, but the error is due as much to Mr. Lyon's youth and experience in the world as it is Mary's presumption. He must become more firmly aware of his place in society, just as Mary must know hers. If he is ever to lead a congregation of his own, he must learn that permitting such familiarity with the lower orders is no real kindness to any of them."

Mr. Lyon made a small bow of concession. "Pray forgive

me for differing with you, My Lady, but my goal as to the welfare of any young person such as Mary—that is your name, isn't it?"

"Yes, sir," Mary said, bobbing another curtsy to signify her willingness to receive more of his welfare. "Mary it is, sir."

"I thank you, Mary," he said. "Regardless of the differences in rank, I regard it as my solemn duty to employ whatever means I must towards furthering Mary's education."

"Oh, sir, you're too kind," Mary said. "For certain, I cannot educate myself, not as you can."

He nodded, raising an admonishing finger beside his nose, where, thought Mary, he must surely—surely!—be breathing the scent of her spending upon his hands. "While some things can be done well enough alone, there are others that do require the participation of another to achieve true satisfaction and success."

"Be grateful, girl, and thank Mr. Lyon for what he wishes to give you," Lady Nestor prompted, jabbing her furled fan into Mary's arm. "There's not many gentlemen so generous at sharing their knowledge like this with a serving girl."

"Yes, My Lady, I am," Mary said, purposefully looking at Lady Nestor instead of Mr. Lyon, from fear she'd laugh aloud at this entire preposterous conversation. "He'll always find me most willing."

"'Self-knowledge is a science to which most persons pretend,'" he intoned, clearly quoting from some other source, "'but, like the philosopher's stone, it is a secret that none are masters of in its full extent.'"

Lady Catherine studied him closely. "Pray, whose words

are those, Mr. Lyon? While I can accept that sentiment is your own, surely the words belong to another?"

"Why, my dear, I wonder that you do not recognize it," cried Lady Nestor, eager to seize the advantage again. "That is the opening line of 'Original Sin,' an essay by that esteemed divine Augustus Montague Toplady. A most wise gentleman is Mr. Toplady, and a righteous one, too, in the Calvinist persuasion."

"Toplady!" exclaimed Mary, astonished, and unable to keep silent as her amusement bubbled within her. "Top-*lady*, sir?"

"Yes, you ignorant, impudent creature," said Lady Nestor severely. "Mr. Toplady is a gentleman of enormous reputation, known for his beauteous hymns. Surely even you have heard *Rock of Ages*?"

"There will be opportunities enough to educate Mary regarding the rewards of Mr. Toplady," Mr. Lyon said, holding up a book he'd taken from the shelf. "But my first responsibility today is this edifying sermon on the nature of mercy, if you will but permit me to read it aloud."

"Mercy," Lady Catherine said with awesome satisfaction, as if she'd invented the concept herself. "What a fine subject for our discourses today!"

A smile from him, accompanied with the prospect of a sermon in the garden, and the two ladies were soon cooing like a pair of plump, contented doves. He bowed them to the door, the two ladies preening with anticipation and having already put Mary from their thoughts.

But as soon as the others were safely in the hall, Mr. Lyon

paused and turned back. Gone was the solemn face, intent for the pulpit. Instead Mary saw the gentleman who'd promised her pleasure, joy, and love—LOVE!—beyond anything she'd known or dreamed. He grinned, and winked, then licked his tongue suggestively over his fingertips to taste her lingering sweetness.

And yet Mary's education had only begun.

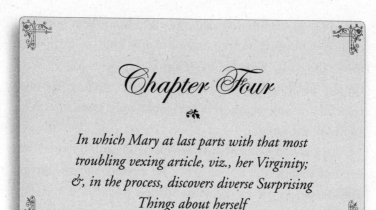

Chapter Four

❧

*In which Mary at last parts with that most
troubling vexing article, viz., her Virginity;
&, in the process, discovers diverse Surprising
Things about herself*

W ith the last grate in the front room swept clean,
Mary hurried downstairs to the kitchen. It
was nearly nine, the hour Lady Catherine
expected breakfast served for her and her guests. Mary would
need to shift her apron and cap and wash her hands of the
grate's soot before she could help carry the dishes upstairs,
where Mr. Lyon would be first to appear. If luck and fortune
were with her, she might even be able to steal a few moments
alone in his company. She'd not seen him alone since their
luscious exchange in the library three days before, though
there had been a good many scorching looks exchanged in
unaware company, and a single kiss—oh, what a rapturous
kiss!—stolen in the kitchen garden whilst Lady Nestor was
in the privy.

But beyond that, their opportunities were painfully few.

Clearly their betters were determined to keep them both too occupied by their various tasks for any kind of intriguing about the house, whether by design or accident. Mary's frustration and longing had grown with each passing day and wakeful, tossing night, and she could only guess that Mr. Lyon felt the same.

She grabbed her skirts to one side so she could hasten her steps, dropping the bucket with the cinders and sweepings outside the kitchen door. She hurried past Cook and the kitchen maid Susannah, already scrubbing vegetables for the servants' nooning.

"I'll wash, ma'am, and return for the breakfast trays." Mary untied her soot-smudged apron as she hurried towards the scullery to wash. The kitchen seemed strangely quiet for finishing the upstairs breakfast, and empty enough of waiting dishes that she began to fret. "Mr. Punch hasn't sent the footmen ahead, has he? He hasn't begun to serve?"

Cook made a small snort of disgust. "Where's your head, lass? Her Ladyship and the others took their breakfast an hour ago, each in their rooms, on account of riding out for the day."

"Riding out, ma'am?" Mary stopped, her apron hanging forgotten in her hands. "They're not here?"

"Oh, they left long ago." Cook pointed out the window with her knife. "Off to look at churchyards and headstones, Mr. Punch says. There, Mary, you can see the grooms tidying up the yard with the carriage and horses gone, and a sight less work for us today with the fine folk gone off, I say."

Disconsolate, Mary stared out towards the now-quiet stable yard. "They have all left? For the day alone, or longer?"

"The two ladies, and that pretty young fellow Mr. Lyon, what Her Ladyship brought with her, and as for how long they'll be away peeking at the dead folk in their graves, they're not about to tell me." With her doughy arm resting over the front of her apron, Cook regarded Mary curiously. "Now why should you be caring, Mary? Why should the to-ing and fro-ing of Their Ladyships matter to you?"

"It doesn't, ma'am." Yet the to-ing and fro-ing of Mr. Lyon mattered to her very much, enough to make tears of frustration sting her eyes. She knew how the gentry were, and how Lady Catherine and her party could just as soon decide to call upon another house, and remain there as guests for a fortnight, even longer. It wasn't inconceivable that Lady Nestor could decide not to return to Worthy Hall at all, but carry Mr. Lyon with her back across the county to her own house, where Mary would never see him again. Then what of love? What of passion?

"Mary?" Cook asked. "What possesses you, hussy?"

"Nothing, ma'am," Mary blurted. "Nothing—nothing!"

At that, she lowered her head to hide her tears, and bolted into the scullery to nurse her misery free from Cook's prying eyes and sympathy Mary did not want. She hurled her balled-up apron at the wall and buried her face in her hands, giving free rein to her misery. Last week she'd been eager to prove her industry in this new position, but now her place above stairs seemed as nothing, a worthless place that held no attraction.

Mr. Lyon was like a fever, a sickness, in her blood, and she could think of nothing beyond him.

"What is this, Mary?" Susannah entered the scullery, gently closing the door behind her. "Where is your usual cheer? What ails you, to weep so grievously?"

"I—I cannot say," Mary said, with fresh tears gushing down her cheeks. "It—it is not my sorrow to tell."

"Nay, but I can guess who's it is." Susannah took Mary by the shoulder and turned her about, forcing Mary to confront her. "I heard the footmen speaking of you and Mr. Lyon, how you permit him to kiss you, and to put his hands on you whenever Their Ladyships turn their backs."

"And what if he does?" Mary shook off the other woman's hand. "Mr. Lyon loves me, and I him."

"Love!" Susannah seemed to spit the word, as if it were the vilest sound in all the world. "Have you lost your wits? Consider your place, and then consider his, and ask how such a man could ever feel love for the likes of you."

"He is a gentleman," Mary insisted, "with a gentleman's fine regard for my well-being."

"All he's regarding is between your legs," Susannah said bluntly. "Has he had you, then?"

Mary raised her chin defensively, neither wishing to see her love for Mr. Lyon dragged through the tawdry tattle of the scullery, nor wanting to confess how little there actually was to it. "That's my affair, mine and Mr. Lyon's, and none of yours."

"Yours and Mr. Lyon's, not that he cares," Susannah

scoffed. "Why, you've no right so much as to speak your name together with his. That one looks after himself, and no one else. Do you think he'd toss aside everything he gets from Lady Nestor for you? Mr. 'Lyon,' hah. He's more like a flea, if you ask me. He'll ride on Her Ladyship's back as long as he can, until he can hop to another what's richer. Mark me, Mary. He's looking for a match that will make his fortune, and not some nameless little fool like you, neither."

"But he loves *me*," Mary insisted. "He swears to it."

Susannah clucked her tongue with disgust. "And what of that oath you swore to Lady Catherine about staying a maid? If the footmen and grooms are talking, then it won't stay a secret long. Once Her Ladyship learns that you've let that rascal tumble you, she'll turn you out directly, and you'll lose the sweetest place in this entire county."

"Mayhap I'm meant for more than this county," Mary said, for just as Mr. Lyon dreamed of playing his life on a grander stage, so now had Mary. "Mayhap I'm meant to find my fortune in London."

"In *London*!" Susannah exclaimed. "Sweet Heavens, Mary, where are your wits? There's only one way a woman makes her fortune in London, and no respectable female would ever choose it. Ruin and damnation, that's all that unwed women find for themselves in London."

"Not if Mr. Lyon and I go together," Mary said confidently. "Then I won't need—"

"Here you two are, idle as usual." The housekeeper Mrs. Able flung open the door. "Her Ladyship don't pay good wages so you hussies can loll about like the Queen o' Sheba. Susannah, tend to Cook's wishes. Mary, a fresh apron for you, then upstairs and make up the beds."

"Myself, ma'am?" Mary asked, surprised. Previously she'd only been permitted to make beds under the strictest supervision, to be sure that she'd follow Lady Catherine's orders and make the sheets tight and the tufted counterpane smooth.

"Aye, yourself, Mary, and who else would it be?" Mrs. Able shook her head with dismay, then clapped her hands briskly. "Hurry, hurry, you lazy chits! Just because Lady Catherine's not here don't mean her work's not to be done."

Swiftly Mary found a clean apron and hurried up the back stairs. Lady Nestor's chamber would be first, in the front of the house. Through the windows she could see the long drive, where Lady Catherine's carriage would have driven, carrying Mr. Lyon away from her, and as she turned to begin the bed, she sighed forlornly. Just knowing he wasn't under the same roof with her made her sorrowful, she thought, thumping and smoothing the pillows. At least the day matched her mood, gray and overcast and threatening rain, and a fine, grim day for viewing dead folk in churchyards, too. What possessed Their Ladyships to judge that as sport?

Mr. Lyon's chamber made her sadder still for being so empty. It was much smaller than Lady Nestor's rooms, for though he was visiting Worthy Hall as a guest, he was still considered only slightly more than a servant, and considerably less than a true gentleman. Still he slept in a proper bedstead, with proper hangings and pillows and a soft woolen coverlet, with beeswax candles in the candlestick beside his bed and scented soap beside his washbowl, and for Mary, at that time, it all seemed as luxurious as a palace.

Yet as soon as Mary flipped up the sheets, she was struck by his bodily scent, rich and masculine, that still clung to the linen. She closed her eyes, breathing deeply and imagining he was there with her. The picture in her mind's eye was so strong, so vivid, that she groaned aloud with her longing, and threw herself onto the bed. She buried her face in the sheets, rolling wantonly across the bed as she imagined him in this same bed, his beautiful manly body in repose as he slept. If only she could find a way to creep down here at night to join him, and together find the bliss that both so desperately desired, if only she might—

"Mary?"

She gasped and sat bolt upright, convinced she must be still imagining. But there in the doorway stood her own dear Mr. Lyon, his handsome face as astonished as her own must be.

"Oh, sir, forgive me," she said, sliding from the rumpled bed. Apologies for trespassing came without thinking to maidservants like her. "I was only making up and tidying, sir, and didn't expect you to come back so soon, or—"

He smiled, to put her at her ease, and also to show he understood the enormous good fortune that seemingly had tumbled into their laps. "Are you alone, sweet?"

"Oh, aye." Mary nodded eagerly, for good measure. Already her initial guilt was subsiding, replaced by an altogether different emotion. To have him here now, in his bedchamber with her, was like one of her most delicious dreams come to life. "The others are working below stairs today, on account of you and Their Ladyships being abroad. Or did they return with—"

"I left Their Ladyships at an inn, drinking tea," he said. "I was sent back to gather warmer cloaks for them against the coming rain."

He closed the chamber door and latched it. "And so, Mary, we are quite, quite alone."

"So we are." She grinned, settling back on the edge of the unmade bed. "You will not be missed?"

"In time, I suppose." He tossed his cocked hat, then his jacket, onto a nearby chair. One by one, he began to unfasten the small thread brass buttons on his long waistcoat. "But until then, we've time enough."

Fair bubbling with excitement, Mary eased herself farther back across the bed, resting on her elbows to watch him undress. The shoes, the stockings, the waistcoat, and the breeches all were shed with astonishing speed, and she chuckled with delight to see parts of him that had been so long hidden now to her finally revealed. His legs were strong and brawny, his calves and forearms knotted with muscle from riding. As he unwrapped his neck cloth, she could glimpse the curling hair on his chest. She could see, still hidden by the long tails of his shirt, the proud, blunt outline of his prick jutting out stiffly from his body.

For *her*.

"Come, lass, don't leave everything for me," he said, already breathing hard with anticipation. "Or must I do all the work, eh?"

She laughed again, tugging away her cap so her hair uncoiled, spilling over her shoulders. Then she raised and bent one leg gracefully, letting her skirts fall back over her coarse dark thread stockings to silken pale skin above. Inexperienced though she was, she'd already come to understand the effect that such gestures had on him. Without looking up, she heard him make an appreciative little grunt. She smiled at him over her bent knee as she reached down to unbuckle her shoe, but his patience was gone.

"Come here, Mary," he said, the words little more than a rough growl of desire. "Holy fire, I'm hard as steel for you."

He was on her before she scarce realized what was happening, and pushing her back into the tangle of sheets. He kissed her with an urgency she'd not yet seen from him before: no sweet finesse, nor gentle wooing, but only a man driven towards possession. He was heavier than she'd imagined, too, heavy and large and much, much stronger than she.

Yet as she twisted beneath him, the first shock of surprise faded into something altogether different, her blood heating and her heart racing. This was different from all the teasing torment of the past, all the stirring and diddling that had kept her so on edge. *This* was what she wanted, what she craved, and as he shoved her petticoats over her hips, she in turn pulled his shirt clear. After so many days of preliminaries, he'd little left to squander on her now. He drew back for a moment, opened her with his fingers, stroking her quickly to ease his way as he directed the head of his cock to her cunny.

She caught her breath, both with pleasure and amazement. She'd caressed his member and the heavy sac beneath it with her fingers before, of course, but his staff felt entirely different this way, pushing into her, filling her, stretching her open. He slipped his arms beneath her legs, lifting her hips to drive with a more determined rhythm. She caught her breath at the heady, unfamiliar sensations racing through her, and arched up to look to where their bodies were joined. She watched him flex his hips, burying himself impossibly deep in her, only to slide out, glistening with her juices before plunging back inside her again. Surely there could never be a more fascinating sight, and she gasped, left without words to explain what she was feeling.

Without a thought she began to move with him, following his motions as neatly as if he were her dancing master. To her surprise, the more she responded to him, the more her own pleasure built, the same pleasure she'd come to crave so much when he touched her. The same, yes, but a hundred times—a thousand times!—better.

She felt none of the pain that virgins were supposed to experience, and none of the weepy regret that plagued the innocent in ballad songs (and in that single much-thumbed romance in the servants' quarter). A quick sting, and her maidenhead was gone, with no further trouble than that.

Instead there was only that delicious tension, spiraling from her quim through her entire body, more and more tightly. Now, when he groaned as he worked her harder with his cock, she answered with cries of her own, her legs wrapped tightly around his body and her fingers digging tight into his shoulder, desperate for the release that seemed to just elude her.

"Here, Mary, here," he gasped, taking one of her hands between their bodies, to feel the sticky flesh where they were joined. "Make it better."

Holding her fingers in his own, he rubbed her hand over her swollen lips and the little nub between, and at once she felt as if she'd exploded with delight, her body thrashing and tossing beneath his with the power of their coupling.

"Ahh, sir," she said afterwards, with her eyes still blissfully shut, "have we time to do that again?"

"Permit me time to recover my resources, sweet." He rolled off her to one side, propping his head up on his bent arm. He was breathing as hard as if he'd run a footrace, his hair clinging damply to his forehead. "And tell me true, Mary Wren. You told me you were a maid, that I'd be your first."

Her eyes flew open. "I am," she said indignantly. "Rather, I *was*."

He smiled, though not perhaps with the openness nor the charm that she could have wished. "Forgive me, sweet, but there was a ... ah ... a *freedom* to your performance that I cannot countenance as that of an innocent."

"You dare to doubt me!" She pushed free of him, clambering up onto her knees. She pulled her skirts up again, and there was the unspoken proof she needed in her defense: a streaky smear of blood mingled with his own seed to stain the white linen. "Now tell me I lie, sir. Tell me I tried to deceive you!"

He stared down, his face full of fresh wonder. "That is truth, Mary," he said slowly, "for I happened upon you by accident, and such a thing could not be planned. I must beg your forgiveness."

"'Tis granted, sir," she said, though barely mollified. "Though well I might ask you if you're in the habit of debauching virgins, to be so knowing?"

"Hardly." He reached out to trail his fingers over her bare thigh, unable to keep from touching her. "But for you to show such a gift for the arts of Venus, that my mistake must be forgiven."

"A gift, sir?" Mary frowned, not sure if this were a compliment or not. She'd enjoyed herself famously, that was true, and if he would but stop chattering, she was eager to repeat the exercise again. "I do not understand, sir."

"'Tis simple enough," he said thoughtfully. "Some women are adept at making quince jam, or embroidering the covers of footstools. But you—you fuck like a goddess, Mary."

"I do, sir?" Surely being likened to a goddess was a compliment, and her humor improved. "A goddess?"

"Venus or Aphrodite, whether you prefer her Roman incarnation or the Greek," he said. "The rapturous goddess of pagan love."

"Love, sir," she repeated fondly, ignoring the pagan part. "So you do love me, sir?"

"I just proved that, didn't I?" he asked. "Ah, Mary, Mary, I've never had another woman like you."

That made her chuckle happily. Fancy her being a goddess of love! All her life she'd been faulted for what she couldn't do properly and for what she lacked. It was a wondrously fine thing finally to be told she had a gift—a rare gift, too—that set her apart from other women. To be sure, it was hardly the sort of gift that would be widely recognized by others, but if it pleased Mr. Lyon, well, then, that was well enough to start.

Her hair trailed around her face and his as she leaned down to kiss him. "Perhaps it was only you, sir, that made me seem so skillful," she suggested shyly, "being an excellent teacher."

"That could have much to do with it, aye," he admitted proudly, puffing out his chest like the rooster who has just hopped from a hen's back. "Yet there's a rare quality to you that I cannot put into words, Mary. You are beautiful, to be sure, but the world is full of beautiful women who are cold as turnips beneath a man. Not you. It's how you're fashioned, as if you were born to please every sense."

"Maybe I was," she said thoughtfully. "I've no knowledge who my parents are, or what they meant me to be. Lady Catherine found me without any markings or notes at all."

"Well, then, blood from Mount Olympus explains it," he said, idly slipping his hand inside her bodice to fondle her breast. "You're a lost by-blow of mighty Zeus himself, cast upon the English countryside to wreak havoc on mortal menfolk. I'd wager this cunning little heart of yours is proof enough, a kiss from the deity himself."

He followed his actions to his words, and kissed her birthmark, and he teased her roseate nipple, too, for good measure, and to make her sigh and wriggle afresh with delight.

"You burn so hot, sweet," he murmured, "that it's a wonder I'm not reduced to a cinder."

"Fah, sir, that would be a pretty waste," she whispered, laughing as she began to stroke his cock back to attention.

"I'd have to sweep you up with the rest of the dust when I cleaned the grate."

He smiled, his eyes turning hazy. "No more 'sir' between us, sweet. Call me John, as others do."

"Then I shall call you Johnny," she said, "to be unlike any other you've ever known."

He laughed, even as he began to move against her hand. "You are that, my dear Venus."

She watched him through her lashes, delighted by this new familiarity. "I'll always be what you— Oh, merciful Heavens, sir, listen. Listen! I hear Mr. Punch calling my name!"

She could not recall ever moving so swiftly. In an instant, she'd twisted back her hair and restored her cap, and shaken down her skirts, while John had collected his clothes from their scattering on the floor, and bunched them in his arms before he ducked inside the tall clothes press. The door opened, and all Mr. Punch saw was Mary snapping the sheet back in place over the feather bed.

With the corners of the sheet in her hands, she curtsied demurely. "Yes, Mr. Punch?"

"Have you seen Mr. Lyon, Mary?" the butler asked crossly. "Has he been here?"

She widened her eyes. "Not here, Mr. Punch." She wasn't exactly lying, either. John wasn't exactly *here*, but over *there*.

"Blast that infernal young fellow," Mr. Punch grumbled. "He came up these stairs to retrieve certain belongings of Their Ladyships, and has yet to return, while the carriage still waits for him at the door."

"I cannot imagine where he might be, Mr. Punch." She

didn't have to imagine, because she *knew*. Lord, how ever was John keeping from laughing aloud, to hear himself discussed in this way? "But if I see Mr. Lyon, you can be sure that I'll tell him he's wanted."

"That's a good lass, Mary," Mr. Punch said. "I can't keep that carriage waiting all morning on his pleasure. Tell him that he's to come directly, mind?"

Mary smiled serenely, as if beneath her skirts she wasn't still dripping wet and swollen eager for more of whatever Mr. Lyon could offer her. She was the goddess of love, wasn't she?

"Oh, aye, I'll do exactly that," she promised. "I'll be certain to see that Mr. Lyon comes directly, and no mistake."

And la, how she meant to make him do it. . . .

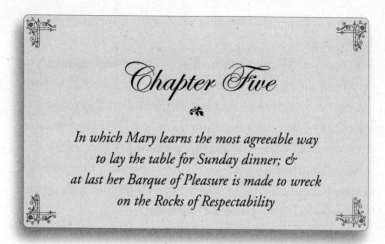

Chapter Five

*In which Mary learns the most agreeable way
to lay the table for Sunday dinner; &
at last her Barque of Pleasure is made to wreck
on the Rocks of Respectability*

A n old saying in the country states that there's no
use weeping over spilt milk. Meaning, of course,
that after something has been done that cannot
be undone, all the lamentation in the world will be of little
avail, and that it is far more useful to continue onward in life
without looking back.

So it was with Mary in the fortnight that followed her
deflowering by John Lyon. Not once did she lament her own
spilt milk, or lapse into melancholy reflection over what she'd
given up with such eager abandon. Instead it was as if by losing her innocence, she'd been granted admission to a far
greater world of sensual pleasure and adventure, with John as
her agreeable guide. Her long-ago pledge to Lady Catherine
was as forgotten as if it had never been sworn. To Mary, it

seemed as if there was nothing whatsoever to regret and every-thing to glory in.

These two weeks became a constant adventure of excess, made all the more exciting because she and John had to keep at least a modicum of decency. He would read sermons and poems to Their Ladyships one moment, then steal away to consort with Mary. Because all their time together was stolen, they squandered little of it on conversation or pretty compli-ments, but instead flung themselves at once into each other's embraces like wild, possessed creatures.

One afternoon he'd taken her in the dairy, where her hot flesh had warmed the chilly marble sill beneath her, there amidst the earthy scents of fresh cream and butter. Another evening, they'd met in the apple orchard, where on a whim Mary had curled herself inside a gardener's wheelbarrow and flipped her skirts over her raised bottom, gleaming in pale invitation in the moonlight.

More daring still, they'd returned to the library one after-noon when the ladies were resting in their rooms before din-ner, and while John had sprawled in one of Lord William's leather armchairs, Mary had swiftly unbuttoned the fall of his breeches to free his rampant prick. She'd climbed aboard with groans of pleasure that she smothered into his shoulder, her knees spread wide over the padded arms of the chair as she rode him deeper, deeper. Wickedly he'd called that frolic "Mrs. Toplady," after Lady Nestor's favorite clergyman, and doubled the sinfulness by reading one of that learned gentle-man's sermons aloud after dinner, when Mary was helping clear. The danger of discovery was the added spice to their couplings, and only served to spur them on to be more daring, more reckless.

It was, of course, an ill-kept secret among the staff. Within days there were few who had not guessed that Mr. Lyon was dallying with Mary Wren. Though none spoke to Mary directly of it, she could tell readily enough by how they'd fall silent when she entered the room, or send looks of disgust or scorn in her direction, with the housekeeper Mrs. Abel the most scornful of all.

But likewise Mary realized that Mrs. Abel would much rather ignore her intrigue with Mr. Lyon than turn her out because of it, and then be forced to find her replacement. Further, for the housekeeper to reveal to Their Ladyships what everyone else knew would cause great suffering to both Lady Catherine and Lady Nestor, and likely end their long acquaintance, and for what purpose? No, Mary would have wagered a week's wages with confidence that Mrs. Abel and Mr. Punch had decided to keep their silence in the matter so long as it was possible, for the good of Her Ladyship.

Yet the fact that Mary could comprehend her situation so thoroughly, and with such cynical common sense, demonstrated how much she'd altered since she'd become Mr. Lyon's wanton. She'd become more worldly, albeit more worldly for her tiny corner of the world. Likewise his praise had given her her first taste of true awareness, and she found she worried less of the opinions or judgment of others, and more for simply pleasing herself. She'd not become bold or slatternly, or begun painting her cheeks or lips, or stopped working hard at completing the tasks about the house that she'd been given to do.

It was a more subtle change than that. While she dressed in the same modest linen gown and kerchief that belonged to the Hall, her every movement had acquired a languid grace and confidence that made her plain dress more alluring than the golden silks of a pasha's houri. She'd ceased to be flustered at silly things or giggle nervously. It was as if she'd changed from girl to woman in a matter of hours, rather than years, and had at last grown into the rare beauty that before she'd worn like a tied-on mask. Half in jest and half in despair, John had predicted that men would willingly ruin themselves for a night in her cunt. She had smiled, but she hadn't laughed, and for the first time she'd begun to dream of a life far beyond the warm brick walls of Worthy Hall.

So potent had her attractions become that Mr. Punch was loath to send her unattended on errands, from fear she'd be kidnapped by Gypsies. Mr. Lyon was the envy of every man, high and low, in the county, or at least those who'd heard he'd come to possess such a jewel. The other maids who'd long been Mary's girlish companions now shied away from her, as if fearful of being tainted.

But Mary knew otherwise. She wasn't tainted; she was blessed and happier than she'd ever been in her entire life. She was, after all, a goddess of LOVE, and she'd only begun to discover her power.

* * *

On every Sunday, the entire household of Worthy Hall was expected to attend the small church nearby together for worship. Lady Catherine felt most strongly about this, and no excuses were tolerated. Of course, the house and its fires could not be left alone, especially not with Sunday dinner to be served at the old-fashioned country hour of three of the clock. Thus, one house servant was designated each Sabbath to remain at home, a different servant each week, so as to make sure no one person's soul was put in undue danger.

At the end of the month, it fell to Mary to remain alone at home. From the front window, she watched the carriage with the two ladies and John Lyon, followed by a wagon with the female servants and Mr. Punch, and the footmen, gardeners, grooms, and stable boys loping along behind on foot. It was not a long way to the church, and because the day was warm and bright, the air of the party was more festive than reflective, especially among those farthest from the carriage, and as Mary watched them leave, she wished she, too, were among them. Though she was now more at ease in the rooms upstairs, she'd never liked being alone, perhaps from being a cast-off orphan at birth, and she found the house a vastly echoing and lonely place when she was the only one in it.

Dutifully she did everything about the kitchen that Cook had left for her, and adjusted the weights on the clockwork spit to make sure the roast continued to turn evenly before the fire. She fed bread crumbs to the three canaries that were Cook's pride, there in the hanging bamboo cage by the window. She poured a dish of tea and spread Mr. Punch's London newspaper out flat on the table to read, devouring the news of the grand folk, and what they'd worn to which ball at the palace.

Would those be the kinds of balls John would attend when he went to London? she wondered. He'd sworn that was what his life would be like, once he'd left Lady Nestor and made his own fortune. Would she be invited, too, hanging on his arm in a rich silk gown with rubies around her throat? Ah, how much more pleasurable this time alone in the house would be if only she'd her Johnny to keep her company!

When she heard the tall clock in the hall upstairs strike the hour, the chimes thudding twice in the empty house, she put the paper away, and latched the kitchen door. Her last responsibility could not be avoided any longer, and reluctantly she climbed the stairs to lay the table for dinner, whistling as loudly as she could to give herself courage in the empty house.

Painted in shades of green with yellow coverings on the chairs, the dining room overlooked the flower garden. The tall windows were open to catch the breezes, and the richly indolent fragrance of roses warming in the summer sun filled the room.

Mrs. Abel had left a fresh cloth on the table, still folded from the press, and with great care, Mary spread it across the polished mahogany top. Lady Catherine was most particular about presenting a perfect, pristine tablecloth, particularly on the Sabbath, and Mary used the flats of her palms to smooth the cloth even on every side, and to avoid making extra creases or rumples in the snowy linen. She took the chairs from the walls, carrying them as she'd been taught so as not to scratch the floorboards, and set them at the table: Lady Catherine's at the head, with the others for Lady Nestor and John, and for Reverend Graver, who, so long as his sermon was pleasing to Her Ladyship, was always invited to join them for dinner. With no one to see, Mary bent and kissed the seat of John's chair, a secret little tribute that made her smile wickedly. If she longed for him to amuse her now, how much more he'd wish for her when he'd be trying to keep awake in this solemn company!

Next she began to lay each place with pieces from the sideboard: a fork, a knife, a spoon, set with the shining bowl turned upwards, a square plate of creamware with a folded napkin upon it. At last she stepped back critically to consider her work, and as she did, she glimpsed the figure of a man in the round looking glass over the mantle, her Johnny, stepping through the garden door behind her.

She was always struck anew by how handsome he was each time she saw him, for surely if he judged her a goddess, then he in turn could have posed for a young Adonis, his features were that regular, and full of manly beauty and charm. The sunlight licking at his golden hair like a halo, with small curls clinging moistly to his forehead from the heat of the day.

"Ah, love!" she exclaimed, turning swiftly about to throw her arms around his shoulders. "I didn't hear the carriage."

"That's because I couldn't wait to see you again, Mary." He tipped her back into the crook of his arm, kissing her as hungrily as if they'd been apart for weeks instead of hours.

"You left church for me?" she asked breathlessly, titillated more than she'd admit by him taking such a risk on her behalf.

"The service was done," he said, sliding a deft hand inside

her bodice to caress her breast. "Her Ladyship had invited another to dine, and I offered to return to the house ahead of the rest to make sure you'd set another place at the table."

"How kind of you," Mary murmured as she arched into his caress, relishing the heat that he was already stirring within her. She shifted her own hand lower, to the front of his breeches. He was already hard for her, and languidly she rubbed against him, feeding her own arousal as well as his. "Another lady, or a wicked rogue like you?"

"Only a dry, pompous stick of a fellow, a captain from the Indies trade." He caught his hands low on her hips, his fingers spreading over her buttocks as he pulled her closer and fitted himself against her. Eagerly she separated her legs, and even through the tangle of her skirts she could feel the heat of his cock pressing against her cunny. "Captain Tidwell will have nothing to interest you, sweet. Nothing like this, eh?"

"Why should I so much as glance his way, when I have you?" Lightly Mary nipped at the lobe of his ear. "Have we time, my Johnny? Have we time enough?"

"There's always time." He kissed her harder, more deeply, making her dizzy from the taste of him. "Hell, Mary, I can never keep away from you."

"Then don't," she whispered. Blindly she began unfastening his fall—hah, the new skills she'd acquired!—her fingers nimble over the double row of buttons. Her reward sprung forward through the tail of his shirt, his cock sleek and velvety and hot, its winking eye weeping for her. She dropped down to her knees, meaning to lave and torment him with her tongue, but instead he caught her in his arms and pushed her backwards.

"Here," he said, lifting her onto the edge of the dining table. For one dreadful moment, all she could consider was how she was sitting on Lady Catherine's fresh Sunday cloth, wrinkling it beyond salvation and use, and at the empty end of the table dedicated to Lord William's memory, too.

Then John was easing her legs apart, sleeking his palms along the insides of her thighs, and she forgot the crumpled linen beneath her. He feathered her open, finding her passage already slick and ready for him. She reached down between their bodies to help guide him in, and shuddered with pleasure as he pushed hard, filling her in a single deep thrust. She tilted her hips, rocking back on the table with her bent arms for support, and curled her legs high over his arms to take him deeper still.

Her cap had slipped forward over her brow, and as she shoved it away, she had a quick, bewitching sight of the two of them in the round mirror, her blue skirts spread like an open flower against the white tablecloth, her pale legs crossed over the back of his dark dress coat as he pumped into her. She was aware of the scent of their sex mingling with the heavy perfume of the roses, of her cries and his groans and the dull drone of the fat bumblebees bobbing at the windows.

His thrusts grew shorter, more relentless, and she gloried in his strength, flexing her own muscles to caress him from within. He bent his head over hers, his eyes squeezed shut as he concentrated, and a single bead of sweat dropped from his forehead to her cheek. She could feel the inevitable pleasure tightening within her, and her hands clutched the tablecloth beneath her, making unconscious, exuberant rosettes of the white linen between her fingers.

She was closer now, so close, the glittering prize almost within her reach. She opened her eyes again, meaning to watch their reflection in the glass as they spent.

And instead saw the horrified faces of Lady Catherine and Lady Nestor, and her own ruin besides.

That same day, Mary was turned out from Worthy Hall.

Her last time before Lady Catherine was not pleasant. Her Ladyship was so angry that her chins shook with rage as she sputtered every third word, yet still it was enough to curse Mary soundly as the worst kind of ungrateful, blasphemous, unrepentinent, wicked, whoring, Devil's own bitch. Mary was permitted to keep the blue gown, not from any generosity, but because Lady Catherine wished none of her other girls ever to wear such a foul, filthy, defiled garment.

She was given only a handful of minutes to collect her few belongings from her room into a worn linen bag, and then forced to watch as Mr. Punch searched through those same belongings to make certain she'd stolen nothing from the house. She was offered no parting wages, nor a letter of reference or introduction towards future employment. She was forbidden to say farewell to any of the other servants, for fear she'd corrupt them, and as Mr. Punch marched her down the back stairs for the last time, it was as if the house and everyone (as much home and family as she'd ever known) in it had already forgotten she'd ever existed.

Yet as she walked alone down the side of the long road towards the nearest town (scarcely more than a village, really, but because the place was called Worthington after Lady Catherine's family, it was likewise called a town, a peerage among villages), she resolved to keep her head high, and her spirits, too.

Truly, matters could have gone far worse. She'd not been beaten, whipped, or branded, all of which Lady Catherine would have been perfectly in her rights as her mistress to do. She'd not been given over to the county magistrate to be tried for licentious behavior and condemned to the stocks, or even transported to some fearful distant colony. Her only punishment seemed to be her freedom, which was, in truth, no punishment at all.

Doubtless, John had been tossed from his comfortable situation as well, for the wrath of Lady Nestor had burned even hotter than Lady Catherine's. Mary's last glimpse of him would be one that she'd never forget: his being dragged from the dining room by a pair of footmen, even as he tried to hold his still-unbuttoned breeches in one hand and deflect the vigorous blows of Lady Nestor, acting far more like a Billingsgate fishwife than a peer's relict.

Mary sighed, and wiped away a stray tear from her eye. It wasn't fair, of course. None of this was. To be punished and cursed for doing no more than what they'd all been put on this earth to do was cruel, barbarous cruel. But now she and John would have a chance to chart some new course together, the way he'd always promised to her. The stage stopped at the tavern in Worthington, and from there every brave journey must begin.

To London, she hoped, and Mary's spirirts rose just to imagine it. Glorious, glorious London, a place more welcoming to a goddesses (and gods) of love than Devonshire had been.

She heard the little cart coming up behind her, the donkey's hooves and the cart's two wheels crunching on the gravel, and she stepped to one side, onto the grass. As she did, the cart slowed, and stopped.

"Mary Wren!" Old Abraham, the most ancient of the grooms from Lady Catherine's stables, motioned for her to climb into the cart with him and a half dozen baskets of apples from the orchard. "I'm sorry it come t'this, Mary Wren, that a lass so fine as you must needs walk."

She hesitated. "If Her Ladyship ever learns you stopped for me, Abraham, then she'll turn you out, too."

"Nay, she won't dare," he scoffed, shifting his pipe from one side of his gums to the other. "I can take you so far's Worthington, if that's where you be bound."

"Thank you." Mary scrambled up onto the board seat beside him, her little bundled bag in her lap. "I pray that Mr. Lyon has someone so generous as you, carrying him there to meet me."

"Ohh, Master Lyon won't be meetin' you, nor any other lady for a good long while, Mary," Abraham said. "Didn't they tell you that at th'house?"

"Tell me what?" Mary asked, her uneasiness rising. "What has happened to Mr. Lyon?"

"Nothing, Mary," he said, sliding a little closer to her on the bench. "Only that if you're bound for th'town, Mr. Lyon be bound for th'Indies. Lady Nestor gave him over t'that sea captain Cap'n Tidwell for his crew."

"The Indies!" gasped Mary, horrified. Even here in Devonshire, she knew that the Indies lay clear on the other side of the world. "How can she do that?"

"Ahh, Mary, Mary, you know the noble folk can do anything they please with the rest o' us," he said, resting a bony, consoling hand on her knee. "In Her Ladyship's eyes, he sinned mightily, an' now must pay."

"But it was only because he loved me!" she cried. "It was my fault, not his!"

"There now, there now, it's not the end o' th'world," he said, taking advantage of Mary's distress to slide his gnarled hand higher, from her knee to her thigh. "Leastways this be better than if she gave him to th'press gangs. Now they say th'poor young gentleman's locked in th'gaol for th'night, then off to sea on th'morrow. You was his last frolic ashore, Mary."

Mary shook her head, unable to believe that such a grim fate could befall her dear Johnny. "Oh, I cannot believe that such a— Hah, Abraham, *Abraham,* enough of *that*!"

She shoved his hand from her leg, glaring at him.

"Don't be so high an' mighty wit' me," he said, unperturbed. "We all knows what you are now."

"I'm Mary Wren, thank you," she said tartly, "and that's no different than it ever was."

"And I'm thinkin' it is, Mary." He glanced at her shrewdly. "You'll see. I'll not be the only one what thinks that once th'loaf's been cut, then another slice shared here or there won't be missed."

"And I say you're wrong," she declared. She grabbed the little bundle of her belongings, and jumped down to the road from the lurching donkey cart. Astonished, the old man looked over his shoulder to see her making a mocking curtsy in the dust behind him.

"Good day to both you old asses!" she shouted, turning about to reverse the curtsy and flip her petticoats towards him with her bottom in the air towards him. "I'm Mary Wren, aye, and I'll do whatever I please, and whatever pleases me!"

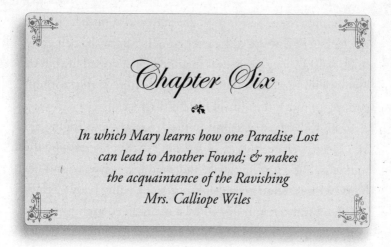

Chapter Six

*In which Mary learns how one Paradise Lost
can lead to Another Found; & makes
the acquaintance of the Ravishing
Mrs. Calliope Wiles*

I t was dusk by the time Mary reached Worthington, the fireflies darting through the tall weeds and the stars beginning to show in the dark blue sky. At once she repaired to the gaol, with the hope of seeing John. The gaol was a tiny building not far from the blacksmith, a stout brick box that housed the gaoler as well as two cells for prisoners, poachers and drunkards being the usual occupants. Before this night, it had struck Mary as neither ominous, nor gloomy, but now as soon as she'd entered, she understood the sorrowful truth of everything Old Abraham had told her of her lover's fate, and felt the bleakness of the gaol's despair.

"So you're the Jezebel that ruined that young gentleman, eh?" The gaoler seemed to stand seven feet tall at the very least, his feet wide spread and his arms folded over his mountainous chest as he blocked Mary's path. She edged to one side, hoping to see past him to the cells, and at once he shifted to block her view, the ring of keys jingling from the belt at his thick waist. "They say he was intended for a blessed life before he met you. Haven't you done enough to him, harlot, without coming to mock him further in his disgrace?"

"No, sir." Mary was already tired, hungry, and frightened of a future that seemed to be growing more uncertain by the moment. She'd lost her lover, and she'd lost her place and her home with it. She'd been called every vile name Lady Catherine could muster, and pawed by a man old enough to be her great-grandfather. To add this great hulking bully of a gaoler to the rest seemed more than anyone should be expected to bear, and she fought against the sharp sting of tears welling from within. "That is, I've no wish to mock Mr. Lyon."

He grunted. "How old are you, hussy?"

"Sixteen, sir," she answered. If she wished to see John, she'd have to use her wits with this man, and now he'd just given her the key she'd needed. She bunched her skirts at her sides and dipped into an awkward, girlish curtsy to seem younger still. "Just, sir."

"Sixteen." He shook his head with disgust. "That bastard should've known better than to dawdle with a lass so young as you."

"Yes, sir." The gaoler was relenting—she could sense it—and he'd chosen her side over John's. She wasn't surprised, either. For all his righteous palaver, the man had been ogling her as freely as any other male from the instant she'd opened the door.

She sighed piteously, clasping her hands together with what she hoped was a suitable display of contrition. "Be merciful, sir, oh, I beg you! A few last moments with Mr. Lyon is all I ask, a few minutes to beg him his forgiveness and mercy for my—my wickedness."

"Wickedness, eh?" he said, his interest growing. "How much will you offer me to see your sweetheart again?"

Mary swallowed, unsure of how far she was willing to play this game, even for John's sake. "I've no coin, sir."

"It's not coin I want." He reached out towards her bodice, his fingers like greasy, fat sausages. "Are those bubbles of yours as pretty as your face, eh?"

"Aye, sir, they are," she said carefully. "But you've told me yourself that I've already ruined one man's life today, and I'll not add yours to my conscience, on account of tempting you too far."

His hand froze, just over her breast. "Temptation," he muttered, warring with himself. "The chit's temptation."

"I am, sir," Mary quickly agreed. "I'd be worse for you than Eve was for Adam, sir."

"Spake like Eve in the Garden." He groaned with regret. "I should make you beg for mercy on your knees for that, chit, I should. But I won't. Come, this way."

He led her through the door to the next room, divided into two mean cells by an iron grate. There, sitting on the straw-covered floor, was her bedraggled captive lover. By the single hanging lantern, she could see that his clothes were wrinkled and dirty, his golden curls had lost their habitual black silk ribbon, and there was a bulging plum of a bruise on his left cheek from where he must have battled with one of the footmen, or perhaps Lady Nestor herself.

"Mary!" he cried, rushing to the grate to her. "How did you come to be here?"

"That doesn't matter, not now," she said, pushing her arms through the iron bars to reach him. "Oh, Johnny, my Johnny, what's to be done? What's to become of us?"

Behind them the gaoler laughed cruelly. "You should've thought of that before, hussy."

"A few moments alone with the lady, sir," John asked, drawing himself up to be as imposing as he could. "That's not so much to ask, is it?"

"A few moments, sir, please, oh, please!" Mary cried, letting her tears finally spill over. "A few moments alone together, and then no more!"

"Ah, you break my heart," the gaoler scoffed. "But this I'll do for you. I'm off for my dinner, across the way. That time is yours, until I return, with a small condition."

"Anything, sir," John vowed, but Mary, who'd learned better, laid a cautionary hand on his through the bars.

"It's only a small precaution, you see," the gaoler explained. "I cannot leave your harlot here on this side of the grate, where she could cause any mischief, but I can't put her in there with you, either, because she's never been given over to me as a prisoner. But I've an answer."

He took a set of wrist irons down from the wall, and before either Mary or John could protest, he'd clapped one cuff around Mary's left wrist, threaded the chain through the bars, and locked the other around John's right. Then he set an hourglass on the head of a barrel nearby, where they both could see it.

"I'm a hungry man," he said, turning the glass so the tiny grains began to race downward, "and I don't linger at table. When this glass is done, rest assured I will be, too, and your time with it."

He laughed then, delighted with his own solution, and was laughing still as the gaol's door closed after him.

"Oh, Johnny, my Johnny." Her words were rushed, driven by her awareness of the racing grains of sand. Through the haze of her tears, Mary looked at her hand doubly joined to John's, their fingers twined together with the heavy iron cuffs dragging down their wrists. "How can I ever tell you how sorry I am to have brought you to this?"

"You did nothing, Mary," he said softly, "except be my own weakness."

If he tipped his face, he could just reach her lips with his through the bars: not the most satisfying of kisses, but still Mary found it wrenchingly romantic, and more arousing than she would have guessed. She pressed closer, desperate to reach more of him as her cheeks were crossed by the chilly bars.

"But if I'd never met you," she whispered, "never tempted you, then you'd not be here."

"If I'd never met you, Mary, I'd be less a man." He reached through the bars, tracing the curving underside of her breast. "This isn't the way I'd have chosen it to end, but it's not so bad as it could have been. They say there's plenty of ways for an Englishman to grow rich and sleek in India. I could return to cover you with rubies and sapphires, and an elephant to ride upon."

"But it will be so dangerous!"

"Life can be dangerous anywhere." His fingers spread beneath her breast, cradling it, as his thumb unerringly found her nipple, rubbing until it stiffened through her linen bodice. "Perhaps this is what Fate has intended for us from the beginning. The French are better at partings like this than we English: they never say good-bye, but *au revoir*, until we see one another again."

"I *will* see you again, Johnny," she said with poignant determination, even as she arched her breast through the grate to meet his teasing fingers. "This will not be the last time, not for us, not in this life or the next."

He nodded, kissing her again. "I'll sail to India, and come back a Pasha, while you will go to London, and become a queen."

"I'll wait for you," she said breathlessly. "Until you come back."

"No talk like that, now," he said softly, "nor swearing other promises you cannot keep, nor will I burden you with any such from me. We've each of us our fortunes to make in this world, however we can. I could be gone for years, or never return at all. How could I expect you to keep all this lovely flesh of yours locked away in cotton wool for me until then?"

Sadly Mary nodded. Neither of them had been graced by the happy accidents of wealth or rank, or families of any sort. If she wished the glorious future in London, then it would be by her own doing, and no one else's. Her only dowry was her beauty, and the passionate nature that had come with it, and that was even now making her rub herself so shamelessly against his hand.

"If I were the heroine of a ballad song, I would be true to you, Johnny," she said, slipping her unshackled hand inside the band of his breeches. "I would wait and wait forever for you, if I had to."

"If you were the heroine of a ballad song," he countered, pulling her bodice lower to free the aching flesh of her nipple for his tongue, "then you'd have brought me a magic key to open these locks, and a horse with wings to carry us to freedom, or at least Scotland."

"But I've better than that, don't I?" With her single free hand, she pushed the fall of his breeches open, freeing his cock. She curled her fingers around its warm, hard, familiar length, brushing across the blunt, velvety head, and sliding down to cradle the heavy sac beneath. "You see, I have a magic sword."

He chuckled, pressing into her hand. "Magic, is it?"

"Oh, aye," she said, teasing him as he'd teased her. "From next to nothing, it can grow to the most prodigious length. It can change from being as soft as warm butter, to the strength and mettle of Sheffield steel."

"It won't carry us from this place." His breath was quickening, his eyes heavy-lidded by the lantern's light.

"Not to Scotland, no," she admitted, "but it's always taken me to a most fine place before."

He glanced at the spilling hourglass and grinned wolfishly. "You are certain, Mary? Here?"

"If it pleases you." She flicked her tongue against the edge of her upper teeth, a suggestive small gesture that she'd discovered inflamed him no end. "We did not finish this afternoon, and I would give you something better to recall me by until the next time when we—we— What was that pretty French word?"

"Au revoir." Link by link, he used the cuff on his wrist to pull her closer to the grating. She closed her eyes, trying to remember everything of this moment for the time they'd be apart, and he kissed her hard, with purpose. She gasped as her bared breast with the tiny heart birthmark brushed against the cold iron bar, her nipple tightening further.

"You like that," he whispered. Before she could answer, he'd pulled the other side of the bodice down as well, then drawn her close to the bars again, letting her feel the chill press into her warm flesh as he kissed her again. She fluttered against him, her pleasure feverish and palpable, and in return she felt how his hips jerked, pushing his cock more firmly into her hand to show he wanted more as well.

It must be a dance now, she realized, a dance between partners. Deftly she raised their joined hands, the chain clattering between them, and dipped beneath, releasing his hand long enough for the cuff to spin on her wrist. As soon as her back was turned to his chest, he reached through the bars to her petticoats, lifting and shoving the linen aside to reach her. She slid her feet apart, opening her legs to him, and as he threw her skirts over her hips, she felt the cool air, her skin prickling with the chill and the anticipation.

She bent forward, giving him more access to her most intimate self. He stroked her, opening her, and she shuddered, knowing he'd found her cunny swollen with longing, wet for his cock. He knew, too, how aroused she was to be doing this here, by the light of a smoky tallow lantern in the cell of the Worthington Gaol, and oh, how she was going to miss his cock and his devious inventions for inflaming her like—

"Lower, Mary," he ordered hoarsely, and she obeyed, raising her shackled hand higher to give him the angle he needed. She felt the head of his cock pushing into her, claiming her with delicious thoroughness until he could go no further. With his free hand on her hips to steady her, he began to move. She cried out with each thrust, letting him know how much she needed this and him. It wouldn't take long, no matter what the hourglass said, and as she felt her crisis nearing, she arched her back to take him more deeply.

And it was then she finally saw the jagged piece of a looking glass, propped on a brick in the opposite wall. The glass was set there and angled for a purpose, so that the gaoler might be able to sit in his front room and only needs glance up to survey his prisoners, without leaving his chair. But now the gaoler was using the scrap of glass to spy on them, his face mottled and intent in the reflection as he watched, and worse, other men were with him, shadowy faces in the mottled glass, all turned to watch and desire *her*.

With that, she came, the pleasure ripping through her so keenly that she would have fallen.

She never learned if John had realized they'd been watched. They'd scarce time to catch their breath when, with a great amount of bluster and heartiness, John's new master, Captain

Tidwell, fair burst into the gaol. He was weary of land and had decided to leave for the coast now, traveling by moonlight, instead of waiting until dawn, and he'd come to collect his prisoner. He'd frowned mightily when he'd discovered Mary there, too, and the gaoler's mischief of chaining them together. The captain declared that doing so was as good as binding a bottle to a drunkard's hand, or tossing a diseased libertine into the pox house.

Yet all it meant to Mary then was that the moment of farewell had finally come, and as soon as the gaoler freed her wrist from the heavy cuff, she felt only the first agony of separation. As John was released and led away, she struggled to reach him one last time, for one final embrace, but the gaoler himself held her back.

"Johnny, my love, my love!" she wailed frantically, tears streaming down her face. "Oh, please, I beg you. Do not take him from me!"

Unable to resist, John tried to turn towards her, but the captain's sailors held him firm. He, too, wept, not caring who saw the tears on his cheeks as the two burly-armed sailors hauled him to the top of the carriage.

"Be strong, lad. Don't weaken now," the captain advised sternly as he climbed inside. "Better to cut away the poison clean than to let it fester any longer."

"Don't forget me, Johnny!" Mary cried as the driver flicked his whip over the backs of the horses. "I'll always love you, my own Johnny!"

"*Au revoir,* Mary," he called, his voice breaking with the burden of his emotions. "*Au revoir,* my love!"

She wrenched free of the gaoler, running after the carriage. She'd a final glimpse of Johnny's golden hair in the moonlight as he turned back to see her one last time, her first love, her Johnny; then she caught her toe in a wheel rut and fell forward to her knees in the dusty road. The carriage was rumbling beyond her reach, and so was John Lyon.

She rose unsteadily, not caring who saw her cry, staring inconsolably after the vanishing carriage. Why should she, when she'd not a friend left in all England to care what became of her now?

"Are you the maidservant dismissed by Lady Catherine Worthy, of Worthy Hall?"

The lady—for she did appear to be so—was standing in the road beside a tall liveried footman, holding a lantern like a beacon. She was not much older than Mary herself, and rapturously beautiful, with silver-white hair and a kittenish face, and even more rapturously and beautifully dressed. Even by the wavering light of the lantern, Mary could see clouds of pale blue satin and creamy lace, darker blue ribbons clustered like scattered flowers, and pearls as big as gooseberries around her throat and hanging from her ears. Since the lady had appeared so suddenly beside her on the darkened road, Mary wasn't even sure if she were real or imagined.

"Perhaps you did not hear me," the lady said again. "Are you the maidservant everyone's speaking of at the tavern, the one so cruelly dismissed this day by Lady Catherine Worthy?"

"Aye, ma'am, I am." Belatedly Mary curtsied, unsure of what else to do. Of course they'd be speaking of her at the tavern, and speaking the vilest of calumny, and she flushed with misery to imagine it. But what could they have said among so much foul slander that would possibly interest a lady such as this?

"Well, then, so you are the ill-famed maidservant," she said. "That is good. Fitz, raise the lantern so I might view her more properly."

Obediently the footman stepped forward, washing Mary in light, and making her squint and raise her hand to shield her eyes from the brightness.

"No, please, don't hide your face," the lady said. "If you're to be of any use to me as my friend, I must see if you're as lovely as they say."

Mary dropped her hand. "Use, ma'am?" she asked warily. "What use could I be to you? And how can I be your friend?"

But the woman was too occupied in studying Mary to answer her question. "Smile, so I might see if you've all your teeth. A small thing, I know, but gentlemen can be most demanding about that."

Dutifully Mary smiled, for, because she was country-bred, her teeth were as white and even as the pearls around the other woman's throat. With the hem of her sleeve, she wiped away the mingled tears and dust from her face, trying to make as brave a show as she could.

"They said at the tavern that you were a foundling," the lady continued. "Is that true?"

"Aye, ma'am," Mary said. "But I do not see how—"

"No inconvenient brothers or uncles who might appear to defend your dubious honor?"

Mary shook her head, bewildered by this questioning. "Forgive me, ma'am, but I do not see what—"

"What is your name?"

"Mary Wren, ma'am. Lady Catherine named me that herself, from want of knowing what my mother intended."

"No doubt what she intended was for a better Fate than to fall into the intolerant hands of the righteous Lady Catherine," the lady said wryly. "But we shall change that now, won't we?"

"Forgive me, ma'am," Mary said, thoroughly confused by now, "but I don't know if we'll be changing anything, or how, either."

"If you agree, we will," the lady said, and smiled, a smile full of promise and delight. "My name is Mrs. Calliope Wiles, and you will but place your future in my hands, I can assure you that you'll do nothing—nothing!—but prosper."

Chapter Seven

In which Mary begins her journey to London;
&, whilst traveling, learns significantly more of
her beauteous new Benefactress, Mrs. Wiles

A s can be imagined, Mary had no notion what to make of an offer such as this. "Are you offering me a place, ma'am?" she asked. "Because if you are, you must know I've no references nor character to offer, on account of Lady Catherine not giving them to me."

"But the very fact that this odious Lady Catherine gave you none proves to me that you are most deserving to me." Miss Wiles drew a fan from the deep flounce of her sleeve and languidly began to flutter it before her face. "I have been looking for a young woman exactly like yourself for my household."

"You are, ma'am?" Mary could not believe her good fortune, finding a new place with such ease. "You would wish me?"

"I would." Mrs. Wiles smiled again, and might even have winked, though Mary doubted so grand a lady would ever resort to something so low and sly as winking. "I stopped here only so long as to change my horses, and now you see what good fortune has befallen us both!"

Thus it was that Mary soon found herself exactly as John Lyon had: sitting on the top of a carriage, sandwiched between two others as she rode away from her disgraced past in Worthington, and cheerily towards a new-minted future. Mary's two companions on the front bench were the carriage's driver, who wisely cared only for his horses and the road, and Mrs. Wiles's lady's maid, Turner, who seemed to wish nothing more than to sleep, swaying gently back and forth with the carriage's motion to lull her dreams.

Their silence was welcome to Mary. In half a day's time, she'd lost her place, her home, and her love, with nothing to replace any of it. Her whole being seemed to ache with loss and loneliness, more than she'd ever imagined possible, and far more than was right for any would-be goddess. She'd impulsively thrown in her lot with Mrs. Wiles, even though she'd still no notion of what her place or her duties with that lady would be. All she knew for certain was that she was being given her meals and a place to sleep for the next night, and that with every turn of the carriage's gold-trimmed wheels she was coming closer to London.

But for now, for Mary, nodding in the summer sun, that was enough.

"Careful with that, Mary," Turner advised, watching Mary pour the last bucket of steaming water into the large tub before the fire. "Mrs. Wiles is most particular about her water."

"Yes, ma'am." Mary nodded, wanting to make a good impression. She'd never been a lady's maid, and she was eager to learn the private niceties of as elegant a lady as Mrs. Wiles.

Certainly Lady Catherine would never have *arrived* at a stage inn with the flourish Mrs. Wiles had. She'd ordered her horses given the finest grain and stables and her servants fed whatever they pleased in the front room. She'd taken the best rooms upstairs all to herself, and had her own linens brought in from the carriage to replace the ones on the bed. She'd ordered a sumptuous dinner brought up to her rooms to dine privately, and a selection of wines, too. With solemn-faced Fitz as her escort, she'd gone out to walk beside a neighborhood river famous for its willows, carrying a fanciful white lace parasol with dangling yellow tassels, which had made others in the inn's yard crane their necks in marveling wonder.

While she was abroad wandering beneath the willows, she'd left orders that this tub be filled with water, as hot as could be managed, brought up directly from the kitchen fires, and of course she'd been obeyed. Mary knew, because she'd helped carry the heavy buckets up the back stairs herself.

"Does Mrs. Wiles wish us to do her washing now?" Mary asked, watching Turner wipe up the few drops of spilled water from the floor. The tub itself was like one of the water buckets grown large, the sloping oak slats bound together with an iron ring, and the inside draped and fitted with a cloth. An extra measure against leaking water, Mary decided, and cleverly done, too. She began to roll up the cuffs of her sleeves, and glanced around the room for the clothes for laundering. "I warrant she's most particular about her washing, to have the water brought up here."

Turner looked at Mary oddly. "Aye, I warrant she is."

"Likely Mr. Wiles feels the same, doesn't he?" Mary asked, in perfect innocence. Any gentleman who indulged his wife as freely as Mr. Wiles clearly did could expect to have his whims obeyed in return, or so it seemed to Mary. "If she is this particular, then surely she must be doing so to please him."

Turner wiped her hands on her apron, her expression carefully revealing nothing. "I'll not tattle about Mrs. Wiles's private affairs," she said. "Nor should you, if you wish to keep with this household."

"What must she do, Turner?" Prettily flushed from her exercise, Mrs. Wiles entered behind them, untying the ribbons of her hat and handing it to Turner. "I'll not have anyone forced against their will, not in my household."

Turner smiled, as if this all were a great jest between them. "She asked of Mr. Wiles, ma'am, and if you laundered your linens in this tub to oblige his wishes."

"Yes, ma'am." Mary made an extra curtsy, unsure of what else she should do. "Forgive me if I erred, ma'am, for I meant no harm by asking."

Mrs. Wiles laughed, a merry, pealing sound like bells. "Dear Mary! The water's not for washing linens. It's for washing you."

"Me?" Mary frowned, and shook her head. "I've no need of washing, ma'am, not in a great huge tub such as that."

"But you do," Mrs. Wiles said evenly. "You stink like a

brothel. Now come, shed those filthy clothes, and into the water you'll go."

At once Turner stepped forward, briskly beginning to unlace the back of Mary's gown.

"No, ma'am, no!" Mary cried, spinning about and backing against the wall. "That's—that's not washing proper, not like a Christian!"

"Then call me a heathen, for I'll not tolerate you the way you are." Mrs. Wiles's smile was pleasant but determined. "Either you remove all your clothes and climb into the tub, or you leave and do not return. I told you, I'll not force anyone against their will."

Still Mary hesitated. "I've not been naked before anyone," she said. "Not since I was a babe."

"Not even by that handsome beau of yours?"

Mary flushed, more with misery than shame at being reminded of her dear lost Johnny. "No, ma'am, not even by him. Our time together was always stolen, and we'd never enough for that—that freedom."

"Ah, well, I am sorry for that, for your sakes," Mrs. Wiles said. "To lie naked in the arms of an equally unencumbered gentleman, to feel his warm skin pressed against yours and how his member hardens with desire against your bare thigh, nudging into your quim, is one of life's great joys."

"Yes." Mary nodded, startled by the openness of this last speech. She'd never heard another lady speak like this of a gentleman, especially not one so elegant and refined as Mrs. Wiles. Yet she'd also never heard of anyone undressing to wash themselves in a tub, either, but perhaps such things were commonplace in London. London was a different place—nay, a different world!—from Devon, and Mary knew she'd do well to remember that. If her grubby shift and petticoats were the only impediment betwixt her and a lasting place with Mrs. Wiles, why, then she'd be a modest fool not to do as she was bidden.

Shrugging away Turner's assistance, she swiftly undid her lacings and pulled her gown over her head. She unbuckled her shoes, untied her garters, and one by one, rolled down her stockings, shamefully noting how much of the dust of the road had grimed her feet. Next she undid her stays and let them drop to the floor at her feet, and then her petticoats, puddling in a soft sigh of linen around her ankles.

"Go on," Mrs. Wiles said, watching her with more eager interest than Mary had expected. "Pray, do not stop on my account. Believe me, you will feel so much better once you are clean."

Mary nodded, and with a deep breath, she drew her shift over her head and dropped it with the other discarded clothes. Then she sat on the edge of the tub, catching her breath at the warmth of the water as she slid down the side. She slid down far enough to soak her hair, and flung it backwards, scattering droplets of water as she pushed herself back up. Mrs. Wiles was right: she did feel much better now.

"I'll attend you." Turner didn't wait for Mary to agree, stepping forward with a cloth for washing and a large ball of lavender-scented soap. At once she began scrubbing at Mary's hair so vigorously that Mary yelped and tried to duck away.

"Turner, my dear, please," Mrs. Wiles said quickly. "I think we'll let Mary manage on her own. You may go."

"Yes, ma'am." Turner curtsied, but the glance she gave to Mary as she left was oddly knowing. Mary frowned, not sure what to make of that, and began to wash herself briskly to cover her confusion.

"Don't let Turner dismay you, Mary," Mrs. Wiles said, stepping to the sideboard to pour herself a goblet of wine. "Her loyalty to me can become prickly. But now that we're alone, perhaps you'll not feel so shy with me."

"No, ma'am, not that—"

"Ah, you see, that's exactly what I mean," she said. "You must call me Calliope, not ma'am, if we are to be true friends."

"Yes, ma— Calliope." Mary smiled, thinking how vastly different this was from her relationship with Lady Catherine.

"How sweet it sounds on your tongue, my dear." She was pulling the pins from her hair, freeing the silvery locks to fall loose over her shoulders, nearly to her waist. "But then everything would. You are feeling more refreshed?"

Mary nodded, squeezing the water from her hair. She sank down deeper in the tub, watching how her breasts floated and bobbed on the water's surface, her nipples tight and rosy from washing. She could feel the water in her cunny, too, the warmth gently filling her, whispering between her lips in a most pleasing fashion. It was peculiar having a woman study her as avidly as Calliope was now doing, her lips parted and her gaze intent, almost as if she were a gentleman instead of a lady. Peculiar, yes, but also pleasing. Who wouldn't wish to be admired with such interest?

"You're practically glowing with contentment," the other woman said, pouring wine from the decanter into the tall-stemmed goblet. "How delectable you look, all moist and pink! What a shame your poor sweetheart's not here to see you like this."

"Yes," Mary said sadly. "Though most likely I won't see him again for years and years."

"True, true, considering how very far away India lies." She filled a second goblet and handed it to Mary. "You will drink with me, Mary, yes? As friends?"

Mary looked at the goblet. She'd never tasted any wine, let alone with Lady Catherine, but she'd be willing to try it, and besides, she *was* thirsty. She took it, and drank, finding the wine pleasantly sweet and agreeable.

"There now, let me fill your glass again," Calliope said hospitably. "Did you love him?"

"Oh, more than I can say," Mary said fervently. "How I miss him already!"

"That was how it was with my first love, too," Calliope said, her wide blue eyes filled with melancholy. "My gallant was as handsome as sin, and as charming, too, even as he coaxed my maidenhead away without so much as a by your leave. Ah, what a lovely cock that man possessed, and how bravely he knew how to brandish it, and make me spend until I saw Heaven itself!"

"Then what happened?" Mary asked with genuine interest. The wine had flooded through her limbs, leaving a delicious lassitude that made her feel even more at ease in Calliope's company. It was as if they were already old, dear friends, among whom such intimate confessions would be commonplace. "Did he stay true?"

"He was but a man," Calliope said ruefully, "and it's not man's nature to remain constant. He needed to advance himself by a fortuitous marriage, and I could not fault him for it. I faced much the same predicament."

Mary nodded, understanding completely. "So it is with me. We must each of us make our fortunes, with little room for love."

"How true, how true," Calliope said. "But no matter what cruel tricks Fate will play upon us, I have kept him always in my heart, here."

Impulsively she pulled open her bodice, baring one perfect white breast, and pressed her palm over her heart, as if pledging her fealty to her lost love all over again.

"What he gave me, what he did for me—that I shall always have, in my heart," she continued, her voice quavering with emotion. "He taught me of love, and he showed me the pleasure, the joy, to be discovered within myself."

Her voice dropped lower, reverential, and as if by explanation, she curved her fingers beneath her breast to cradle the flesh like a lover would. She brought her forefinger and her thumb together, and light lightly tweaked her nipple, making it stand at once.

"Yes, yes!" Mary exclaimed. "So it was with Johnny and

me! He took my innocence, true, but I gave it gladly in return for the pleasure he brought me, and taught me to seek for myself."

"Then you understand the complicated delights of the flesh," Calliope said, dropping to her knees beside the tub. "I knew from the moment I first saw you, Mary, that you and I were of a mind, destined for friendship."

She leaned over the edge of the tub and kissed Mary, sweetly, yet seductively, and it seemed not shocking, but the most natural thing in Creation. Without hesitation, Mary closed her eyes and parted her lips, and gave herself over to Calliope. Her tongue was quicksilver against Mary's own, her mouth velvety soft, and when Calliope reached forward to caress her breast, Mary mirrored her touch, brushing aside the long floss of her hair to reach the small, firm breast beneath.

"A moment, a moment," murmured Calliope, pausing to shed what remained of her own dress. She slung her bare leg over the side of the tub and slid down into the water, facing Mary. She leaned forward to kiss Mary again, her pale hair drifting over the surface of the water to tangle with Mary's darker locks.

"This is very cunning," Calliope said, lightly touching a fingertip to Mary's heart-shaped birthmark with unabashed fascination. "Clearly you've been branded by Venus, a sister of her wanton family."

"That is what Johnny said, too," Mary said shyly as the other lady traced her finger over and over the tiny heart, as if for luck. "He said it showed I was meant to be a goddess."

"A goddess of love, indeed," Calliope murmured. "Come, let me worship you, yes?"

She leaned closer to rub her breasts against Mary's, nipple over nipple, and Mary was astonished by the new sensations that flooded her body. She thought she'd known everything about carnal delights with John, but now she was realizing she'd only barely begun to experience the possibilities.

And as they kissed, she felt Calliope reaching down through the water to her cunny, opening her, rubbing her nub even as she slipped two slender, clever fingers into her passage. Mary gasped, clinging to Calliope as the pleasure built. Who would have guessed she'd feel this way not from a man's hand, but from a woman's?

"Here, here, put your legs up," Calliope ordered with breathless urgency. "This way, pet."

Splashing in the lavender-scented water, Mary did as she was told, bracing her feet against the side of the tub as Calliope did the same, their silken legs now intimately interwoven. Then Calliope took Mary's fingers and guided them to her quim, showing her how she liked to be touched. She twisted so she was pressing against Mary's thigh, riding it astride, and Mary followed her lead, twisting to slide the other woman's thigh between her own. She gasped as the unexpectedly exquisite pressure tugged and stroked at her cunny, magnified by the taut muscles of her own inner legs. Calliope grinned, and her head tipped back against the tub, arching her back.

"Together, Mary, together," she whispered as they reached their crisis in unison. "Oh, my dearest, isn't this fine!"

It *was* fine, too, much to Mary's astonishment, as wave after wave of delight racked her body and the bathwater splashed over the sides of the tub. It was different from what she'd experienced with John, yet the joyful, shuddering release was the same, something she'd never dreamed possible with another woman.

"There now, I told you we'd suit one another," Calliope said afterwards with a contented smile, fishing over the side of the tub for her wine. "I can always tell. Such fun we'll have in London!"

"Forgive me, please," Mary said, "but am I to be another lady's maid with Turner, or—"

"You're to be my companion, not a servant!" Calliope exclaimed incredulously. "What gave you such a notion? Have you looked in the glass, my dearest? Beauty so rare as yours should never be wasted on a servant, and when it is coupled with so passionate a nature— La, the plans I have for you, and for us!"

"What manner of plans?" Mary asked. She'd never heard of a place as a companion, but then she'd never heard of women pleasuring women, either. And if that were the most arduous task that she'd be expected to perform, then it would certainly be a step upwards from scaling fish and peeling carrots as a scullery maid. "And what will Mr. Wiles say to me being your—your companion?"

"Mr. Wiles?" Calliope laughed uproariously, sending little ripples across the bath water. "My darling Mary, there is no such article as Mr. Wiles. I've never been burdened with a husband, nor do I ever so wish to be. That title is a courtesy only, with no true goodwife's merits behind it."

Mary shook her head, bewildered. "I do not see how you can live in such a fashion without a husband."

"Oh, Mary, do not be such a noddy," Calliope scoffed. "I'm in keeping to the Earl of Rogersme. He is a kind and generous gentleman, and he makes my life as comfortable and agreeable as possible. Everything flows from him."

"Everything?" asked Mary in amazement.

"My house in London, my carriage, my clothes, my jewels, my box at the playhouse, the money I've put by for the future and that which I send to my mother in the country, even the very food I eat and the wine I drink," she said with a graceful, all-encompassing turn of her hand. "In short, everything."

"Everything?" Mary breathed, scarce able to imagine such a heady degree of everything-ness. "Everything?"

"Everything," Calliope repeated happily. "So long as I please His Lordship in his desires—which of course I do, to an extravagant extent—and play the part of his pretty accomplice sufficiently to make both his friends and his enemies sicken with envy, I'm rewarded."

"But do you love him?" Mary asked earnestly. "To be able to please him as you must?"

"Do you love me?" Calliope smiled slyly. "Yet I brought you great satisfaction, as you did me, yet we were as much as strangers."

Mary blushed, not for the first time. "But that—that was different."

"Was it?" Calliope winked. "It's not so complicated as that, dear Mary. Love is not essential for pleasure, any more than it is for marriage. Useful, perhaps, and certainly more enjoyable, but not essential. You can keep your love for your first sweetheart locked away in your heart, safe as in a strongbox until he returns to you from India, but the rest of you—the rest of your lovely self is yours to do with as you please."

Mary nodded, considering, and remembered how Johnny had advised her much the same thing. She was no fool, and she was beginning to understand exactly what kind of devil's bargain her new friend had struck. And yet, when she saw the rewards and the happy security that seemed to have come her way, it seemed less a gift from the devil, and more sent from Heaven.

"And you *are* rapturously beautiful, Mary," Calliope continued, idly toying with her wine goblet between her fingers and making it float on the surface of the water like a round-bottomed boat. "You cannot forget that, and anyone who tells you that beauty is empty and worthless and a sinful vanity offers false counsel indeed. Instead you must consider it as your bravest talent, like the Lord gave his servants in the parable. To bury yourself away in a dowdy servant's place would be a waste of your God-granted gifts. Far better to take your talent to London, and see how you can make it grow and prosper tenfold, or even a hundred-, just like that clever servant."

"I know that. It's Scripture," Mary said, impressed. Lady Catherine had always employed Scripture when she wished to make a point.

"Aye, it is," Calliope said, drawing the goblet back and forth through the water. "My father was a pious tailor, you see, and spouted Scripture with every stitch he took, all the day long. But recall what happened to that lazy, fearful servant who did nothing with his talent: he was cast out into the outer darkness, where he'd only weeping and gnashing of teeth to comfort him. I've never quite figured what teeth gnashing might be, but it sounds most vile and disagreeable, and I'd not wish it on you."

"I'd not wish it for myself, either," Mary said thoughtfully. All her life she had dutifully followed the path of obedience and righteousness that Lady Catherine had preached, yet the first time she had followed her heart, she'd been cursed and cast away, into as much outer darkness as could be found in Devonshire. She had, in short, always tried to be the good servant, and what had been her reward? Perhaps it was time to venture down that other path—even if only a step or two—to see what else Fate might have to offer an aspiring goddess.

"In London, the gentlemen will worship you," Calliope promised. "You'll see, Mary. They'll be crawling about at your feet, groveling for you to smile their way."

"Truly?" Mary could not quite envision that, but it was still something she'd like to see, just for sport. "At my feet?"

"Truly," Calliope declared. "On their *knees*. In London, you'll have your choice of men, and if you'll let me guide you, I vow by year's end you'll be as good as a queen."

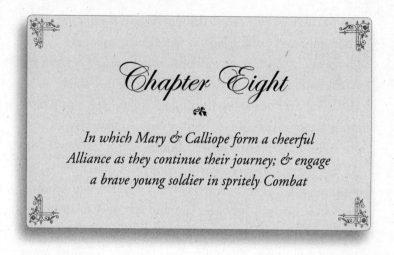

Chapter Eight

*In which Mary & Calliope form a cheerful
Alliance as they continue their journey; & engage
a brave young soldier in spritely Combat*

The next morning, Calliope chose clothes for Mary
from her own trunk. They were of a matching size,
and what had been stitched to fit the one likewise
suited the other, with only the most minor of adjustments.

First came a shift of cambric linen so fine that it high-
lighted, rather than hid, Mary's most intimate charms. Calliope's stays were fearsome constructions of buckram and
whalebone, hidden beneath a beguiling mask of pink damask,
but once they were laced snuggly around Mary's body, her
waist was fashionably diminished, her back drawn tight to
next to nothing, and her breasts raised high and round in the
most winsome offering imaginable. Wicker hoops tied at her
waist swelled her hips, and made her waist seem smaller still.

Over these underpinnings went a gown of cherry red
glazed chintz, scattered overall with roses, with lace about the
low neckline and the deep lace flounces at the elbows to add

grace to every gesture. Heeled slippers gave a seductive sway to her step, and coral beads at her throat, ears, and wrists added a saucy touch of vermillion. Turner dressed her hair in an artful arrangement of curls and knots, with a single love-lock falling over one shoulder. Pinned on top was a tiny cap, more a scrap of ruffled lace, with a flat cartwheel hat of leghorn straw and cockades of red ribbons.

Thus Mary had gone up the inn's back stairs the night before as a maidservant, in grimy linen with her hair braided and pinned beneath her plain cap and a bucket of steaming water in each hand. Yet by noon the following day, she came down by way of the front staircase as the fairest English lady, trussed and bound and powdered and curled and ready for delectable presentation to the world.

The world was ready to receive her. While Mary's rare beauty in its innocent, unvarnished state had always attracted attention wherever she went, this fresh gloss of privilege and fashion lifted her to giddy new heights. Both the innkeeper and his wife curtsied as she came down the steps with Calliope, as if they'd never seen her before, as if they'd not each given her a hard shove and a cross word the day before when she'd been underfoot in their kitchen. The other guests in the dining hall also rose from the benches and chairs to curtsy, and in the yard, as Mary and Calliope climbed into Calliope's carriage, three gentlemen pausing to change horses bowed and tried to engage them in conversation, which Calliope disdained.

"Why didn't we speak to them?" Mary asked as their carriage drove from the inn. "They were gentlemen."

"And what if they were?" Calliope unpinned her hat and settled back against the leather squabs. "The world is full of gentlemen, yet there are only two of us. We cannot possibly acknowledge them all."

"But gentlemen—"

"Do not expect every lady to greet them," Calliope said sternly. "Because we are beautiful, and because they are men first and gentlemen only secondly, they will try to address us. But because ladies seldom acknowledge men they do not know, it is far better for us not to speak to them than to do so, and far less work besides."

"I see," Mary said, though she didn't, and she sighed mightily. "Truly I have much to learn."

"Not so very much," Calliope said, holding up her fingers to tick off her reasons. "Ladies are more desired because they are more rare. If a woman is dressed like a lady and can behave with a modicum of common sense, then gentlemen will believe what they see, and treat her accordingly. A gentleman will always offer more for what he thinks he cannot have, because it will make him feel much the greater man among other gentlemen. It's not difficult, not really."

Where Calliope was concerned, perhaps it wasn't. But for Mary, who in the last fortnight had seen nearly every assumption and certainty in her life turned wrong side out, it *was* difficult, one more complication to unscramble for herself. But she was determined to make sense from it, just as she was determined to make a new life for herself with Calliope as her providential guide.

Her education continued as they rolled along through the

green countryside. She learned that what they'd done in the tub (and afterwards, again, in the large bed, their bodies still moist and smelling sweetly of lavender) was called tribadism, two women pleasuring each other by petting and stroking their cunnies; and that it was also considered wanton and cursed by pious folk, for being an unfruitful union and, worse, as idle witches' play.

To Calliope, the practice was no more than an amusing pastime when there were no willing cocks to offer better, but she swore that there were other women who by nature preferred their own sex to men in everything. She said that it was not only low women worn from brothel work and weary of the demands of men, but also many great ladies, the wives and daughters of peers, who, having been abandoned in the country by their husbands, turned to women friends for comfort.

"Was that why you took me in?" Mary asked. "Because His Lordship had sent you to the country?"

"Oh, hardly," Calliope said with a grin, reaching into a small compartment in the side of the coach for a decanter of wine. "Besides, His Lordship had gone off with his family, and I with mine. Their was no sending involved at all. In Worthington, I heard everyone at the inn speaking of you, of how wicked you were, and I knew we would be friends. And now we are. Lord, how vastly tedious traveling can be! Are you thirsty?"

Mary nodded, leaning from the carriage's window. For her, traveling like this was still a new, luxurious delight, with an ever-changing parade of sights and novelty for entertainment. And what she saw on the road ahead of them was entertainment indeed, at least for two young women who'd yet to see their twentieth birthdays.

"Soldiers, Calliope!" she exclaimed. "It must be an entire company, there are so many of them marching before us!"

"Soldiers?" At once Calliope was at the other window, kneeling on the seat to thrust her entire head and shoulders from the carriage. Blown by the wind, the pins began to pull free from her silver hair, with stray locks streaming out behind her. "I do love the red coats, don't you?"

The soldiers were marching in a neat row, six abreast to fit the width of the road, with three officers on horseback at their head. The sun shone on their bright red uniform coats, and glanced off their chalky white breeches and facings. Their brasses and buttons glittered like gold, and the officers' horses pranced and danced as if they were on review. The company must not have been going far, for they were without the usual ragtag assortment of wagons for baggage and supplies. Instead it was only the soldiers themselves, like the playthings of small boys, and girls like Mary and Calliope who liked soldiers.

"So many, and so handsome," Mary sighed. "And all the same wondrous height, too."

"I've heard they're chosen to match," Calliope said. "They're supposed to be as alike as peas in a pod, except for being in scarlet, of course, and men instead of vegetables. Tall, splendid, brave, and handsome. I wonder if they match in their breeches, too."

"What, their weapons?" asked Mary, laughing. "Their swords?"

"Nay, their *sabers*," Calliope said with relish. "They're British lions, Mary, and ready to display their rampant weapons, whether pike, pistol, or blade. Oh, if only we'd the chance to test their mettle!"

Was it any wonder that the two could scarce remain at their windows, from laughing so long and so hard at their own wit?

"How will we pass them?" Mary asked finally. They were coming closer now, each man becoming distinct from his brother beside him. "Will the driver take the horse about them on the grass?"

"We'll go down the middle, the same as always," Calliope said. "Look, they're already parting for us, just like the Red Sea for Moses. They have to stand aside for us. We're gentry, and for all they know, we could be peeresses, too."

Mary craned her neck, shading her eyes with her hand. "More like the Sea of Redcoats than the Red Sea. Shall we wave, and try to make them notice us?"

"Oh, I can make them notice us." Calliope sat back on her heels on the seat, and with both hands pulled the already-low neckline of her bodice lower still. Her tight pink nipples were bare, the white flesh of her breasts held high by her stays and framed only by a tiny ruffle of white lawn. She laughed gleefully, her breasts quivering in response.

"I'll cheer their spirits," she promised. "No eyes straight ahead for me!"

Giggling with anticipation, she waited until the carriage was passing between the two halves of the company, their peaked helmets as regular as a pale fence as they stood along the sides of the road. At last Calliope popped from the win-

dow, quick as a jack- (or jill)-in-the-box, her pale hair tousled
and her bare breasts bouncing as she waved.

"Huzzah, huzzah, my lads!" she cried merrily, the carriage
sweeping her past the astonished soldiers. "Huzzah, my hearty
fellows, huzzah!"

Not to be outdone, Mary yanked down her bodice to free
her own breasts before she, too, clambered up on the seat to
wave at the soldiers.

"Huzzah for the brave English lions!" she shouted. "Huzzah, huzzah for England and the king!"

The sun warmed her breasts, unaccustomed to such expo-
sure, and the passing breeze tightened her nipples like an invisible caress. But most exciting of all was having so many
men staring at her, a blur of tall, rough, brawny men in their
splendid uniforms, their faces showing admiration, amusement, surprise, and unabashed lust for her—for *her*. They
cheered and roared as the carriage rolled past, and Mary
laughed and waved in return.

Two months before, and she would have perished of shame
at the very thought of making such a display of herself. Two
months before, she would have passed through such a gaunt-
let with her head bowed and her eyes downcast in perfect
modest misery, exactly as Lady Catherine would have
wished.

Now, balanced on her knees in the rocking carriage, her
breasts bouncing like plump fruit in sympathy to the carriage's
motion, she felt like the most desirable woman in the kingdom. She gloried in her power, in the pleasure that her beauty
could offer to these men. In sympathy her cunny felt warm

and ripe as well, her lover's dew swelling within her and spilling down the insides of her thighs.

Hah, what these cheering men would say if they knew that! She'd seen several that had reminded her of Johnny, their golden blond hair so much like his, and she'd wondered if they'd resembled him in other ways, too. How many of them already had a cock stand hidden beneath their long waistcoats? How many would have been willing to put those cocks to use with both her and Calliope, if they'd stopped the carriage to make their choice?

At last they reached the end of the cheering company, the carriage racing onward and leaving them behind. With a happy sigh, Calliope fell back onto the seat across from Mary.

"Oh, mercy, what a lark," she said, exhausted, yet chuckling still. "Have you ever seen so many handsome rascals in one place?"

"I know," Mary said with a great sigh of longing. "But I find I'm monstrous *lonely*."

Calliope laughed, languidly stroking her own breasts. "*Lonely?* Is that what you call it?"

"Very well, then," Mary said, watching her friend touching her nipples, lightly strumming the hard little peaks with her fingertips, weaving beneath her tumbled pale hair. It was strange for Mary to realize that watching, too, aroused her, and she sighed again, restlessly wriggling her bottom against the soft leather cushions beneath her. "I'm warm."

"You're wanton," Calliope suggested. She raised her leg,

pointing one slippered foot until her skirts slipped up over her knee, showing off her yellow-striped garter. "*Very* wanton."

Mary nodded, and grinned. "Impassioned."

"Lusty." Delicately Calliope squeezed one of her nipples as if testing a berry for sweetness.

"Inflamed."

"Your blood's on fire."

"Yours would scorch any man who touched you."

"Lascivious."

Mary laughed. "Lord, that's a mouthful!"

"Here's another," Calliope said, raising her brows with relish. "Lubricious."

"Where do you learn those words?" Mary demanded, laughing. She couldn't tell if it was the words themselves that sounded so arousing, or the way that Calliope was saying them.

"From His Lordship," she said. "He's a clever, learned gentleman, and it amuses him no end to teach me new words for old things, especially when— Why are we stopping?"

"I don't know." Not sure of who or what could have caused the driver to stop, Mary hastily drew her bodice back in place before she leaned from the window. "Why, it seems to be another soldier."

Calliope did the same, and poked her head up through the window to look up at the driver. "Why are we stopped, Smithson? What is the reason?"

"Forgive me, ma'am, but it's my doing." A lieutenant stepped from the front of the carriage into view. He bowed stiffly, his face nearly as red as his coat. "I've been sent ahead of the rest of the guard on orders, yet my horse has gone lame, and I've been reduced to foot. If it pleases you, ma'am, I'd like to join your party and ride on the box into Tilham, the next town along this road."

"Gracious!" exclaimed Calliope with a great show of surprise. "Are you under orders from the king himself?"

The lieutenant's round cheeks seemed to redden even further. He was very young, perhaps even as young in years as Calliope and Mary, though it was abundantly clear to them both that he was much their junior in worldly experience. His babyish jaw had only a hint of downy beard, his voice broke despite his best efforts to control it, and his nails were gnawed to the quick.

"My orders have come from my superiors, ma'am," he said carefully, "and thereby ultimately from the Crown."

"Then we must obey you, too, mustn't we?" Calliope said, making her eyes nearly as wide as his. "I'd never wish to stand in the path of the duty of His Majesty's own officer."

"Thank you, ma'am." He touched the front of his black cocked hat, and began to climb up onto the box with the driver.

But Calliope had another notion. "No, sir, no, I won't hear of it," she called. "I cannot permit a loyal servant of the king to ride outside. You must ride in here, with Miss Wren and with me."

She waved to the footman, who jumped down and opened the door, also giving the lieutenant a full, inviting view of Mary and Calliope waiting within.

"Forgive me, ma'am, but I could not presume," he said,

swallowing so hard that his Adam's apple quivered in his throat. "I could not."

"Oh, yes, you can," Mary said softly. She'd drawn her fan from her pocket, and now opened it slowly, blade by blade, and smiled over the arching top at the officer, the way she'd learned from Calliope. "You wouldn't be presuming at all. You'd be our guest. Our most honored and courageous guest."

He made a wordless strangled sound of discomfort, his hand clutching at the hilt of his sword. Having ridden ahead, he'd no idea of the wicked mischief they'd just committed before his comrades. To him, they were only as they seemed, two young and innocent ladies in their carriage.

Mary's smile widened. This was almost *too* easy, really, but so amusing that she didn't dare look at Calliope. "Please come with us, sir. We'd feel so much more safe having a brave warrior such as yourself riding with us."

"Please, sir." Calliope reached out to lay one of her little hands on his arm, her fingers trembling as if with reluctance. "I'd hate to have to confess to your superiors that you'd neglected the pleas for protection of two ladies. Please us—oh, yes, please *me*—and come with us."

Swiftly Mary raised her fan over her mouth to hide the laughter she was sure was twisting her lips. But the officer had finally given in to their pleas, or perhaps he'd finally divined the prize that was being dangled so winsomely before him. He climbed into the carriage, the footman latched the door, and away they began, in every sense of the expression. He sat gingerly on the edge of the seat beside Calliope, fiddling with the scabbard of his sword as if it were a protective fence between them.

"If you're only with us until Tilham, sir, then we haven't time for ceremony." Deftly, Calliope pushed aside the scabbard so she could wriggle closer to him, her thigh pressed close against his. "I am Calliope, sir, and I am honored to make your acquaintance."

"And I am Mary." Mary changed seats to sit on the lieutenant's other side, making a neat sandwich of him with her friend. "Your servant, sir."

"Ah, and mine as well." Awkwardly he tried to bow while sitting, and only succeeded in knocking his hat from his head.

"Oh, you don't need that," Mary said, picking up the hat before he could and laying it on the other seat. "This way we can see your brave, handsome face more properly, Lieutenant—"

"Lieutenant Alfred Hunt, ladies." He chuckled nervously, his gaze darting from one to the other. "Forgive me for being so slow, but I say, this is dazzling company, eh?"

"Oh, indeed," purred Mary, slipping her hand as if by accident across his shoulder as she leaned closer to him. "The pleasure is all ours, you know. I'd warrant that a gentleman so handsome as you has more sweethearts than he can count."

"Of course he does," Calliope said, resting her hand on his thigh, her fingers spreading lightly as she moved her palm back and forth. "A gentleman like the lieutenant will be quite the gallant with the ladies."

"That must be why I'm all a-fluster, just sitting here beside him." Mary smiled winningly. The poor fellow was practically panting from anxiety and excitement, with little beads of sweat clustered on his forehead and his brows. It was strange, playing the role of the aggressor like this. In the past, with Johnny and with others, she'd let the men lead her, yet this was ... this was *fun*. She understood entirely why Calliope had invited him to join them for the sport of it. But Tilham was fast approaching, and they hadn't much time.

"I *am* a-fluster, too, Lieutenant." Mary took his hand—a damp, meaty paw, but no matter—and laid it over her breast, holding it there with her hand over his. "Can you feel how fast my heart is beating, sir?"

What he felt wasn't her heart, or at least that wasn't what he was likely most conscious of. At once his fingers closed over her breast, filling his hand with the soft, round weight of it. One instinctive shift of his hand, and he'd gone diving into her bodice to find bare skin, her nipple instantly hard against his rough palm. He'd no finesse, no skill, yet still it was a man's touch, and she wistfully remembered what she'd had with John Lyon, and what she'd lost, too.

But before she could wallow too deeply in sentiment, he was kissing her, a wet, slobbering kiss that seemed more like to drown her than seduce her. His mouth seemed to worry at hers, as if he'd never have his full, and as she kissed him in return, she thought of what a fine soldier he must make, so ready and eager to launch his attack.

Yet there was more to this kiss than made sense. He was jerking against her, plunging his tongue vigorously into her mouth, and gasping oddly, as if he'd somehow forgotten to breathe while he kissed her. Inexperience could excuse much, but not this, too. With their lips still furiously engaged, Mary opened one eye to see if perhaps Calliope was the reason for his peculiar behavior.

She was. To Mary's astonishment, Calliope had deftly unbuttoned the fall of Lieutenant Hunt's breeches to release his cock, and a tall, handsome cock it was, too. But she'd not been content simply to fondle and stroke his sturdy army musket. No: instead Calliope had burrowed her head in his lap and taken as much of his cock as she could into her mouth, her silver head bobbing up and down as she sucked him in more deeply.

Fascinated, Mary opened her other eye. No doubt Calliope was viewing this demonstration as yet another part of Mary's education (and likely a part of the lieutenant's as well). Who could have imagined such an act was possible? Did the man enjoy it more than spending in a woman's cunny, or was it only another possibility, much as she'd found her frolic with another woman?

Calliope's lips stretched around the young officer's member, his cock engorged and purple and glistening from her mouth as it slid in and out of her willing mouth. Her fingers grasped him at the base, playing over his ballocks, and from the way his hips were rising from the seat, it was clear that his crisis was near.

Abruptly he broke away from Mary's mouth, his face contorted as if in the utmost pain. His fingers tightened convulsively over her breast, hard enough to make her yelp with surprise just as he roared his release. Bellowing and thrashing his limbs, Calliope held him steady, taking his spurting seed into her mouth.

Mortified, it took him only a moment to realize what he'd done, and as quickly as he could, he pulled himself free of her mouth.

"Oh, forgive me, ma'am. That is, that is, ah, both of you," he stammered, trying to stuff his member, now limp and dejected, back into his breeches.

Calliope smiled wickedly, unperturbed, and wiped her mouth with her lace-hemmed handkerchief.

"There's not one jot to forgive, sir," she said. "Unless you find it unpatriotic to take your pleasure in the French fashion. If that is your concern, then you may simply tell your friends you met two English ladies willing to demonstrate their loyalty to the Crown."

The carriage had stopped, and the driver knocked on the roof overhead. "Tilham, ma'am."

"I must go," the lieutenant said, throwing open the door and half falling from the step. His shirt was still half untucked and his scabbard flapping against his thigh. It was a good thing that his superiors would not be here to greet him, for they'd guess at once what he'd been about.

"Your hat, sir," Mary called, reaching out to hand it to him. She'd yet to repair the disaster he'd made of her bodice, and as he took the hat, he stared at her breast like a man bewitched, his expression dazed and his mouth slack.

"There now, sir, make yourself proper." Trying not to laugh, Mary took the hat back from his hands and set it squarely on his head, then brushed her hands along the front of his coat to make him as spruce as she could. "Mind, you've orders to deliver, don't you?"

"Yes, ma'am." He gave himself a little shake, as dogs will do, and bowed to them. "Yes, of course. Your servant, ladies, and good day."

They watched him shamble off down the street, still trying to put himself to rights: as sad a sight as any well-spent man had a right to be.

Mary sighed as she restored her bodice. "Was that truly in the French manner, or an invention of your own?"

"Not even I could invent that," Calliope said, running her tongue along her lip for extra effect. "I've heard that is the only way that the French will love one another. But English gentlemen do enjoy it to distraction, too, as should you, for the power it will give you over them and their cocks."

"Does His Lordship like it like that?" Mary asked curiously.

"He is a man, no more, no less. Of course he likes it." Calliope shrugged extravagantly, still watching the lieutenant. "Consider that sorry, bedraggled fellow. What a tale he'll tell his fellows this night!"

"They won't believe a word of it." Mary smiled slyly. "Or perhaps they will. We shall be famous, you know. The wanton harlots of Tilham!"

"Oh, bah," scoffed Calliope. "You wait until we reach London, and then, Miss Wren—then!—you'll learn exactly what fame can be."

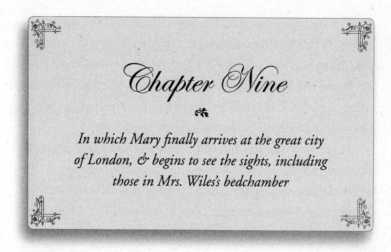

Chapter Nine

❧

*In which Mary finally arrives at the great city
of London, & begins to see the sights, including
those in Mrs. Wiles's bedchamber*

Before this week, Mary's sole experience with town life was what she'd seen among the handful of houses and shops that had constituted Worthington. Nothing had prepared her for London, and as the carriage slowly approached that great city, she began to realize exactly how ignorant she was.

"I hate this last part of the journey," Calliope grumbled, slumped against the squabs with her arms crossed over her chest in the very picture of boredom. "I vow we could travel twenty miles in the country in the same time it takes us to crawl twenty paces once we've reached the city. Not that I would, of course, but it's almost enough to make me walk the rest of the way."

"I've never seen so many people in one place," Mary marveled at the carriage's window. "I've never seen so many people in all my *life*."

The carriage's speed had ground to nearly nothing as the driver did his best to maneuver the horses through the crowds that filled the road. It was not only that the road itself had narrowed, hemmed in on either side by an unbroken barrier of houses, shops, taverns, and churches, but the sheer number of other travelers all crowding into the same space.

There were wagons full of baskets of apples and crates of honking geese, bound for the city's markets, and from the other direction came other drays burdened with boxes carried by ships from faraway ports. The din was staggering, from the shouted abuse between frustrated drivers and their passengers, to the long brass horns employed by the stages, to the lowing of the terrified cattle on their way to market.

Stagecoaches, donkey carts, and single-horse chaises jockeyed for their places beside Calliope's carriage, along with still more travelers on horseback. The greatest number were on foot, milkmaids balancing tall tin cans on their heads, apprentices hurrying with a sheaf of their masters' orders under their arms, tattooed sailors with long tarred queues and their dunnage in canvas sacks on their backs, peddlers and rag pickers, seamstresses and carpenters, fiddlers and farmers' daughters, all on their way into the greatest city in the kingdom.

"Where do you think they're all going?" Mary wondered aloud. "I mean beyond London. Where will they go once they arrive?"

"I do not know, nor do I care," Calliope said with grumpy disdain. "So long as they don't appear on my doorstep, then it's of no concern to me. That is, if I'm ever permitted to appear on my own doorstep. At this snail's pace, I won't be home until nightfall, which will scarce leave me time to ready myself for His Lordship."

"His Lordship will call tonight?" Mary asked. Since joining her fortunes with Calliope's, she'd heard much of Calliope's protector, but little of any real substance, and she was curious to meet the earl for herself.

"He will," Calliope said. "It is Tuesday, and on Tuesday he always dines with his younger sister, makes excuses to avoid drinking with his loathsome brother-in-law afterwards, and comes to me instead, where I will entertain him until precisely three in the morning, at which time he will return home. His Lordship is as prompt and predictable as the Westminster bells, and a fine thing that is in a man, too."

"I cannot wait to make his acquaintance," Mary said. "I've never seen a true earl, let alone been introduced to one."

"Well, you shall not see one tonight, either," Calliope said. "His Lordship hasn't fucked me for the fortnight since I've been away, and I expect he'll be most ardent tonight, and in no humor for other company. Besides, I've not quite decided how I shall explain you to him."

"*Explain* me?" Mary asked, more than a little wounded by that. To be sure, their friendship was of a short and furious duration, but she'd rather thought it was also already of a fondness not requiring explanation. "What is there to explain?"

"Why, everything." Calliope blinked her large blue eyes in wondering disbelief. "I cannot simply appear with you from nowhere, with no other explanation than that I found you in the road."

"But that is true!"

"Yes, but who would believe it?" asked Calliope. "Perhaps that is an acceptable tale for baby Moses in the bulrushes, but not for a personage as sizable and full-formed as you."

Mary said nothing, too overwhelmed with emotion to reply. She hadn't considered their meeting in that way, not exactly. Why should she? As an abandoned infant, she'd been gathered up from the weeds by Lady Catherine, but she'd not realized that her new friend regarded herself as her benefactress, too. To have been cast away and rescued by another's charity twice in one's short life was hardly a pleasing revelation to have thrust in one's face.

"Forgive me, ma'am, for—for taking so much of your time," she said at last, her voice quavering. "I hadn't realized I was such a—such a burden to you, and I'll be happy to—"

"Oh, hush. Don't be daft," Calliope said crossly. "You are not to go anywhere. I only meant that if we are to launch you properly in London, we must make certain that you are ready. The world will only make a fuss over you once, and then the novelty is gone, no matter how beautiful you may be."

"Oh," Mary said, and sniffed dramatically. "That is different."

"Yes, it is," Calliope said, mollified. "First of all, we must devise a more alluring name for you. 'Mary Wren' sounds like dry sticks and virtue."

"That's what Lady Catherine intended for me."

"She succeeded admirably," Calliope said. "Can you imagine the earl would be as enamored with plain Jane Greene as he is with Calliope Wiles?"

Mary shook her head. She couldn't imagine the ethereally beautiful Calliope being called Jane, either.

"Could I be called Marianna?" she asked shyly, remembering the heroine of that long-ago romance novel passed among the Worthy Hall servants. "I have always liked the name."

"Marianna," Calliope mused, testing the name on her tongue. "Marianna, Marianna. We could begin with that. My dear Marianna. 'May I present my cousin from the country, Miss Marianna Wren?'"

Mary—or Marianna, as she became from that moment onward—laughed, and clapped her hands together with delight. "I am honored, Mrs. Wiles."

Calliope winked. "So am I, *Miss* Wren. But that is only the beginning. To be most desired, you must be a virgin. Nothing makes a gentleman more generous than a country-bred virgin."

"But I'm not!" Marianna exclaimed, surprised Calliope would suggest such a thing. "You know that. I'm not at all."

"Yes, but the only gentleman who knows for certain—your Mr. Lyon—is on his way to India," Calliope said with blithe confidence. "The others will believe it because they will wish to, and because you have the glow of an innocent. That, and a simple dip in alum water to tighten your passage. It's easy enough, and the poor cullies are none the wiser."

Mary frowned, considering this well. She'd thought she was willing enough to throw aside the traces that Lady Catherine had used to bind her into obedience, but some of the new freedoms that Calliope was offering to replace the old restraints were more troubling to her conscience than others.

"To lie like that does not seem quite honest," she said finally.

Calliope sighed impatiently. "Is the costermonger who soaks her oranges to make them more plump for market being dishonest? Is the butcher who cuts and turns his chops to make a better display? Or the mercer who glazes his woolens to look like the silk his customers crave? It's all part of the trade, my dear, and no one expects more or less."

"But shouldn't a gentleman fall in love for me as I am, not how he wishes me to be?"

"Is it any different from dressing your hair, and choosing a pleasing gown?" Calliope asked. "Or would you rather venture how many fine gentlemen here in London will look your way if you go about dressed in your old servants' livery, with your hair screwed back like a dairymaid's?"

She leaned forward, resting her hand on Marianna's knee. "I know it must sound queer, but it's how the world goes round. The gentlemen understand there's a certain amount of deception from us, but then they will dissemble about the beauty of their wives, or the cleverness of their children, or how bravely they fought in a battle they didn't attend, or how bold a figure they cut whilst speaking in the House of Lords."

"That is true," Marianna said slowly. "Gentlemen do not always speak the truth, or act with honor."

Calliope sniffed, not hiding her contempt. "Always never," she said. "All's fair in love and pleasure, Marianna. I've lost my maidenhead three times, with three different gentlemen, and only the first brought me nothing but sorrow in return. Ah, here we are at last, my own little house."

The carriage stopped and the footman opened the door, swinging open the small metal step. Calliope hopped down, clearly glad to be home, but Marianna followed more slowly, staring up in awe at her friend's "own little house." To her, the house was unfathomably elegant, three stories of smooth white stone with three rows of narrow arched windows, white marble steps, and a glossy black door with a gleaming brass knocker.

"This is for you?" she asked, incredulous. "You live here alone, with no one else?"

Calliope looked up at the house, holding her hat in place with her palm on the crown. "Excepting the staff, I'm alone. And His Lordship, of course, when he calls. And now you. Come, let me show you inside."

She took Marianna's hand and led her inside, past a blur of bowing and curtsying servants and up the curving staircase.

"This is my bedchamber," she said, throwing open the first door. She ran across the room and threw herself on her back on the bed, then looked back at Marianna and laughed. "You can see why I'd grown so weary of those hideous inns. Isn't this a delight?"

"Oh, it is," breathed Marianna, her eyes wide as she gazed around the room. "It *is*."

She'd never seen a bedchamber like this one. Everything in the room was in shades of silver and pale rose—the same colors, really, that Calliope herself was. The centerpiece of the room was the bed, raised up so it almost seemed as if it were on a stage, or the display window of a fine shop. Considering how Calliope had come by this house, that seemed appropriate enough, and like a stage or shop window, the bed's pink silk hangings, silver tassels, and posts carved with silver-painted cupids likewise served to highlight the costly prize that (usually) lay within.

"You like my bed, don't you?" Calliope grinned, kicking off her shoes, and pushing herself up the bed backwards until she reached the mountainous pile of feather-stuffed cushions at the headboard. "It is my domain, my kingdom, my worldly realm!"

She laughed again, then rolled from the bed to pad across the floor in her stocking feet and take Marianna's hand again. "Come, come, come! If I'm to be a proper hostess to my dear country cousin, I must take you to your own rooms, to make sure everything is as you please."

Marianna's bedchamber was directly beside Calliope's own, and though the mahogany bedstead was less grand and the hangings and upholstery a more somber pale blue, the room was far richer and more fashionably appointed than any at Worthy Hall.

"This is for me?" Marianna asked in wonder, running her fingertips along the highly polished wood of the dressing table lightly, as if fearing she'd be singed by so much magnificence. "You would have me stay here as your guest?"

"Well, yes," Calliope said, beaming. "You'll be my very first guest, too. His Lordship gave me the lease only four months ago, so everything's new."

Almost shyly, she searched Marianna's face for a reaction. "Are you pleased? Does it suit you?"

"How could it not?" Overwhelmed, Marianna pulled Calliope into her arms and hugged her close. "You have shown me such kindness—such kindness!"

"Oh, Marianna," her friend said, kissing her on the cheek, "I only give you what you deserve."

Tears of gratitude welled up in Marianna's eyes. "But you scarce know me."

"I know enough," Marianna said, resting her palm fondly on the other woman's cheek. "I acted first on a whim, I know, didn't wish you to come to sorrow for loving too strongly. You are such a pretty innocent, and pretty innocents too often meet uncommonly unpretty ends in London. You could have stepped from the Worthington stage and been swept up by a brothel keeper without even realizing it, until you'd found yourself naked and dosed and locked away in a squalid garret in Covent Garden, bound to fuck any poxed rascal who laid down his coin. I'd not wish that on anyone, especially not you, my dearest."

"That didn't happen to you, did it?" asked Marianna fearfully, and feeling every bit the country innocent that Calliope had declared her to be. She knew only enough of the world to realize that she could well have followed the grim fate that led to the bawdy houses of Covent Garden, and she could never thank her friend enough for saving her. "You never were in Covent Garden, were you?"

"Praise Heaven, no," Calliope said with a visible shudder. "I was 'ruined' the same as you were, and quite happily, too.

But it was my own parents who cursed me as a whore and tossed me forever from their home and their care. I was no wiser than you when I came to town, but I had a friend here, an older girl from my old lane, who took me in and guided me as I'm guiding you. If I am kind now, Marianna, then it is simply my shifting the same kindness she showed me, keeping me from misfortune and helping me to prosper."

"What has become of her?"

"My darling Juno?" Calliope smiled, clearly recalling her benefactress with genuine affection. "Ah, she took what she'd earned from a besotted duke and bought a tavern in Bath. She's now wed to a wine merchant there, where she lives now as the fine, fat model of Christian respectability. Now look here. I've not shown you this yet."

She stepped to the wall that separated Marianna's bedchamber from her own, and to an elaborate chinoiserie shelf that hung there. She pushed a porcelain figure of a dancing monkey to one side of the shelf, revealing a round hold in the wall much like the knothole in a tree. She leaned close to the wall to peer through the hole, then stepped aside, motioning for Marianna to take her turn.

"There," she said as Marianna put her eye to the hole. "You've a perfect view of my bed, haven't you?"

"I do," Marianna said. The peephole was precisely situated to offer a complete view of the glorious pink bed, without any obstructions from the bedposts or other furnishings. "But why would I—"

"Because you wished to know more of His Lordship, didn't

you?" Calliope asked slyly. "What better way to learn of him and his habits than to watch him when he lies with me?"

For the first instant, Marianna was shocked. Most people would wish to perform such acts of intimacy alone and in private, and the notion of spying on the Calliope with her earl struck Marianna as shamefully perverse.

Yet the more she thought of it, the more titillating and less shameful the idea became. She *was* curious. She had the most fleeting glimpse in the looking glass of herself with John on Lady Catherine's dining table, but she'd hardly had time or inclination to consider their postures or their actions. She'd really only been a performer in the sexual act, never the spectator, and yet the knowledge that others had watched her had added a certain extra spice to the coupling, and to her own pleasure.

Again she looked through the peephole at the bed, imagining the coverlet tossed aside and the pillows and sheets in disarray from the writhing, naked couple upon them. What would it be like to be the watcher? Would she share their pleasure by being a witness to it? What would she feel, here on the other side of the wall?

Already she was beginning to experience the warmth of arousal heating her blood, her heart quickening in response to the picture her imagination was creating. She could easily envision Calliope with her lovely white limbs and tangled pale hair, her eyes squeezed shut and her head thrown back in ecstasy, but the earl was a tantalizing phantasm, with too much still unknown.

"You'd like to watch us, wouldn't you?" Calliope said softly, her mouth curved in beguiling smile. "You're flushed from thinking of it. But that will be only the start for us, you know, only the start, and then you will join—yes?"

They both turned towards the footman in the doorway.

"Forgive me, ma'am," he said swiftly, not waiting for any further acknowledgment from Calliope. "But His Lordship's carriage is in the street."

"Not now!" Calliope wailed, clutching at her hair. "How dare he come to me so early? I am a shambles, unfit for him to *see*! Put him in the drawing room and see that he has whatever he wishes to drink and eat. Explain that I'm recovering from my journey, but that I'll come directly, as soon as I'm tidy for him."

The footman bowed and left, and quickly Calliope turned back to Marianna. "I must leave you to your own devices this evening, dear friend. Ask the servants for whatever you need, and tomorrow I promise I'll take you about London. Now I must go."

"But if I—"

"Forgive me, but I cannot keep His Lordship waiting," Calliope said, and winked. "But if you grow lonely, pray, do not forget to spy on us for company."

With a flicker of petticoats, she was gone, scurrying off in her stockinged feet to make ready for the earl. Almost at once, a maidservant appeared with a tray containing a light supper— cold chicken, sweet buns, cheese, and peaches, plus a small bottle of sillery—and briskly laid it out on the table beside the window. Marianna watched her, feeling oddly as if she should be helping; after all, it had not been so very long ago when she'd been the one performing exactly the same tasks.

The girl turned and curtsied to her. She was short and stout, and her flat face was badly scared by smallpox, a combination that, though pleasant enough, would never inspire any gentleman to heights of lustful folly. That was the only difference between them, thought Marianna, and an uncomfortable realization it was, too. She was beautiful, while this girl was plain, and thus she would eat peaches and sip sillery from a crystal goblet, and the other must wait upon her.

"Mrs. Wiles said to tell you there're nightclothes and a dressing gown in the chest, miss," the maidservant said, her hands folded over her apron. "Mrs. Wiles said for you to be at your ease."

Marianna nodded, not sure what else to do. "What is your name?"

"Betty, miss," the girl said with agreeable cheer, and dipped an extra little curtsy. "Will you be wishing anything more, miss?"

What Marianna wished was for Betty to sit and eat with her, and keep her company without treating her like a false lady. But sadly Marianna realized that would not do, and that already her life was considerably changed. The camaraderie of the servants' hall was no longer for her. She'd become Marianna and was rising upward, just as this girl would always remain an earthbound Betty, with no classical transformation of her name. Nor could Marianna imagine who would be more scandalized by such a democratic suggestion: Calliope, or Betty herself.

With that in mind, she finally gave the expected response, rather than the one she wished.

"Thank you, no," she said, sitting before the little table with a graceful sweep of her skirts, copied from Calliope. "That will be all, Betty."

"Yes, miss." The girl curtsied again, closing the door after her, and Marianna was alone for the first time since she'd fled Worthington with Calliope. Worse, she was alone with no responsibilities, and nothing to do.

She nibbled at the chicken, and before she ate the peach, she idly pricked a pattern into its fuzzy skin with the tines of her fork. She drank all the sillery. She turned her chair so she could look out the window, to the street and the small patch of fenced green lawn and trees that centered the square of houses that all matched Calliope's. It was early evening, without much to see: a few carriages, a few people strolling along the pavement with dogs, the moon rising over the rooftops. She'd heard nothing further from Calliope and her lord, and wondered if they'd gone out. From the windows lit in the other houses, it seemed as if everyone else had already retired to their bedchambers for the night, and with a weary sigh, Marianna decided to do the same.

She changed into the night rail left for her, carefully draping her gown over the back of a chair (for old habits did die slowly, and she couldn't quite bring herself to leave it crumpled on the floor for Betty, the way a lady would). She blew out the candlestick and climbed into the bed, leaving the curtains open so she could see the moon through the window.

Yet at first she could not sleep, her mind too jumbled for

rest. She'd never slept alone, and the bed felt vast and empty, the room far too quiet. What would it be like to have a house like this, a home of her own? Foundlings didn't have homes, any more than they had families, and the notion that Calliope possessed this house and everything in it was incomprehensible.

Sadly she thought of John, and how his last advice to her had been to come to this place and become a goddess in her own right. She was only now beginning to realize what that might mean. Would her beauty and passionate nature—her Johnny's joy!—be sufficient to entice a worldly London gentleman? Could she really find a gentleman willing to reward her as thoroughly as Calliope's devoted earl? Would anyone truly find her as desirable, and as worthy of so much?

At last she drifted off into an uneasy sleep, filled with troubled nonsensical dreams of foundering on an enormous feather bed in the middle of a crowded London street, with peddlers and apprentices jeering at her as she struggled in the rocking sheets and pillows.

Finally she jerked awake, her heart pounding. Still frightened, she sat upright, disoriented as to exactly where she might be. By the moonlight that streamed into the room, she gradually remembered where she was, and how she'd come to be there, and to realize that the feather bed was not going to swallow her up. Further, she heard the muted murmur of voices nearby, and Calliope's ringing laughter. The voices came from the next room, Calliope's bedchamber.

The peephole. Marianna slipped from the bed and hurried across the room, and carefully placed her eye close to the hole. What she saw stole away her very breath.

The rose pink bed was lit by a half dozen sterling candlesticks, their wavering light casting dramatic shadows against the walls and bed curtains. In the middle of the bed, facing Marianna, knelt Calliope, naked except for her pink stockings, green ribbon garters, and green silk-covered mules with high curved heels. Tiny brilliants winked and sparkled in her hair, earlier dressed high for evening, but now tumbling loose in wanton disarray. Her pale skin glowed like polished ivory in the candlelight, and her nipples and lips were a dramatically deeper rose, riper by contrast. She knelt with her thighs angled apart, the short curls between her legs glinting silver. Her eyes were heavy-lidded and unfocused, and her lips swollen and parted with arousal.

She made for a beautiful picture, yes, but it was also one that Marianna had seen before. What changed everything was seeing the Earl of Rogersme kneeling on the bed behind Calliope. He was not much taller than Calliope, but bull-chested and powerfully built enough to make her seem fragile before him. With his dark eyes and arched nose, he reminded Marianna of the satyrs in other bawdy pictures that John had shown her, in the same book with Leda and her lubricious swan.

With his cheek pressed against the side of her neck, he had one arm around Calliope's chest, filling his hand with one of her breasts, while the other was gripped around the top of her thigh, his fingers sinking into her soft flesh. He wore nothing beyond the black silk ribbon that tied back his dark hair, and with rapt fascination Marianna watched how the muscles in his arms and thigh tightened and released as he moved his hips against her friend's bottom.

In turn Calliope was undulating up and down, rocking the rounded cheeks of her bottom hard against his cock, still hidden from Marianna's view at the peephole. Bracing her hands on her widespread thighs, she leaned forward, twisting around to look back over her shoulder at him. She grinned wickedly and arched her back to present not just her bottom, but her quim, slowly sliding herself down his hard length.

The earl groaned, and grabbed her hips to hold her still against him.

"Hot little cat," he growled, his voice nigh strangled. "Over the rest of the way, Callie, and let me have you proper."

Not waiting for her to obey, he pushed her forward onto the bed the rest of the way so she was on her hands and knees. She laughed with excitement, low and teasing, and shifted just far enough to offer Marianna a glimpse of the same prize she was granting to His Lordship, her cunny enticingly flushed and glistening with her juices. Now Marianna could see the earl's glory, too, his cock red-purple with his urgency, jutting from the thick bush surrounding his ballocks. He knelt poised before Calliope, relishing her shamelessness for a moment before he aimed his cock and drove deep into her willing body.

Calliope cried out with delight and wriggled against him, drawing him deeper, while he held tight to her hips and thrust again and again, the thick veins and bulbous crimson head of his cock glistening from her juices with each withdrawal. His face was twisted with the raging agony of pure lust, even more like a satyr's, his breathing harsh and grunting with exertion as he worked against her.

On the other side of the wall, Marianna could not make herself look away. She didn't know if Calliope was aware of her there, or if the earl likewise was performing for her benefit as well as his own, nor did she care.

All she could do was watch her friend take her lover's cock, her rapturous expression, her shuddering sighs and nonsensical exclamations of passion, and could not help imagining herself in the same place. To be on her knees with her bottom raised like that, to feel her cunny stretched and filled by the earl's member, to have him reach around her hip and stroke her most sensitive place between her swollen nether lips when she was so open, so vulnerable to delirious sensation.

Marianna was shaking with shared desire, her breath tight in her chest with it. Without looking away, without thinking, she pulled her night rail to one side and stroked herself in sympathetic rhythm with the woman and man before her. She wanted to be possessed with *that* fierceness, to be claimed with *that* passion, to give herself over to being loved with that much fire and force, and as Calliope finally cried out and collapsed as she spent, so did Marianna, her knees giving way beneath her as she sank to the floor.

The tremors of her release racked her body, and though she closed her eyes, she still saw the images of the writhing lovers, still felt the sweet torment of secondhand passion. She could hear their voices on the other side, muffled now, and her friend's familiar, languorous laughter, as she dallied further with her lover. But for Marianna, all she could do was press her forehead against the cool plaster wall, seeking relief for her fevered body.

Somehow she crept across the room to her lonely bed, curling herself into a tight ball beneath the covers. She tried to think of Johnny Lyon, to little comfort and more misery. She'd found no satisfaction in watching Calliope and her earl, and less than that in the false, empty pleasure she'd wrenched from herself. She wanted more than that, much more, and the man who'd give it to her.

She wanted it all, and she would not stop until she got it.

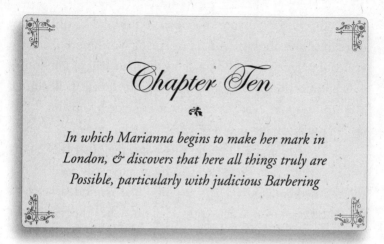

Chapter Ten

*In which Marianna begins to make her mark in
London, & discovers that here all things truly are
Possible, particularly with judicious Barbering*

True to her promises, Calliope began her presentation
of Marianna to London the very next morning. In
Calliope's carriage, they made a tour of the most
fashionable milliners, mantua makers, and jewelers. At each
shop Calliope made certain that everyone learned Marianna
was her cousin, new arrived from the country and eager to
improve her acquaintance. Finally they drove at a genteel
pace through the park, with Calliope gaily greeting every
gentleman on horseback that she knew, which to Marianna
seemed to be nearly every male out of leading-strings.

"How did you ever come to know so many people in London?" Marianna asked as they passed yet another pair of grinning gentlemen. "Lord, it would make my head ache to
remember so many names and faces!"

Calliope laughed gaily, twirling the ivory handle of her
lace parasol between her gloved fingers.

"I don't know everyone, not at all," she said. "It only must seem to you that way after the tiny size of Worthington's society. And pray note that I only know the male half of London, which limits things considerably. The polite female half won't even admit that I exist, let alone that I'm worth knowing."

"But why should that be?" Marianna said in perfect innocence. She *had* noticed how, in the shops, the other lady customers would turn their backs to them and draw away as if they carried smallpox. Their response had reminded her of how she'd been treated at Worthy Hall once the other servants had realized she and Mr. Lyon had become lovers. But here in London, no one would know her, let alone know her past scandals, and yet they'd regarded her with the same scornful disdain. "How can they judge you without knowing who you are?"

"Because they know *what* I am," Calliope said, her lips curving into a sly smile. "They know I'm the sort of woman who can please their men—their husbands, fathers, and sons—better than they can themselves, and find my own pleasure in the pleasing, too. Likely they've decided the same of you. I'm not quite sure how they do it. Perhaps we give off some scent of disrepute that only the overnice can sniff."

"I vow it must be a surpassing sweet fragrance to gentlemen's noses," Marianna said, laughing, too, "considering the way they gawk at us."

"Oh, yes, most rapturously sweet, to give the poor rascals cock stands before they've realized what's happened," Calliope said, rolling her eyes towards the Heavens with feigned dismay. "I'll wager they're trying to figure exactly who you are in every club in town. You'll have the choicest of them to warm your bed soon enough."

Marianna nodded solemnly. Everything they'd done this day had been to that end, and after last night, she hoped that Calliope's "soon enough" would blossom into sooner rather than later. "Whoever he may be, I hope he'll be as fine to me as your earl."

"His Lordship is rather fine, isn't he?" Calliope smiled like the cat who'd purposefully spilled the dairy cream to be able to lick it up. "So you did spy upon us last night."

"You told me to do so!" Marianna exclaimed. "You showed me the peephole yourself, else I never—"

"Hush, hush, dear friend. I only wished to tease you," Calliope said, laying a calming hand on Marianna's arm. "Of course I meant for you to watch. You wished to see His Lordship, and I wished for you to have your wish. Did you take the measure of him as a man, then?"

That was not a question Marianna expected. She knew that while her friend did not consider herself exactly in love with her earl, she did regard him with a certain possessive pride, and thus Marianna answered her query with suitable care. "He seemed to be, ah, a most virile man."

"Oh, yes, His Lordship is *that*," Calliope said, leaning forward on the seat to wave out the window, "else he'd have little use for me. But here, you can offer your compliments to him yourself. Halloo, My Lord, here, here!"

"He's here?" Flustered further, Marianna patted anxiously

at her hair and her skirts. The carriage was already stopping, and she'd a glimpse of the earl on horseback riding beside the window.

"Oh, my own sweetest, dearest lord!" Eagerly Calliope popped her head and shoulders through the carriage window to kiss the earl, then slipped back inside with a *whoosh* of petticoats, so he could do the same in turn and return her kiss, like players in an Italian comedy. At least the earl had the sense to sweep off his hat before he leaned through the window, his florid face filling the space.

"Good day, my dear ladies, good day," he said, his grin wide and wolfish as he turned towards Marianna, so wolfish, in fact, that she felt quite certain he would have devoured her whole if he could.

"My Lord, might I present my cousin, Miss Wren?" Calliope said. "Miss Wren, the Earl of Rogersme."

"A pleasure," he said, reaching out to seize Marianna's hand like a prize. "London is a far more beautiful place now that you are here, Miss Wren. You will be gracing us for a good long time, I hope?"

"Oh—oh, yes, My Lord," she stammered. In spite of everything Marianna herself had done in the last month, she was now blushing furiously. When she had last seen the earl, he had been naked and mounted on her friend, and snorting and rutting like the village bull. To meet him now, impeccably dressed for riding with his hair sleeked back in a tidy queue, the exemplary model of an English peer, seemed oddly more embarrassing than when she'd spied on him through the peephole, as if she were shamed in reverse. Yet when he raised her hand to his lips, his dark-eyed gaze intent on her over their joined fingers, she felt a shiver of desire race through her veins—desire that felt horribly disloyal to her friend. "That is, I shall remain here so long as my, ah, my cousin will have me as her guest."

"That will be as long as you wish," Calliope said, cheerfully unperturbed by His Lordship's reaction. "I do enjoy your company that much, Marianna."

"Who would not, Callie," said the earl, his gaze sliding hungrily from Marianna's face to her provocatively presented bosom, "when your company is as delicious as Miss Wren's?"

He squeezed Marianna's fingers meaningfully, a signal of his interest that she couldn't mistake even through her gloves. Oh, yes, he was most virile. In the pressure of his hand around hers, she was aware of his strength, his resolve, and most of all his lust, and at once she remembered how his aroused cock had possessed exactly those same qualities. She could feel her body shamelessly responding to him, too, her breasts growing heavy and her cunny warming and swelling, readying itself for a male, and she couldn't help pressing her thighs together in a private little caress.

Private yes, but not unnoticed. The earl had seen the shifting of her legs, the slight rustle of her petticoats, the way her snip-toed slippers had arched and pointed beneath her hems, and rightly guessed the cause, and his role in it, too. His smile widened, his expression so much that of a knowing libertine's that Marianna blushed again.

"Pray call on us this evening, My Lord," Calliope said, her voice a velvety purr that was as full of the same suggestion to be found in his single cocked brow. "We shall be a home to you. Both of us, My Lord."

"You may rely upon my attendance. Good day to you both." He released Marianna's hand, and ducked back through the window, where Marianna could see him as if he were framed like a portrait, squinting slightly against the sun as he squared his black beaver hat on his head. He climbed back into the saddle and the skirts of his coat flew up, his close-fitting breeches revealing the neat curves of his buttocks and the tension in his powerfully muscled thighs. Marianna recalled those, too, from last night, and she leaned forward a fraction, greedily looking her fill.

But as he gathered his reins in his hand, he looked back to the carriage and caught Marianna watching him. He smiled, salaciously showing the tip of his tongue between his teeth, then laughed and rode off.

Mortified, Marianna slid lower, her back pressed against the seats. Twice now he'd caught her showing more interest than she should, two more times than he should have.

"I knew you two would have a liking for each other," Calliope said, smiling a thoroughly pleased smile. She took one of her pale lovelocks and began twirling it around her finger like a silken ribbon, teasingly looking down at it as if the curling lock of hair were of far more interest than Marianna could ever be. "I knew you would be beguiled by him from the moment I met you, and la, how intrigued His Lordship was to hear that!"

Marianna gasped. "What else did you tell him?"

"Oh, nothing much," Calliope said idly. "That you were

my cousin. That you were eager to make your mark on the town by breaking hearts. That you were very beautiful, and very young. And, of course, that you were a virgin. I could have told him that alone, and it would have been sufficient. Men like His Lordship will let their fancies fill in the rest of the picture to suit themselves. Or, rather, fancy what it would be like to have his cock fill *you*."

"But I'm not so very young," Marianna protested. "I'm sixteen, almost as old as you."

Calliope shrugged elaborately. "His Lordship is thirty-four, double my years. In his eyes, you at sixteen are the merest new-fledged chick, and he likes you much the better for it, too."

Marianna frowned, thoroughly confused. "You do not mind that he—he showed interest in me?"

"Why ever should I mind, my dear?" she answered, her eyes wide with droll amusement. "I like you. I like His Lordship. You both like me. Therefore it would seem only logical that you should like each other, and vastly more agreeable, too. Consider how pleasurably we can amuse ourselves, we three."

At once Marianna thought of the coupling she'd witnessed last night, and how much she'd secretly wished to be with her friend and the earl.

"But I thought I was to pretend I'm a virgin," she said, not bothering to hide her frustration. "How can I, and join you and His Lordship?"

"Because, my dearest friend, there are many paths to amusement, and to pleasure without full possession." She smiled, and reached out and linked her fingers into Marian-na's. "Surely you must have realized that with me by now."

But what Marianna was realizing was more complicated than that. She thought of how perfectly she and Calliope complemented each other, her dark hair in contrast to her friend's silver, her longer legs and more lissome figure the ideal foil for Calliope's delicacy, and she remembered, too, how Calliope had studied her by lantern light, there on the Worthington road, making sure of Marianna's appearance and that she'd no meddlesome family before she'd show her any kindness. To be sure, she'd shown Marianna a great deal of kindness since then—a very great deal—but the rest couldn't be denied.

"You chose me for His Lordship, didn't you?" she asked softly. "From the beginning. You took me in and brought me here because you knew His Lordship would desire me."

"Dear, clever Marianna." Calliope sighed, and slipped her fingers free of Marianna's. With that sigh, it seemed as if much of Calliope's natural exuberance disappeared, the way a ship's sails hang lifeless when becalmed.

"I won't deny it, for you've guessed true," Calliope contin-ued. "His Lordship has been very generous to me, yes, but it is not easy to amuse so experienced a gentleman. I must al-ways be charming, and amusing, and wanton, and original to keep him beguiled. When first I saw you, I thought only of that. But now that I've come to know you better, why, I wish more for you than to be only my partner in pleasing His Lord-ship. I've my eye on a friend of his, a marquess, of all things, who would suit you most admirably."

"A marquess?" Marianna repeated, not entirely sure of

what that was, let alone whether it was a good attribute or not.

But Calliope misread her uncertainty, and again sighed mournfully. "There, you doubt me, and how can I expect otherwise? Yet it's true as well, though now I would not fault you if you despised me, and left me altogether."

"Oh, Calliope, no!" cried Marianna softly, gently. "I'd not leave you, not over such a quibble as this. You never lied to me, or played me false, and instead have been kindness itself, where other more righteous folk have not."

"Yet you asked me to explain myself," Calliope said, still troubled, "and right you were to do so, too."

"But it was not like that, not at all," Marianna said, once again taking her friend's hand, squeezing it fondly. "I asked because I felt certain ... certain *longings* for His Lordship, yet I'd no wish to wound you through jealousy or envy for his sake."

Finally, happily, Calliope smiled. "But that was what I'd wished from the beginning. A dalliance for pleasure, and nothing more. Dear, dear Marianna! No wonder we've made such splendid friends."

"And so we will continue to be," Marianna said, kissing her friend lightly on the cheek as a pledge. "I've already lost my love to the other side of the world, and I'm not about to cast away my dearest friend as well."

With everything thus resolved between them, the two returned to Calliope's house, entertaining each other with gossip and jesting, and inspecting the purchases they'd made in the shops earlier that day. They ate a light, fortifying supper, and then, dressed in flowing silk dressing gowns, they set to preparing for the earl's visit.

"You know His Lordship might not attend us at all, Marianna," Calliope warned. She was sitting very straight and still on a stool while Turner dressed her hair, stroking the long strands with sugar water, then wrapping them carefully around the iron tongs that had been heated by the fire. It was a perilous venture. If the tongs were too hot, then the hair would be singed and break, and like every other lady of the fashion, Calliope had learned from painful experience what happened if she wriggled, and bumped her neck or forehead against the hot tongs. "No matter how much we tempted him—and surely we did!—he could still be pressed by other obligations that keep him away."

"I cannot believe that," scoffed Marianna, sitting on the bed, her knees tucked comfortably beneath her. Because her hair curled by nature and not by artifice, and because she was to play the artless virgin, she would be spared the ritual of hairdressing. "His Lordship's a great gentleman, a peer of the realm. If he can't do as he pleases, then I ask you, who could?"

"Even a peer has family," Calliope said, sighing dramatically. "Though he claims not to love his wife in the least, and says he was forced to wed her by his father for the sake of joining their titles and properties, he still will always trot to her side if she crooks her little finger to him."

Perplexed, Marianna frowned. She'd never considered whether there was a countess wedded to the earl, or that she'd have certain rights as a wife that would outrank a mistress. It

didn't seem fair to someone; she just wasn't sure if that someone was Calliope, or the demanding and unloved countess.
Most certainly, it was not His Lordship.

"But if he prefers your company," Marianna said thoughtfully, "shouldn't he come here?"

"He *should*," Calliope said severely, a fierce twitching of
her brows the only animation she permitted herself with the
curling tongs so near to her face. "And I vow he would, if he'd
any sense in that delicious head of his."

"I wouldn't let any gentleman treat me so," Marianna declared. "It's not polite."

"It's not a great many things," Calliope said ruefully. "But
that is how all men are with women. They will be the roosters,
ready to crow over nothing and hop on another hen's back."

"My Johnny wasn't like that," Marianna said, her voice
turning wistful. "He never ordered me about, or told me what
I could or couldn't do."

"What a rare gem he must be among men." Calliope
sighed, idly stroking one of the new-curled locks between her
fingers. "Sometimes it seems as if My Lord must heed a flock
of other, lesser masters, for all he is a peer: his fellows in the
House and at his clubs, his overseers and his solicitors and his
bankers, the men who tend his money and his stables and
his estates and his sons and likely even the fellows who blacken
the soles of his boots— Oh, yes, he has a thousand different
demands upon his time, and a thousand different excuses as
well."

"You're the most important, I should think," Marianna
observed, and grinned. "You tend his cock."

"Most likely I do a good deal better job with my responsibility than most of the others do at theirs, too." Calliope held the small-handled looking glass up as Turner gave her hair a final tweak and stepped aside. "That is lovely, dear Turner. Quite perfect, as always."

"Thank you, ma'am," Turner said, tucking the tongs back into a bucket of sand by the hearth to cool. She paused to adjust the curtains at the window, for it was late enough now that the last of the sun's light had finally faded.

"Shall I bring the razor now, ma'am?" she asked as she began to light more candles against the dusk.

"Is it time?" Calliope asked, her eyes bright with excitement. "Now?"

"Yes, ma'am, I believe it is," Turner said. "Everything's as you wished."

"A razor, Calliope?" Marianna asked, curious. "Whatever do you need a razor for?"

"In time, my dear, in time you'll see," Calliope said.

She rose gracefully from the stool, her blue silk dressing gown billowing about her bare legs as she walked across the room to the washstand. When she returned, she sat not on the stool, but on the armchair, taking care to angle it first so that she would be directly across from Marianna, still on the bed. In her hand was a small porcelain cup with a squat silver-handled brush resting inside. Briskly she began to stir the brush around in the cup, whipping up a froth of sweet-smelling suds in her familiar fragrance of lavender. Now she held the brush upward like a fluffy flower, and grinned over it at Marianna.

"His Lordship had this brush made specially for me, you know," she said proudly. "It's badger hair, not common boar bristles, the softest to be had, and the handle's silver."

"It's a pretty toy, yes," Marianna said, still mystified. "But I do not see what—"

"Oh, you shall see," Calliope said, "and you shall feel Master Badger's wicked tickle, too."

With a dancer's finesse, she pointed her toe and artfully lifted one leg into the air, before draping it over the arm of the chair. She pushed open the front of her dressing gown, leaving her cunny bare and exposed to Marianna's view. The short silver curls and pouting lips were set off to more wanton display by the crumpled blue silk around them. Despite their warm friendship, Marianna found herself blushing at the frankness of Calliope's pose, and aroused, too, from wondering what would come next—for as she had learned by now, with Calliope, there would always a "next."

She hadn't long to wait. With her mouth curved in a sly and knowing smile, Calliope slid a fraction lower on the chair, opening herself farther. She took the brush, laden as it was with the sweet-smelling bubbles, and daubed it over her nether hair. Then she worked the brush's soft hairs all over her mound and her cunny in teasing little circles, building the soap into a snowy froth, and building her own pleasure, too. Her lips parted as her breathing quickened, her eyes grew heavy-lidded as she relished the touch of the brush and Marianna's reaction.

"Does it tickle?" Marianna asked, her voice turning husky. She leaned forward on the bed, towards her friend, and smoothed her hair back behind her ears. "Does His Lordship like you to wash yourself so thoroughly?"

"I don't mean to wash myself, my dear, though I suppose that's part of the sport, too." She dropped the brush into the cup and set them both on the floor beside her. Waiting beside her was Turner, and she now handed Calliope a small pearl-handled razor. With the same assurance that she would employ opening a fan, Calliope deftly opened the razor, the sharpened-edge steel gleaming dangerously beside the glossy pearl. "Rather I mean to play not the laundress, but the barber."

As she spoke, she brought the blade to her mound, and with short, careful strokes, began to shave away every last curl of her silvery fleece. Fascinated, Marianna watched yet held her breath, fearing what might happen if the blade slipped in her friend's fingers. When at last Calliope was done, with the final stray soap bubbles wiped away, her mound was smooth and sleek, her cunny below it now fully, shockingly, enticingly exposed.

Calliope tipped her looking glass between her legs to survey her work. "His Lordship prefers me this way, and I do it to please his tastes. He says it's in the ancient fashion, that the great ladies of Rome and Athens were all hairless as new babes, and he's shown me the statues in the galleries as proof. It's also a great deal more wicked this way, isn't it? I vow those ancient ladies knew what they were about with those ancient gentlemen. But come, here, it's your turn."

"Mine?" asked Marianna, startled by such an unexpected

proposal. "But I've never used a razor before, let alone in such a tender place!"

"Then I shall be honored to serve you myself," Calliope said merrily, rising from the chair to offer her place. She patted the cushion by way of encouragement, the gleaming razor still brandished in her other hand. "Come, come. Hasn't our friendship been filled with first delights?"

Yet still Marianna hung back, unsure and more than a little frightened by the blade. "I do not know, Calliope."

"Be brave, my darling," Calliope said, coming to the bed to take her friend's hand and lead her. "I can assure you that His Lordship is not alone in his tastes. Every gentleman of my acquaintance finds even the notion of a well-shaven cunny wildly inflaming. It is as if the last veil of natural modesty has been removed for their gaze."

Marianna gave a small anxious sigh. She did *so* like to inflame gentlemen, and besides, Calliope's advice where such matters was concerned had always proved most instructive, and often pleasurable, too.

"Very well, then," she said, marshalling her courage as she took Calliope's place in the chair. "Do your worst."

"Rather you should hope that I do my best, and take the greatest care imaginable," Calliope said, laughing as she pushed back Marianna's gown. "Turner, pray hold a candlestick low, so I might have extra light. There, there, that is fine."

She knelt down before Marianna, guiding her as she took the same pose with her legs widespread over the chair. She pushed her dressing gown aside, baring her, and smoothing her palms along the taut tendons of Marianna's thighs to calm her.

"You have the most lovely cunny, my dear," said Calliope softly, stirring the brush in the soapy cup to make fresh lather. "How I'll envy the gentleman who'll make you his!"

"I wish I knew who he might be," Marianna said with a sigh. "No, I wish he were here, now."

Calliope laughed. "Oh, I warrant he'll be here soon enough."

With great care she covered Marianna's mound entirely with the lavender-scented froth. The badger hair was as soft as Calliope had promised and, combined with the bubbled soap, made for a gentle, teasing caress, and Marianna couldn't help but shift restlessly, moving her hips in pleasing sympathy.

"You can't do that, my dear," Calliope scolded gently as she traded the brush for the razor. "As much as you might wish to move, you must stay perfectly still when I start with the razor, for Turner makes certain the blade is as sharp as blazes."

At once Marianna froze. Calliope's gaze was intent as she began to shave her with short, sure strokes. Marianna gasped as the blade moved over her most private flesh, the slightest tug and scrape of the razor against her skin. She'd expected the process to be unpleasant, even painful: she'd never imagined it would be so strangely ... *arousing.*

The rasp of the sharp blade and the scent of the lavender, the open vulnerability of her position, Calliope's focused attention to her cunny and her own concentrated effort not to move, even having the impassive Turner holding the flickering candlestick close, as if lighting Marianna as an actress on a most private stage: all combined in a way that was so uniquely pleasurable that Marianna had to close her eyes against the lusciously intimate scene, her head falling back as she fought against the irresistible urge to raise her hips and seek release from the delicious torment rippling through her body.

"There you are, my dear," Calliope said. She closed the razor against the flat of her palm with a click, and reached for a fine linen cloth to wipe away the last traces of the soap. "We're done, and you survived, with nary a scratch, nor drop of blood spilled. What other barber can say the same? I ask you that."

Marianna's eyes flew open, and she looked down at her new-shorn parts. Her familiar dark curls had vanished, the skin beneath sleek and gleaming white. She'd never looked more unabashedly *naked* in her life, and she blushed, not from shame, but delight.

"There now, I knew you'd be pleased," Calliope said, tossing the cloth aside. Lightly she ran her fingers along the inside of Marianna's thigh, and winked cunningly up at Marianna. "Now let me show true pride in my craft, dear friend, and kiss my own handiwork."

Yet as Calliope leaned forward on her heels, the chamber door behind her swung open. Marianna shrieked with surprise and embarrassment, scrambling from the chair as she jerked her dressing gown over her nakedness. But Calliope merely rose, not bothering to cover herself, her hands jauntily on her hips and her smile widening in a mischievous fashion. Indeed, she seemed as unperturbed as if she'd been expecting this visitor from the start—which, in truth, she had, as had Turner, who was even now slipping from the room.

"Be easy, Miss Wren, be easy," said the Earl of Rogersme, kicking the door closed behind him as he tore his arms free of his coat's sleeves. He'd already undone the long row of buttons on his coat and on the waistcoat beneath it, and his neck cloth was likewise untied and hanging free. His face was flushed, his erection jutting unmistakably against the front of his breeches. "I've heard your sighs, your pleas for a lover, and I'm here to oblige."

Chapter Eleven

❧

*In which the binding ties of Friendship are sorely
(if pleasurably) tested; & Marianna learns the
wondrous calculation of making One from Three*

Shocked and stunned and likely feeling a good many other emotions besides, Marianna fell back on long practice, and offered an awkward curtsy to the earl.

"My—My Lord," she stammered. "Forgive me, but I—I was not expecting you."

"You weren't?" Lord Rogersme scowled, stopping with one coat sleeve still turned halfway wrong hanging from his arm, and looked at Calliope. "What is this, Callie? You told me the girl knew, and was willing. Damnation, she will be rewarded."

"She's quite willing, My Lord," Calliope said quickly, coming to stand before Marianna to reassure her. "It's the knowing part where she's perhaps a bit lacking. Marianna, my dear, sweet innocent, I know you can be, ah, *astonished* by how we do things here in London, so I thought it best not to tell you everything just yet."

But by now Marianna had already guessed the truth without being told. The careful placement of the chair opposite the bed and the timing of Calliope's "barbering," as suggested by Turner, were ready clues she couldn't mistake.

"There's another peephole, isn't there?" she asked, swiftly scanning the wall behind the bed. "In the other bedchamber opposite mine, for His Lordship to watch us here?"

"You're a clever lass, Marianna," Calliope said with happy admiration, and not a hint of contrition or shame. She took Marianna's hands playfully in her own, trying to coax her into taking no offense. "I didn't wish you to feel shy, you see. Dear cousin! I knew you'd give a better performance if you didn't realize you'd an audience."

"Your dear cousin's performance was admirable enough," the earl said, coming to stand behind Marianna. "More than admirable for a novice. After a session or two of skillful tutelage, who knows how high she'll fly, eh?"

At once Marianna turned as still as when Calliope had wielded the razor. She wore a silk dressing gown and nothing more, not even the fleece that had once masked her cunny. Her dark hair was loose and rippling down her shoulders like a bacchante's, and her cheeks were painted with circles of rouge that would have marked her as a wanton, professional beauty anywhere in London. A single black taffeta patch in the shape of star—the very apex of fashion!—was affixed near the corner of her mouth, like a question mark to whatever pretty words of love slipped from her lips.

Before her stood her dearest friend, perhaps her only friend, who was now inviting her to frolic in the most delicious sport. Behind her, so close she could feel his hot, lusty breath on her shoulder, stood the other party in this proposed adventure, fair snorting and pawing at his traces to begin. There was certain to be great pleasure if she agreed to join them, and, as His Lordship had promised, there would also be rich rewards.

She still could leave now, if she wished to. They would not stop her. She could leave this room, this house, this city, this life, and not look back.

If she wished to.

Thus did our heroine pause at these crossroads, with a choice to be made. One fingerpost pointed to a brave and bold new life in this city, a life of ease and pleasure and wanton delights, supported by the kind of reward His Lordship had only now dangled before her. The other sign pointed back whence she'd come, to a stern, hard life of unending service to others, with the only reward being the meager wages paid on quarter days, and the knowledge that whatever was done would never be enough.

Marianna's old benefactress Lady Catherine would have declared that her choice was plain: a dutiful decision not to sin. To some, surely, it would have been. But like any good heroine of a novel such as this, Marianna knew the choice before her was not quite so easily made.

Wickedness, or virtue.

Pleasure, or toil.

Wanton, or penitent.

Goddess, or servant.

What she'd been taught, or what she was learning.

"You're a beautiful creature, my dear," the earl said, his voice seductively low. He circled his arm around Marianna, and slipped his hand inside her loose silk gown to cup her breast.

She gasped with surprise at Rogersme's audacity, yet at once her nipple rose in response to his touch, and she made no move to struggle or pull free. Why should she, when this—*this*—was what she wanted, what she craved? She arched against the earl's hand and let her head drop back against his shoulder, her body moving sinuously back against his.

And without any further thought, her decision was made.

"An eager student, too, I see," he said, chuckling at her response. "I like that, Miss Wren."

He rubbed his thumb across her nipple to tease her more, and circled his other arm around her waist, the muscles as unyielding as an iron band. Rogersme was a strong man, with arms and chest more fit for a blacksmith than a gentleman, and Marianna relished how she could feel that strength vibrating between them. It fascinated her, that certainty that he could overpower her so easily if he chose. It didn't frighten her so much as make her feel like a ropedancer, skipping along on the edge of constant danger, relying on her wit and agility to keep herself safe.

"I told you she was ardent," Calliope said, her voice an eager whisper. "I told you she was *perfect*. Oh, my dear cousin, how divinely delectable you are!"

She released Marianna's hands, and leaned forward to kiss her on each cheek, as cousins would. Gently she brushed Marianna's long hair to one side, over her shoulder, and then,

with the nimblest of fingers, she unwrapped the front of Marianna's silk gown, easing the edges apart to free her breasts.
One, of course, was still covered by the earl's hand, his swar-
thy arm, shoved free of his fine linen shirt, making her skin
even more luminously pale by contrast in the candlelight.

The other rosy-tipped breast was the one with the birthmark, and with a trill of contentment, Calliope bent down to
kiss the little heart.

"Have you ever seen anything so rare, My Lord?" she said,
teasing the nipple beside it with her fingertips. "To be marked
by Venus like this!"

He twisted to look, chuckling. "Likely your entire family's
marked that way, Callie."

"Only the beautiful ones," she said, laughing with him.
"Ahh, dear Marianna, surely you were meant for passion, and
for love."

Cradling Marianna's breast in her hand, Calliope now began to lick the nearest nipple as if to worship at that fleshly
shrine to the goddess of love. For Marianna, to see her friend's
pale blond head dipping low over one breast, her artful tongue
at its tormenting work, while the earl's hand offered his own
attentions to her other breast, was almost more than she could
bear. She sighed as her blood began to simmer and the pleasure swept over her. Luxuriantly she reached back to rest her
hands on his broad shoulders and offer her breasts more fully
to her two supplicants, like the very goddess whose name Calliope had conjured on her behalf.

Yet she was not alone on this journey to rare arousal. Lord
Rogersme's caresses had grown more demanding, his breath-

ing more ragged, and impatiently he'd begun to nibble at the side of her throat. He'd found the precise spot below her ear where her pulse beat, grazing and nipping at the sensitive skin with the very edges of his teeth, then soothing the same place with a tender lave of his tongue. To have both the earl and Calliope licking her, caressing her at once—ahh, was there ever such bliss?

"Do you know how you tempt me, girl?" His Lordship asked, his voice so close to her ear that she could feel the words as much as hear them. "Do you know how ripe you are for plucking, how much you need what I could give you this very night?"

She did not answer beyond a shuddering sigh of desire. She'd sworn to Calliope that she'd hold him at bay, and preserve the mockery of her restored virginity, but the more they did this, the more she wondered if she'd made yet another vow she'd be unable to keep.

With his other hand, he'd pulled her bottom back against his groin, letting her feel the hard, thick rod of his erection through his breeches. Instinctively she moved against it, caressing him herself by drawing him into the musky cleft between her cheeks. His rumbling groan reminded her of what she'd watched last night, of how well that same thick cock had served her friend, thrusting in and out of Calliope's swollen quim. She remembered how Calliope had writhed and screamed her ecstatic release, tumbling forward onto the bed as her knees had given way before the relentless force of his onslaught.

And now it could be hers, too, that force, that cock, that driving, delirious possession.

She turned her face to kiss him, her lips seeking his. He wasted no time on tenderness, but pushed his tongue deep into her mouth to duel with hers, mimicking the act he so clearly wished to complete. His caress narrowed into a sharp pinch of her nipple. He caught her jaw in his fingers, holding her face steady as he kissed her with an urgency that she equaled, each nearly devouring the other. She was so lost in the kiss that she was only vaguely aware of Calliope slipping between her and Rogersme to unfasten his breeches, to open his fall and release his springing member to her own ministrations.

"Enough," he rumbled. He grabbed Marianna around the waist, and before she quite realized what had happened, he'd hauled her onto Calliope's bed. She sank on her back deep into the feather bed, the rope springs creaking beneath her. He followed at once, climbing onto the bed and shoving her legs apart with her knees. She struggled against him, trying to rise to embrace him, but he'd trapped her by kneeling on the trailing skirts of her dressing gown and pinning her to the bed.

She pushed herself up on her elbows, her eyes wide as she watched him now just as she'd watched him the night before. The fall of his breeches hung open, his cock jutting outward and glistening with his first seed, his cods hanging heavily beneath. His breathing was harsh and rough as he whipped his shirt over his head and threw it from the bed. His chest was covered with dark, curling hair, as were his forearms, and she thought again of the ancient satyr, ready to ravish her as his woodland nymph.

Now he loomed over her like a very colossus, his face mottled with lust, and all his primal masculine energy concentrated on Marianna. Marianna could feel it even though he'd yet to touch her again, as if the raw power of his heat had already penetrated her. She could think of nothing beyond drawing him in, enticing him to take her in the most primal way possible. She shook her hair back from her face and smiled slowly, shifting her legs even farther apart so that he'd a beguiling view of her new-shaven cunny and the rosy petals within, and the hot, sweet honey of her desire that she could already feel gathering within her.

He reached down and grasped her thighs, opening her more widely, and Marianna dropped backwards to signal her willing surrender, her arms widespread across the bed and her heart racing with anticipation.

At once Calliope joined her, scrambling across the bed to kneel over her. Without any shred of shyness left between them, she'd shed her dressing gown entirely. She smiled as she smoothed Marianna's hair from her face, fluttering little kisses over her cheeks and forehead.

"This is what I wanted for you, my dearest," she whispered, her pale hair falling like a curtain around their faces. "This pleasure, this joy!"

She blocked the earl from Marianna's sight, but Marianna could feel him there, sleeking his palms along the muscles of her trembling thighs. She held her breath with anticipation, ready to welcome his cock. Instead he shocked her entirely by lifting her hips and burying his face in her cunny, kissing her nether lips with the same greediness with which he'd kissed her mouth.

His heavy head of dark hair brushed the insides of her thighs, and the shadow of his bearded jaw grazed her softest skin, yet neither compared to the impossibly wet heat of his tongue on her newly shorn cunny. As a preliminary, he ran the flat of his tongue along the length of her slit. With his thumbs on either side, gently he parted her swollen lips like a split fruit, finally dipping his tongue inside to taste her juices. He licked her and lapped at her and nipped at her besides, a thousand new sensations she'd never felt making her twist and buck against his restraining hands.

"I knew it would be like this, my dear friend," Calliope said breathlessly, her kisses more feverish as she rubbed her breasts shamelessly across Marianna's. "I *told* you it would be so with us!"

Marianna cried out as he found the sensitive nub of her pleasure and circled it, suckling her hard until her body bowed tight and her heart drummed in her breast. She'd never been so wet, so open, the honey flowing from her. Desperate for any anchor, she clung to Calliope as she ground her hips against the earl's face and whimpered and begged for release. Slowly she realized that Calliope, too, was now stroking her, another kind of torment. No wonder she could feel the spasms gathering deep within her belly, with Rogersme's relentless tongue driving her mad with wanting.

This is all for my pleasure, she thought with the last

fragment of her brain that still could think. *They would do this for me, to me, for my delight....*

Yet when she was sure she could bear no more, he thrust his tongue deep into her passage to fill her that way. She cried out; her hips rose. Deftly Calliope pressed her little fingers over Marianna's slippery nub, and at once Marianna exploded, her whole body rocking with the force of her spending.

When at last he let her go, she curled on her side, panting, and pressed her thighs together, savoring the last spasms as they faded through her aching limbs.

"Now," Rogersme ordered sharply, and at once Calliope was on her back beside Marianna. She'd scarce time to open her legs before he was on her, driving his too-ready cock into her in a single thrust. Calliope curled her legs over his hips, taking him deep, and crossed her ankles over his back.

Fascinated, Marianna watched them, her eyes wide at such a sight so close beside her. The chamber was ripe with the musky scent of sex, as intoxicating as any wine. Without thinking, Marianna reached out to touch them as they'd touched her. When Rogersme drew back on his knees, pausing for a moment to relish the heat and the caressing grip of Calliope's cunny, Marianna slipped her fingers between them, feeling where they were joined.

"Around me, lass," rasped the earl. "Circle your fingers around my cock, there at the base. Tighter, sweetheart, tighter. Ah, that's it. That's *it.*"

She couldn't begin to encompass the entire breadth of his shaft, but it was clearly enough to excite him further. He seemed to thicken in her fingers, plunging even more forcefully into Calliope. His thrusts made Marianna touch Calliope as well, to the other woman's considerable delight, and soon her fingers were sticky with their juices. After so much dalliance, their pleasure couldn't last, and soon after, they spent together, collapsing in a sweat-soaked tangle of satisfied lubricity.

Twice more that night they entertained one another, though by the third time the earl, as robust as he was, preferred to watch the two young women engage each other, directing them as if they were players performing for his own private amusement—which, in a way, they were. The sky was beginning to pale with dawn when he finally left them, kissing each good-bye in turn before he returned home.

Exhausted, Marianna did not bother to return to her own room, but remained instead in Calliope's bed, the two twined around each other, as close as friends could be after such a bawdy night. As Marianna finally drifted off to sleep with Calliope's arm draped protectively over her waist, she marveled at how her life had changed, and so rapturously much for the better, too.

It was well past noon when Turner brought them their breakfast of hot chocolate and oranges, toasted muffins and honey. With the impassive expression that she maintained so perfectly, no matter what she witnessed, she retrieved the two dressing gowns that had been tossed to the floor the night before, turning the sleeves right side out before she held them up for Calliope and Marianna in turn.

"I think I should much rather go about naked than to bother with dressing," Calliope said, holding out her arms for Turner to slip the gown over her and to tie the ruffled front closed. "It would be so vastly much less work, and so vastly amusing, too. Imagine me in my carriage, riding down Bond Street as naked as a lie, with only a parasol to keep the sun away. Hah, the world would gawk at me then, wouldn't they?"

"Pray sit, ma'am, so I can begin to dress your hair," Turner said, more of an order than a request. "What a rat's nest you've made of it, I'm sure. It will take a good hour to brush it clean."

"More like a bad hour, the way you pull it," Calliope said glumly, sitting on the stool and bracing herself for the worst. Last night's exercises had wreaked considerable havoc upon her baby-fine hair, tangling it so it looked more like spun sugar or cotton wool than the fashionable curls and loops with which she'd begun the night.

"You wouldn't want to be completely naked." Marianna surveyed the breakfast tray before choosing an orange from the silver wire basket. She had never tasted an orange before she'd met Calliope, oranges being costly and exotic and reserved for the table upstairs and not in the servants' hall. Now that she'd discovered them, however, she was mad for them, eating them whenever they were offered. "You'd want to keep your jewels, wouldn't you?"

"Jewels don't count, because I could never go without jewels." By way of example, Calliope flicked one of the pearl-and-sapphire drops that hung from her ears.

"Sit still, ma'am, please," Turner said sternly, brandishing the hairbrush as if it were a fearsome halberd meant for destruction rather than a piece from a lady's dressing table. "I can do nothing if you do not sit still."

"Very well, very well," grumbled Calliope, her pout fit for a chastised student in the schoolroom. "I might not wish to give up my slippers, either, Marianna, or my stockings and garters, because they're so amusing, and because I have such cunning pretty feet and ankles. But away with everything else, and give over being sister to being Eve in the Garden."

"If I'd any ready money of my own," Marianna said, "I'd lay a wager with you, to see if you'd truly do it."

"That would be money lost from your pocket, for certain," Calliope said, laughing, "because I'd do it. You *know* I would. I'd toss aside every other stitch without a thought."

"You'd be monstrously popular if you did, at least with the gentlemen." Marianna broke away the last of the orange's peel and held out half of the fruit to Calliope. "Likely all the ladies in London would despise you even more for it, if such a thing were possible."

"La, I doubt that, nor do I give a fig for their judgment," Calliope said, adding a derisive little snort for emphasis as she took the offered orange. She began to pull the segments apart with her thumbs, then stopped, and laughed wickedly. "Look here, Marianna, look. Does this put you in mind of anything in particular?"

Holding the orange up for Marianna to see, she purposefully split the two segments without separating them, instead rolling them back with her thumbs with a gentle, stroking caress. She brought the fruit up to her mouth, lasciviously poking and waggling her tongue between the plump segments, squeezing the fruit so the sweet juice ran over her lips and dripping down her chin.

Marianna shrieked with laughter, rocking back on her chair as she pressed her hand to her mouth. "Oh, Calliope, if His Lordship could see you do that—"

"If he did, we'd both be on our backs with our skirts tossed up in an instant, ready for him to oblige us again," Calliope said, laughing, too. "I suppose I should have introduced you to the French manner of loving earlier, between the two of us, but I knew Rogersme would wish to taste you for himself, and I thought you'd enjoy it more if at least that was for the first time."

Marianna's cheeks grew hot, and she shyly looked down at the orange on her plate. She so clearly remembered the delicious sensation of His Lordship's tongue tormenting her that she felt herself growing moistly ripe all over again, her cunny still greedy for more even after the exhausting night's sport.

"There now, how you blush, you goose," Calliope said fondly. "No gentleman will ever doubt your virginity, not when you color like that. But isn't His Lordship's tongue the most wondrous thing you've ever had between your legs? Well, that is to say, perhaps the second best, after a good stiff prick, but la, you understand me."

"It was ... very fine, indeed," Marianna said, at a loss for what more to say. A spending as glorious as the one she'd experienced courtesy of His Lordship's tongue made her realize exactly how much more she had left to learn of worldly carnal practices, and also how eager she was to continue her education.

"Oh, yes, I'll warrant it was *fine*," Calliope teased, popping the orange into her mouth. "The earl was born with a rare talent for pleasing women that way, and a taste for women's privates, too, the exact way that other gentlemen are discerning about wine or horses or pictures."

"Not quite the same," Marianna said, thinking of how the earl's rare taste was one that could hardly be displayed like a picture or a horse.

"Do not scoff," Calliope said, wiping the orange juice away with her sleeve. "Not every man is so blessed, as you'll doubtless one day learn to your sorrowful disappointment. I must teach you to reciprocate, too. It is the surest way to make any man your slave—they do love it that much. We can practice first on dildos, until you've mastered what to do with your teeth."

"Dildos?" asked Marianna, thoroughly shamed for not understanding. She felt like the most ignorant creature in Christendom, asking Calliope to explain yet again.

Not that Calliope objected. "A dildo is a pretend cock, devised by wicked Italians," she said cheerfully, "and fashioned from ivory, or stitched and stuffed leather, or carved from a carrot, if that is one's fancy. They're pretty playthings when the real toy is not to be had, for lack of love, or money, or readiness."

"I see," Marianna said faintly, her imagination happily supplying the rest of the definition. A dildo could be a great comfort in place of a flesh-and-blood cock, and she felt her cunny tighten again at the possibilities. It was all too easy to picture herself employing such a device, stretching wide to accommodate its teasing thickness, controlling the thrusts to please only herself.

"Not that you will often have need of a dildo, not with all the gentlemen who will come clamoring to please you," Calliope said, unaware of Marianna's thoughts—or perhaps she was. "You, my friend, are like His Lordship. You also have a rare talent for pleasure, for giving it as freely as you take your own. I saw it that first day in the tub with you, and His Lordship remarked it last night, too."

Sadly Marianna remembered how Johnny Lyon had said the same to her, advising her to take her gift to London and, as it were, to market. "You are not the first to tell me so, Calliope."

"Nor, I wager, shall I be the last, not when— Oh, a pox on that brush, Turner! Must you pull out every hair I possess, and leave me bald as an egg?"

"Forgive me, ma'am, but we are nearly done," Turner said, unperturbed, as she drew the brush briskly through Calliope's long, once again silky hair. "It would not be such a trial if you wouldn't insist on dressing your hair with sugar and pins before you entertained His Lordship."

"Oh, yes," Calliope said, "and can you imagine me entertaining His Lordship with my hair in modest plaits? 'Goodwife Calliope, yer humble servant, sir.' "

She rolled her eyes with disgust, trying to stretch her hand to reach the plate of muffins while Turner had claim to her hair, like some forest savage grasping his enemy by the scalp lock. "But it is your passion, dear Marianna, and your cleverness, and, of course, your beauty, that makes me believe you could be the one finally meant to capture the interest of Lord Blackwood."

Swiftly Marianna handed her friend the muffin she craved. "Lord Blackwood? Tell me, my dear, tell me! Who, pray, is Lord Blackwood?"

Turner sniffed, an ominous sign, yet one Calliope chose to ignore.

"The Marquess of Blackwood is an old acquaintance of Lord Rogersme," she began, nibbling daintily at the muffin. "He is a gentleman of rare learning and discernment, of exquisite taste and sensibilities."

Turner sniffed again, more loudly, and again Calliope ignored her.

"Lord Blackwood has the most fashionable acquaintance imaginable," she continued, enumerating the marquess's attributes with every bite she took from the muffin, "including several in the palace itself. He has numerous estates and residences, including the largest, finest house on the north side of Blackwood Square, so grand as to have made the Duke of Bedford quite ill with jealousy when he saw it."

Marianna nodded, dazzled by this catalogue of so much splendor and accomplishment to be found in a single gentleman. No matter how her friend assured her, Marianna couldn't fathom how she could possibly be equal to such a paragon.

"He has never wed," Calliope blithely continued, "which means there is no sour, unpleasant wife hovering about like a pall to one's pleasure. And yes, yes, before you ask, he is most fantastically wealthy, with a fortune quite ready to be plundered by a clever lady."

"I wouldn't have asked that, not first," Marianna said. "I'd rather know if he's well favored. Is Lord Blackwood a handsome, comely gentleman? Is he young and agreeably made? I'm not sure I could share his company if he weren't."

"Oh, the richer a gentleman is, the more handsome he'll begin to look," Calliope said with a wise, experienced smile. "It's quite a wonder, really. But you needn't worry about Lord Blackwood. He's handsome as sin itself, and if— What is it, Fitz?"

The footman entered bearing a tray with two leather-covered boxes, such as contained the finer examples of jewelers' wares. Like the foretop man on a frigate who could identify another ship's colors as soon as they broke over the distant horizon, so Calliope could recognize not only these boxes for what they were, but also the shop whence they'd come, and most likely the contents, too. Now, with a whoop of triumph, she spotted them on the tray, and prepared to make her capture.

"Release me, Turner, at once, at once!" she cried, wriggling free of the hateful hairbrush. She didn't wait for the prize to be brought to her, but raced boldly across the room to seize it as her own. "Look, Marianna, I told you Rogersme was generous. How I must have pleased him mightily last night for him to send me *two* boxes from Sanderson's!"

With considerable interest, Marianna hurried to join her, leaning over her shoulder to watch. The most lavish present she'd ever received had been a ragged bouquet of flowers that Johnny had filched from Lady Worthy's flowers. A gift from a gentleman by way of a jeweler was an unknown spectacle for her, and she was nearly as excited as her friend as Calliope tore away the white satin ribbon that wrapped around the first red leather case.

"Oh, Marianna, look at these ear bobs!" she exclaimed gleefully, holding one up to catch the light: sapphires and pearls set in silver to make dangling forget-me-nots. "Oh, are those not the most perfect tokens ever a gentleman sent to his love?"

She pulled out the card tucked inside, and read it aloud:

For my wicked little cat, Callie, who sings sweeter in her spending than all the other Muses combined.

With regard & devotion from

R.

"How dear of him," Calliope said with a heartfelt sigh. "Forget-me-nots! As if I'd ever forget His Lordship!"

She clasped the card to her breasts in an excess of fondness, and permitted herself a few precious seconds to bask in the joyful glow of her romantic affections for the earl.

Then she reached for the larger, second box on the tray.

"Forgive me, ma'am," Fitz said. "But that's not for you."

"Not for me?" Calliope asked, drawing herself up straight with indignation, or at least as much indignation as she could command whilst clad in a half-open dressing gown. "It's from His Lordship. Therefore it must be for me."

"Forgive me, ma'am, but it's not for you," the footman

said. "The man at the door was most particular, and the card tucked in the ribbons will say so, too. That box is for Miss Wren."

"For Miss Wren, not me?" repeated Calliope with disbelief. "From Lord Rogersme? *For Miss Wren?*"

Marianna was as shocked as Calliope. Surely there must be a misunderstanding, a grave miscarriage of the tributes of love!

"I cannot believe this is so, Calliope," she said hesitantly. "Perhaps the man made a mistake and—"

"There is no mistake," Calliope said, her voice brittle and clipped, and all her earlier joy in the ear bobs gone. "Pray open the box. *Open the box.*"

With fingers that trembled more with emotion for her friend's condition than any anticipation for the waiting gift, Marianna unwrapped the white ribbons and opened the hinged leather box as warily as if it might burst in her face— and in a way the earl had never intended, it most certainly could.

The card lay on top, where they both saw it and read it together:

*For the divine Miss Wren, to welcome you to London, &
with the expectation that our acquaintance will only
grow deeper & more pleasurable with time.*

Your s'v't in all things,

R.

There was no mistaking the meaning to his words, or how exactly he expected to deepen their acquaintance. With growing trepidation, Marianna raised the card, and gasped.

The bracelet was at least an inch in glittering width, a wrought-silver cuff encrusted with rubies and diamonds. Marianna knew less than nothing of jewels, but a blind beggar at the fair could have seen the extravagance of this bracelet, and guessed the cost of it, too. Overwhelmed, Marianna could only stare at it in the box, bereft of the words to express herself.

But beside her, Calliope suffered no such affliction.

"Rubies," she said, fair spitting the word like the vilest imprecation possible. "Clearly, my dear, it is time you made the acquaintance of Lord Blackwood."

Chapter Twelve

*In which Marianna makes the acquaintance of
that Most Celebrated Gentleman (A Learnèd
Rake), the Marquess of Blackwood; & with him
explores Art, in every Form*

It was, decided Marianna, a most peculiar way to study
pictures.

The gallery was as large as a barn, yet far more crowded
with those who pretended to worship art than any barn ever
was with cattle. On every wall were hung pictures of every
description, stacked one over another until they reached the
ceiling (which was itself glazed like a gardener's glass house,
the better to nurture the tender shoots of painterly inspiration
below). Thus the pictures that were hung low enough to be
comfortably seen received a great deal of attention and admiration, while those banished to the upper regions earned next
to no notice at all.

Yet to Marianna's untutored eye, there seemed to have
been no decision for the plum spots made on either merit or
subject matter. Instead, the portraits of peeresses in their er-
mine and coronets, painted larger than the ladies themselves,

vied with scenes of Venetian sunsets and ruined castles. Favorite hunting dogs hung cheek by jowl (as it were) with ancient gods and goddesses wearing diadems and little else, and gory battlefield heroics held sway beside sentimental Madonnas. There were even a handful of statues, too, lurking in the corners of the gallery, strapping young athletes and swooning maidens, all in the classical mode.

Yet as interesting as all these pictures and statues might be, the true exhibition consisted not of what was hung to be viewed, but those strolling below and doing the viewing. The gallery was packed with those who were fashionable, and those who wished to be, those who were more handsome or more beautiful than anything portrayed on the walls, and those who were sadly deluded into believing that a surfeit of money could compensate for an absence of grace, or worse, of youth. All mingled freely, to ogle one another and engage in the fine arts of flirtation, avoidance, contempt, or fawning admiration.

Into this heady stew plunged Marianna and Calliope, arriving later that day at the most fashionable hour for viewing. Like every good general planning an assault, they had spent much time on readying their arsenal for their attack: their hair was piled extravagantly high, and crowned by even more extravagant wide-brimmed hats, with plumes so long they dipped past their shoulders. Calliope's gown was the bright blue she favored, as brilliant as any exotic's plumage, while Marianna had chosen to dress in black and white stripes, boldly tailored to highlight the narrowness of her waist and the lush fullness above and below.

As was befitting professional beauties, their breasts were on proud display, raised high and barely covered by the gauziest of kerchiefs, with necklines cut so perilously low that Marianna could feel her nipples graze the stiffened edge when she moved her arms. She would have to take care not to move with haste, or risk having them pop scandalously free: though if matters with Lord Blackwood went as she and Calliope hoped, then perhaps such an accidental indiscretion might be just what was needed in the end to secure His Lordship's attention.

"I do not know where they can be, Marianna," Calliope said, her smile pleasant without being encouraging as they slowly made their way around the gallery. "Rogersme assured me that he and Lord Blackwood would be here at this hour. Rogersme doesn't care a fig about pictures, beyond those of the usual lewd goddesses and harem bath scenes, but Blackwood is a true connoisseur."

"A cunny-sir?" Marianna asked with astonishment, mishearing the word. She'd learned many new words from Calliope, but in public company that seemed brash indeed, even for her friend. "Though of course I can guess what that might be, I wonder that you would call him that here."

"I said *connoisseur*, goose, not the other," Calliope said, laughing merrily as she jabbed Marianna with her furled ivory fan. "Though I vow the other would apply just as well. A connoisseur collects pictures and statues and other rare old things, and knows something of them, too, not having them just to cover the stain in the plaster over the mantel."

"Mr. Lyon admired pictures, too," Marianna said, letting

her gaze wander over the offerings on the wall before her. "He liked to show me engravings of his favorites in the books in Lady Worthy's library."

"Did he, indeed?" Calliope murmured, only half listening as she searched the crowd. "You can impress Lord Blackwood with your learning. Only mind you don't tell him how you came by your knowledge of pictures, or mention Mr. Lyon at all. You'll be vastly more interesting to him for being a virgin."

Marianna frowned at that, for she still found the notion of her reconstituted maidenhead to be a foolish and grudging deceit. "Do connoisseurs pride themselves on collecting virginities, as well?"

"Many do," Calliope admitted. "You know how gentlemen are, all mad to be the first up a woman's cunny, and the gorier the taking, the better."

"I shouldn't see why they should care," Marianna said. "I scarce bled at all the first time."

"You'll bleed like a slaughtered cow the second," Calliope said confidently. "It's most easily contrived, and when the time is ready, I'll arrange it for you to make a proper sanguine showing. The crowing fools believe it's proof of their own glorious manhood, you see, and boast about their conquests no end. Blackwood is as bad about it as any of them. Rogersme swears that on a long week at the Abbey, the club will go through three score of virgins, procured just for the gentlemen's sport."

"For *sport*?" Marianna's voice squeaked high with her uneasiness. There were a great many questions raised in that last most casual sentence, and a great many reasons for her to be made uneasy. "What is this Abbey? What club?"

"You'll learn it all in time," Calliope said with a breezy lack of concern that did little to comfort Marianna. "Besides, you wouldn't ever be among that lot of bespoke virgins. They're plain country girls bought for the night and no more, and in truth they're likely as much virgins as you or I."

"But what is—"

"In time, my dear, in time," Calliope said, looping her arm through Marianna's to draw her closer. "This is not the place for explaining such things. Suffice to say that, because you are so beautiful, and so passionate, Lord Blackwood will regard you as a rare and precious prize, to be savored and enjoyed."

She lowered her voice further, though it was unlikely anyone would overhear in the crowded gallery. "I tell you, Lord Blackwood would treat you like a queen—a *queen*. No matter how exuberant the other celebrants become at the Abby, he wouldn't share you. That's how Rogersme is, too. He doesn't take me with him for fear that others would demand a go or two. Not that I would object, mind, not when I've heard of the handsome young bucks brought for the use of the ladies, or for gentlemen with a letch for sodomy. All for sport, yes?"

Marianna thought again of the ruby bracelet—a gift she seemed to have been given simply for letting her cunny be licked.

"But I was with you and His Lordship last night, and he did not seem disinclined, or disapproving."

"No, he didn't, did he?" Calliope sighed impatiently, her

cheeks flushing a deeper, crosser red beneath the painted circles of rouge. "But then, that was to amuse *him*, which makes all the difference with gentlemen. What makes for a succulent sauce for the goose does not necessarily taste so fine for the gander, and I do not believe— Oh, there are the gentlemen are now, near the far door."

Eagerly Marianna craned her neck to look over the others' heads, the plume on her hat bobbing over her shoulder. She was perishing of curiosity about Lord Blackwood, and desperate to see if he truly was as Calliope had claimed and handsome as sin.

"Marianna, please!" Calliope grabbed her arm, and forcibly turned her about, and away from the gentlemen. "Don't shame me now, I beg you! You must not wave or halloo at peers, as if we were vulgar tavern maids off to meet the butcher's apprentice. You let them come to us, and believe it was all their notion in the first place."

"But I don't see why we must—"

"Because we *must*, my dear, and let that be an end to it." Calliope squeezed Marianna's arm more tightly, clearly fearing she might still act on an impulse that would humiliate them both. "Here, consider this foolish picture before us instead, and let us discuss precisely why the raging tiger's eyes are crossed. Yes. Do you believe the original beast actually suffered from such an ill-favored condition, or is it instead due to the incompetence of the artist?"

Marianna tried to concentrate on the tiger, but she'd little interest in either the wild beast or pictures in general, not beyond the bawdy pictures that Johnny had showed her. Instead she tried once again to imagine Lord Blackwood: how exactly was one "handsome as sin"? What, really, did that mean? Would he be young, tall, dark-haired or fair, or—

"Ahh, Mrs. Wiles, good day to you," Lord Rogersme said, and swiftly she turned to face him. He was impeccably dressed and impeccably polite, exactly as any well-bred English gentleman should be, as if he'd not been grunting and worrying his tongue deep in her cunny not twelve hours before. "I'd dared to hope you would be here. Miss Wren, good day to you as well. How pleasant to see you both!"

"We are honored, My Lord," Calliope said, sinking into a respectful curtsy. Belatedly Marianna joined her, bowing her head as if she were still on the staff at Worthy Hall. But unlike those days, now a man's hand clasped hers to help draw her back upright. Startled, she looked up, and directly into the face of the Marquess of Blackwood.

At once Marianna understood what Calliope had meant by calling the marquess handsome as sin, for if sin ever had a handsome face, then surely it would look like this. Lord Blackwood was tall and lean, almost to the point of seeming ascetic, as if there were no place on these bones for the plumping satisfaction of ordinary pleasures and comforts. His features were what the world thought proper for an aristocrat: regular and balanced, his jaw strong, his nose pronounced, his eyes wide-set and clear.

Yet those same eyes were of such a faint blue as to seem gray, even icy, and his complexion, too, was pale, without any of the ruddiness that gave most Englishmen (and -women) the reputation for jollity and good nature. There'd be no such humor in this man—only an intensity that would burn white-hot, and a focus that could not be broken. When he chose to be good, he would be more holy and righteous than all the saints in the firmament combined, but when he turned towards wickedness, he would outpace the devil himself.

"You must be Mrs. Wiles's cousin," he said softly, as if he and Marianna were the only two in the room.

"She is, My Lord," Calliope said beside her, yet she could have been twenty miles away, for all that Marianna heard her. "Might I present my cousin to you, Miss Marianna Wren. Miss Wren, Lord Blackwood."

"I've heard much of you, Miss Wren," he said, her hand still captured in his. "Yet none of those first reports have prepared me for the absolute perfection of your beauty. Before it, I am awed, and honored."

He raised her hand to his lips. At the last moment, he turned her hand in his, her fingers curling loosely upwards like the cupped petals of a flower. He pressed his lips to her palm, his dark brown hair falling heavily over his brow, his kiss so fervent that she nigh forgot to breath. His power, his intensity, his focus on her, had done that to her. She lost all sense of passing time—nay, simply all sense. She was vaguely aware of the comments of the others around them, of ladies' nervous laugher and the jeering suggestions of young men.

It mattered not. Marianna felt her knees weaken, her spine soften, her blood coursing like fire through her veins. Her heart raced and her cunny was warm, to swell and ready itself for him.

She had never been so thoroughly aroused by so appall-

ingly little, and she didn't know whether to be delighted or
alarmed.

"You can let the sweet creature go now, Blackwood," Lord
Rogersme said dryly. "That web you've spun around her is
becoming a bit sticky."

"Yes, My Lord, do," Calliope said, coming more forcefully
to Marianna's rescue. "You've confused her mightily, the poor
sweet dear. My cousin is country-bred, and not accustomed
to gentlemen like you, any more than you are easy in the
company of innocents like her."

"Too true," Blackwood said, finally releasing Marianna's
hand. His bow to her was precise and courteous, a dancing
master's joy, and his gaze never left hers.

"Pray, forgive me, Miss Wren," he continued, his manner
a curious mixture of gallant charm and overweening self-
mockery. "I was overcome by your beauty."

Marianna made another, smaller curtsy, accepting his apol-
ogy. She wasn't certain whether this was what was done in
such circumstance or not, but from her days in service, she
had learned that extra obeisance often eased matters along,
and besides, it was never, ever shunned by the recipients.

"I am sure you intended me no harm, My Lord," she said,
her voice sounding oddly hollow to her own ears. "I took no
offense."

"Oh, of *course*," he murmured with the same withering
self-mockery. He crooked his arm and offered it to Marianna.
"Will you view the pictures with me, Miss Wren?"

She nodded, and rested her fingers on his arm to let him
guide her. The others would follow, and in a room so crowded,

she'd be safe enough, and besides, so long as she studied the pictures, she'd have no reason to meet his gaze.

There was no denying that she felt drawn to him above all the gentlemen in the gallery, just as a honeybee is drawn to the most exotic flowers in the garden. But likewise she felt too vulnerable in his company, too fuddled by his pale-eyed gaze, making her pretty role of the simple country cousin seem uncomfortably true. In half jest, Lord Rogersme had called Blackwood a spider spinning his web, with Marianna the hapless creature caught within: not a fitting Fate for any honeybee (or Heroine, either).

She took a deep breath to clear her head, and shake away the influence he'd had on her. There was nothing wrong with desire, or how her too-weak flesh had responded so boldly to his. He *was* as handsome as sin, and as tempting, too. But before she'd tumble into his bed, she must make sure to recall what Calliope had hinted to her of his ways, of strange practices and careless conquests by the score. Her beauty and her passion would not be enough if she wished to make any lasting connection with a gentleman such as Lord Blackwood. She would need her wit as well, every scrap of it, else suffer the sad Fate of that honeybee in the spider's web.

"Do you enjoy pictures, Miss Wren?" he asked, calling her back from her own thoughts.

"Oh, yes." Beneath the curving brim of her hat, she smiled as if it were true.

In return, he smiled as if he believed her. "I am glad to hear it. Pictures mean a great deal to me. I have a particular fondness for the works of the Italian masters, and have journeyed there myself to add to my collection."

"Indeed, My Lord." John Lyon had taught her much of Italy, there in Lady Worthy's library, and Marianna knew it as a luxuriant, alluring country, given much to venal excess: the land of the Aretino and his sexual postures, of Messalina and Lucretia Borgia and the infamous courtesans of watery Venice, of dildos and prints and paintings so shameless that most sturdy Englishmen flung them away as the work of the Devil.

But not if the Englishman were Lord Blackwood, the Devil himself, nor this Englishwoman the infinitely curious Miss Marianna Wren.

"Indeed, I do," Lord Blackwood said. "I should be loath to learn you considered this no more than a silly exercise to humor me."

"No exercise is silly, My Lord." With studied indifference, she traced her fingertips lightly along the curving edge of her bodice's neckline, over that fascinating territory where her breasts did threaten to burst free of their whalebone restraints.

"No?" He cocked a single dark brow, enough to convince her that he was imagining another exercise entirely between them, one of a decidedly Italianate flavor. He wanted her as much as she wanted him—that was clear. "Then humor me additionally, Miss Wren, and name to me your favorite painter."

"It is so difficult to choose only one, My Lord," she said, gazing about the gallery as if narrowing her choices. In truth there was only one that she knew well enough to name, but even that, she suspected, was one more than he'd expected from her. Ah, the education she'd had in Lady Worthy's library!

"I only ask for one, Miss Wren," the marquess said indulgently. "Nor need you oblige my tastes, and chose an Italian. Any common English artist will do as well."

"But my choice is Italian, My Lord." She smiled, relishing his surprise. "And I've not a single favorite, but two: Correggio and Titian."

He paused, his pale eyes studying her with new appreciation. "You surprise me, Miss Wren. Such vigorous artists are not often to the taste of ladies."

"But they are to mine, My Lord," she said. "It is their classical subjects that intrigue me most."

"In my experience, most ladies prefer portraits." He made a slight, disparaging gesture, as if to dismiss those other ladies and their hopeless taste. "I've always believed it was the jewels and rich clothing that attracted their eye."

"What, as if all ladies were scavenging magpies?" she asked, incredulous. "Attracted only to shiny bits of rubbish?"

"Attracted to bracelets of rubies and diamonds," he said, watching her face closely for her reaction, "given to them by gentlemen in return for certain favors."

She blushed, not with shame, but surprise. She should have known that Lord Rogersme would have shared his exploits from the previous night, nor should she have been offended by the sharing. Hadn't she and Calliope done exactly the same? But she'd a trump for his wretched magpies, and now was the time to play it.

"What a pity that there are no bracelets to be seen in the pictures I like best, My Lord," she said. "In fact, they are devoid of those very features you believe that ladies prefer."

"Can you name these pictures, Miss Wren?" he asked. "If they are truly by Correggio and Titian, then I am certain they will be familiar to me."

"I am sure of it." She smiled, a certain serene yet knowing smile she had learned from Calliope. "My favorite picture by Correggio is *Io and Jupiter*."

If he was shocked, he masked it well. She'd grant him that. "There is no finer representation than Correggio's," he agreed. "The moment of Io's surrender to her lover, the glow of her flesh as she opens herself to receive him has never been more fully captured."

She nodded, her heart quickening as she recalled every detail of the erotic painting, and remembering, too, how she had spread her legs wide and assumed the swooning young Io's exact pose while Johnny had played her Jupiter. She glanced sideways at Blackwood, beneath the veil of her lashes, all beguiling seduction.

Did that memory show on her face now? Could Blackwood tell what she'd done, what she remembered? Had he already guessed that she wasn't the maid that she and Calliope pretended her to be? Was that why he was studying her with such interest now, her eyes narrowed as if to focus their intensity more keenly?

He circled his arm lightly around her waist, a familiar gesture for so short an acquaintance, and one that could have been protective or possessive.

"You must tell me, Miss Wren," he said, "if that is your favorite Correggio, then what, pray, is your favorite Titian? *Sacred and Profane Love,* perhaps? *The Judgment of Paris? Venus and*—"

"Leda and the Swan," she said, her words spilling out in an impulsive rush, yet with not one whit of coyness. "The figure of Leda is so well described that I can fair *feel* her ecstasy as Jupiter as the swan ravishes her, and fills her maiden's passage with his cock, and his divine seed. I can feel how—"

"This way," he said abruptly. He half led, half dragged Marianna from the gallery, heedless of the others who turned, curious, to watch them pass. He took her down one hall, then another. Though not so outwardly muscled as Lord Rogersme, the marquess was every bit his equal in strength, and Marianna doubted whether she could have broken his grasp, even if she'd wished it.

She did not ask him where they were going, or what would happen when finally they stopped. Yet she was excited beyond measure to know that she'd driven him this far, aroused him so fully that he'd been forced to act upon it, and now upon her, and she could scarcely bear to wait.

Finally he drew her into a small, narrow room filled with tall, dark cabinets of ancient pots and other gloomy crockery, locked away behind glass doors. At this late hour in the day, there were no other visitors, and they had the hall to themselves. He took her to the far end of the room, between two of the cabinets, where they'd not be spied at once if any others should happen upon them. He turned her about to face him, squarely, so nothing could be avoided, or dissembled with a sidelong glance. Her heart racing, she expected him to use the privacy of the situation for a more personal conversation, or to inquire more closely after her well-rewarded evening between Calliope and Lord Rogersme.

Alas, on occasion even the expectations of a Heroine are mistaken, and thus it was now with Marianna, and most especially with Lord Blackwood.

For His Lordship was no longer in a humor for conversation.

Instead he curled his hand around her nape, tangling his fingers deeply into her hair to hold the back of her head in his palm. Before she could react, he'd bent down beneath the sweeping brim of her hat and kissed her fiercely, possessing her mouth as completely as he could. He bumped the brim of the hat, and impatiently he pulled it from her hair, letting it fall forgotten to the floor.

He pulled her kerchief from her bodice, and with brisk efficiency freed her breasts as well, her heated flesh spilling from her bodice. He tugged on one nipple, and when she gasped into his mouth, he squeezed harder, making her yelp with the sharpness of the sensation, to the very edge of where her delight would change to pain. She writhed against him, in thrall to the demand of his mouth on hers, and he pushed her back against the rough wall, grinding his hard cock against her. With so much concentrated attention, she'd no doubt that she was aroused, or that it would have taken little more to make her spend, there where anyone could have seen her.

Yet as relentlessly as Blackwood sought to stir her desires— and successfully, too—she'd the disturbing feeling he'd kept his own in tight control, and the chilly distance she'd first noted in his pale gaze now seemed part of his caresses as well. It was almost as if everything he did to her was only for him to observe her reaction, rather than to share the pleasure with her.

When she'd bantered with him in the gallery, teasing him with her bold talk of Io and Jupiter and Leda being ravished by the swan, she'd believed she'd evened the balance between them, or even led. Now she realized what folly that was, for clearly the Marquess of Blackwood always—always—expected to be the master in all things, the one in control.

Unsettled, Marianna tried to draw back and couldn't, a fresh rush of desire filling her as she fought with him, and herself. Oh, she was weak, too weak! Again she tried to pull free and mustered only a sorry flutter of her hands, like sad little birds caught in a snare.

She moaned into his mouth with mingled frustration and desire, and that, it seemed, was enough for him. He let her go so suddenly that she fell backwards, against the wall. Behind him, she glimpsed her reflection in one of the glass-fronted cabinets: her hair disheveled, her mouth so swollen it seemed bruised, her breasts bare and quivering above her stays and her nipples as red and bright as the rubies with which he'd taunted her earlier.

He stood and watched as she repaired her dress, her hands trembling as she pulled her bodice back into place and twisted her tangled hair to support her hat.

"I am sorry for that, Miss Wren," he said at last, softly, and once again taking her by surprise. "But I wanted to be sure."

She paused warily, a hairpin in her hand. "Forgive me, My Lord, but what surety did you require?"

"That you were a virgin, as you claim to be," he answered. "Rogersme swore to me that you were, that he'd touched your maidenhead himself, but the man is an oaf in such matters, and not to be relied upon."

"Lord Rogersme is not so great an oaf as others," she said.

He chuckled, though there was no mirth to it. "Why don't you speak freely, Miss Wren, and say my name aloud?"

"Because I cannot lay any blame at your door without doing the same to myself," Marianna said evenly. "Were you satisfied, My Lord?"

"What, as to whether you are a virgin or not?" he asked. "I would venture that you are."

"How gratifying, My Lord." She jabbed her hatpin into the straw crown of her hat. "I congratulate you."

"I would take care, Miss Wren," he warned, smiling still. "Most gentlemen do not care for a woman with a tongue as sharp as yours."

"Good day, My Lord," she said, not deigning to give more of a reply as she slipped past him to rejoin Calliope in the gallery.

He caught her arm, less roughly this time, and held her back.

"I believe you are a virgin," he said, "though it doesn't matter to me whether you've had a prick up your cunt yet or not. What is the value of a scrap of gristle and blood? No, Miss Wren, it's your soul that remains as yet pure and untouched, unmarked, unviolated by any man, and that—that is what intrigues me far more."

If he were a footmen or groom and she had still been a scullery maid at Worthy Hall, then she would have called him a foul name and spit on him for his trouble. But he was a peer and a gentleman, and though she'd risen from what she'd been, her rank was still far lower than his: and thus the best (or worst) she could do was a perfunctory curtsy, and bitter-tasting silence.

And save the worst curses for herself for letting him play her for such a fool.

"I can't believe His Lordship was as ill-mannered as you say, Marianna," Calliope said the following afternoon, as they slowly began to greet the new day. They had slept apart, or rather, Calliope had shared her bed with Lord Rogersme, and Marianna had not, with both friends agreeing that perhaps it would not be wise to tempt the earl's restraint too sorely. "Though surely you recall I'd warned you how peculiarly demanding gentlemen can be about virginity."

"The demands themselves were bad enough, Calliope, but they were only the beginning." Marianna sipped her chocolate, glad to claim even that small comfort wherever she could. Her breast was bruised where Lord Blackwood had pinched her too sharply, and though there seemed no lasting injury, she considered herself fortunate to have learned the truth of him so cheaply. "He used my person most barbarously ill, and dared to call it his test of my innocence."

"Oh, my poor dear!" Calliope exclaimed. "There are those persons in this world who find the greatest pleasure to be in giving pain to others, in various ways, just as there are those who will also relish receiving that pain. I'd not known the marquess's personal tastes ran that course, though I suppose I should have guessed. Rogersme has told me that there are many opportunities for such complicated amusements at the Abbey."

Marianna sat upright, her cup resting on her crossed legs. "Now that we're alone, pray tell me more of this Abbey, and what occurs there."

"Oh, the Abbey." Calliope sighed dramatically, as was fitting for such a subject. "I could speak of that place all the day long, and not begin to tell you everything there is to tell, and that only what I know is from Rogersme and others, not having visited myself."

"Does Blackwood own it? Is it on his lands?"

"Oh, yes, it's his, in every way possible," Calliope said, settling back against her pillows. "You know how gentlemen will create outrageous clubs to help them keep away tedium, groups of friends who gather for drinking and whoring and gambling and general mischief."

Marianna shook her head. La, there was so much to learn of the fashionable world!

"Well, they do, and small pots of wickedness they are, too," Calliope said eagerly. "The one that Blackwood started is called the Hell Hounds Club, and in addition to the usual activities, its members are said to mock the Church through pagan rituals that are so depraved that members are sworn to secrecy regarding their practices. Rogersme has been a guest, though not a member, and tells me tales of costumed monks and nuns and orgies that last for days, and special rooms that cater to the whims of each member."

"Nuns and monks!" Marianna exclaimed. "So that is why their house is called an Abbey?"

"That, and because it once *was* a genuine abbey," Calliope continued, "before old King Henry disbanded the Romish church, and long before Blackwood bought it for the use of his club. But that is how I know of the gentlemen who blur their pleasure with pain. Rogersme says there are 'nuns' who specialize in caning and whipping, and that when the House of Lords meets, certain members can scarce take their seats, their asses are so raw from a week of flogging at the Abbey!"

"I do believe that would suit Lord Blackwood," Marianna said thoughtfully. "He spoke of not so much wishing to have my innocence, but my soul, as if he truly were the devil himself."

"Well, that's rubbish, isn't it?" Calliope said, speaking plain as usual. "No mortal can take another's soul, and even if they could, who would wish the thing? But think of what sport it would be to wear one of the nun's habits, and put aside ranks and proper names, and fuck and frolic with whomever one pleased! Though I suppose they'd all guess me on account of my hair, but still, I could end up sucking the cock of some famous personage, or fucking a royal prince."

Marianna's eyes widened with her usual curiosity, and as they often did with Calliope. "You would do that? You would go there, and join the Hell Hounds as one of their nuns, and let yourself be taken by strangers?"

"I would," declared Calliope. "I would indeed. I'd wager you would, too, once you've accustomed yourself to the idea. Whenever else would we women have the same chance to be as wicked and wild as gentlemen?"

Marianna nodded, letting the idea settle and grow. For Calliope, it might seem to be great sport and no more, but for Marianna, a week of such openly licentious and blasphemous behavior was a very large step to take, either backwards or forwards, depending on one's point of vantage. And for a Heroine, the burden would be doubly great, to bear both the responsibility of this story along with the considerably sized conscience necessary for rationalizing such wild and unrestrained behavior.

Yet likewise a week at the Abbey could be viewed as a natural step in her journey away from the strictures of Lady Worthy. For Marianna, whose very name was not the one with which she'd been born and whose history and family were forever a secret, assuming another identity for amusement did not seem such a great thing to do, nor, when she recalled how John Lyons had implored her to explore every aspect of her desires to learn what pleased her best, did it seem unduly lubricious, either.

"Would Rogersme take you with him, a guest of a guest?" she asked.

"What, my dear, so you could be my guest of a guest of a guest?" Calliope laughed ruefully. "*That* will never occur, not in this life. Rogersme would never take me, fearing that I would both spoil his fun, and find another gentleman to replace him. Not that I would, of course, but there it is. Besides, I've heard that all the nuns must be ladies, either by birth or by marriage, which would quite omit us, wouldn't it?"

"I don't believe we could look to Lord Blackwood for invitations, either," Marianna said with a sigh. "After yesterday, I do not believe he will wish ever to see me again, nor I him."

"Oh, my dearest of dears," Calliope said, and winked slyly. "I should not be so sure of that, you know. I should not be sure of that in the least."

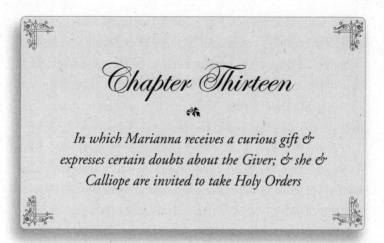

Chapter Thirteen

*In which Marianna receives a curious gift &
expresses certain doubts about the Giver; & she &
Calliope are invited to take Holy Orders*

Three days later, Marianna stood on the small gilded footstool in Calliope's drawing room, her arms in a graceful oval before her, as she'd been instructed as being ladylike, and tried not to shriek as the mantua maker's assistant jabbed and pricked her with needles and pins.

Madame du Précis hovered around Marianna, scowling with fierce and critical determination as she smoothed this pleat, and plucked at that ruffle, striving to mold the emerald green silk lute string into a gown that was both in the latest style as determined by the French *modistes*, and also alluring to the eye of whichever English lord would in time receive her bill.

The first dress for a new customer was the most important, establishing as it did a partnership that could span many years and many, many gowns. It was especially important to please a young woman who was going into keeping. From long experience, Madame du Précis knew that such women would order far more gowns than her more respectable sisters, and equally that their gentlemen tended to be far more tolerant of costly trimmings, extra embroideries, and that final length of Flemish lace than ordinary fathers and husbands, even when the gentlemen were one in the same.

"The waist could be a fraction more refined, yes?" Madame pinched the fabric, judging how much could be subtracted yet leave Marianna enough room for breathing (though not too deeply). "Miss Wren, it is possible for your maid to lace you more tightly, yes? Another inch smaller, only an inch, and Miss Wren will have the most sublime figure in London, in England, in—"

"Miss Wren's waist is already so small as to make the rest of us feel like fat sows," Calliope observed, sprawled on the chaise to watch, her ankles delicately crossed to display her own new pair of red-heeled mules. "Pray don't torment her any longer, Madame, before she becomes so vastly beautiful that none of us will be able to speak to her ever again."

Marianna laughed, glad to have her friend with her. Having a gown fitted to her body was torment, one she'd never dreamed when she'd had but one linsey-woolsey gown to her name. But Calliope assured her it was essential to have her gowns fit as tightly as possible over her stays, the better to reveal the niceties of her figure to gentlemen. It was, Marianna decided, rather like a farmer's wife laying her roundest apples to the front of the market stand.

"Next the flowered silk," Calliope ordered, yawning as she

waved a languid hand towards the assistants. "Along with you now. Miss Wren and I are most barbarously busy, and we can't— Oh, enter, enter."

Marianna twisted around on the stool to see which footman had come, and what he was delivering. An entering footman was generally the harbinger of an exciting delivery to the house: an invitation, a letter, or, as now and as best, a box from a gentleman.

"For you, Miss Wren," Fitz said, holding the tray with the box up for her on the stool. She took it and hopped down, eagerly unwrapping the ribbons. The box was too large and square for a jewel, yet still too small for much else.

"So long as it's not another gift for you from Rogersme, I am content." Calliope rolled from the chaise to join Marianna (doubtless to make sure of the giver), her high red heels clicking across the parquet floor. "There are times when that gentleman shows no sense in the least."

Marianna hopped down, and sat on the stool, ignoring the concerned warnings for the gown from Madame and her assistants. She opened the shop's pasteboard box carefully and unwrapped the packing cloth inside, finally revealing a small oval box of finest French porcelain with gilt-brass fittings.

"What a perfect little patch box," Calliope said with approval. "Most appropriate, whoever sent it. I know you still don't wear many of them—nor should you, at your age—but it's a suitable gift nonetheless."

But Marianna wasn't really listening to Calliope discuss the box's pleasingness. Instead she was staring at the picture enameled onto the box's lid, which wasn't suitable by anyone's standards—except, perhaps, the gentleman who'd sent it.

At first glance, the miniature picture was blandly respectable, a young lady sitting in a bower of flowers. Yet when a tiny button on the side of the lid was pushed, a clockwork mechanism was triggered from within, and the picture changed.

"Hah, Calliope, look," Marianna said, giggling. "Mark what happens."

Marianna pushed the button, and the lady's skirt flew up and her legs parted, revealing her minuscule cunny. She pushed the button again, and a giant, ardent swan suddenly appeared from beneath her cast-off skirt to lunge between her open thighs. Finally, if she pushed the button in rapid succession, the swan's wings flapped as he thrust in and out, while the lady rocked back and forth beneath the force of the swan's attentions.

"Well, *that's* a lewd little piece, isn't it?" Calliope said, but she laughed as well. "Is there a card? Who would send you something like that?"

"I'm sure it's Lord Blackwood," Marianna said, searching for a card in the cast-off wrappings. "We spoke of Leda and the swan while we viewed the pictures."

"You *did*?" squeaked Calliope, agog. "Leda and that infernal swan?"

Marianna nodded. "And of Io and Jupiter, too. We were speaking of pictures. Italian pictures."

"Yes, but, oh, my, what kind of pictures!" Calliope exclaimed with admiration. "I'd not expected that of you, my country cousin."

"Neither did he," Marianna admitted. "Here is his card."

Adventure is wherever you find it.

"I vow, that's even more curious than the box," Calliope said. "He must be plotting and planning something rare, the rogue. A gentleman like His Lordship would do that. But there's no doubt that His Lordship remains intrigued with you."

"That would seem clear." Carefully Marianna replaced the porcelain box in its wrappings, and sighed. "But I am not certain whether I remain intrigued—or even interested—in His Lordship."

Perplexed, Calliope frowned, her arms akimbo and her hands set at her waist, the deep lace *engageantes* of her dressing gown (for that, as was her habit at home, was all that she again was wearing) fluttering at her elbows.

"Madame de Précis, the fitting is done for this day," she announced. "Miss Wren is weary, and needs to rest. Leave us, all of you, at once. At once!"

The mantua maker and her assistants gathered their work and their baskets and fled, leaving the two friends to sit side by side on the settee, with a decanter of canary and a dish of sweet biscuits between them for fortification.

"Lord Blackwood is handsome and rich and clever, but most of all, he would appear sufficiently interested in you that he has sent you a most personal gift," Calliope said, filling the goblets. "Yet you profess not to like him in return. Why is that, my dearest? What could make you doubt such a prize?"

Marianna shook her head, troubled. "It's most difficult to explain, because I do not know exactly why myself," she began. "When first I met him, I was thrilled beyond all measure by his company. His commanding air, his impetuosity, his kiss and his touch—all aroused me to a nigh-feverish state that was unlike any other in my experience."

"Then why ever would you deny him, or yourself?"

"Because the further affairs progressed between us, the less agreeable he became," Marianna confessed. "I do not ask that I love His Lordship, nor that he love me in return. Mr. Lyon will be the only one who ever has my heart and my love. But if I am to share Lord Blackwood's company and his person, then I should prefer to like him at the very least."

"What has happened, dearest?" At once Calliope was ready to defend her. "What has the rascal done to you?"

"It's not precisely what he has done," Marianna explained slowly, searching for the words. "It's rather what he hasn't. When we were alone together, when he kissed me, it was as if it were more important to him to be the master, than to find any pleasure with me."

"Why would he wish that?" Calliope asked with righteous indignation. "What use is there to having another party in your entertainment, if one takes no joy in it?"

Marianna nodded miserably. "What was worse was how he made me feel that the fault did lie with me. It was as if I were once again at Worthy Hall, where I never could do enough to please my betters. With His Lordship, I felt if I were somehow more agreeable to him, then he would have had satisfaction with me."

"Oh, my dear friend, that is not true," murmured Calliope. She slipped closer, putting her arm around Marianna's shoulder. "You are not only beautiful and full of passion, but clever as blazes, too. What other woman would speak to him of Leda and the swan? That was monstrously clever of you."

"It was?" Marianna asked, pleased that her little attempt at coquetry had succeeded. "I did nothing but answer his question. He asked me my favorite pictures, and I told him the ones I liked best."

"But they're such famously lewd pictures, and you're an innocent, and there's nothing that beguiles a gentleman more than an innocent who's unwittingly displaying a taste for wickedness." Calliope nodded sagely. "You'll see. It makes them positively giddy, imagining how they'll corrupt you in other ways, too."

Marianna sighed forlornly. "Do you think that was what he meant by claiming my soul?"

"Most likely," Calliope said. "Gentlemen will blather on in the oddest ways sometimes. And why else would he have sent you this particular box? Because he is trying to prove himself worthy of *you*, Marianna, and you must never forget that."

"That is true," Marianna said with a sniff that betrayed how close she'd been to tears. "It is for me to make the most of my gifts. That was what Johnny told me, and he was wise and right."

"He was right to tell you that," Calliope said, handing her

friend her own lace-bordered handkerchief. "But I expect you knew it yourself already, else you never would have dared to leave Worthy Hall."

"I did." Marianna nodded again, her confidence beginning to return. "I *did*."

"That you did," Calliope agreed. "Now you must decide what pleases you, else you'll never be able to please anyone else. Though I vow that with all his fortune, His Lordship does have enormous resources with which to please *you*."

Marianna raised her chin. "His Lordship may have all that, but he'll not have me, not until I wish it."

"No, he shall not," Calliope said, then glanced up at Marianna, waggling her brows with her usual mischief. "Unless, of course, he perceives your secret weakness, and should contrive a way to change himself into a great raging buck swan and swoop down upon you one afternoon in the park. Now *that* would be a proper adventure, wouldn't it? What better way to make all London speak of you than— Oh, what is it now, Fitz?"

The footman had appeared again, this time with two large bundles in his arms. "These were brought to the door, ma'am," he said. "There is one for you, and for Miss Wren."

"Well, now, at least there's one gentleman in this city who knows enough to reward us both." Eager (or greedy) as always, Calliope hurried forward to take the bundles, tossing one to Marianna and beginning to open the other. "I vow, it's certainly a lumpy sort of tribute. What can it be?"

"I've no idea." Marianna held up the contents of her package: a long hooded robe of white satin, stitched with a delicate pattern of red flames along the cuffs, and a red satin half mask. "I'd venture we've been invited to some sort of masquerade."

"Oh, my dearest dear, this is no common, two-penny masquerade," Calliope said, gleefully holding up the card that had dropped from the folds of satin, a card that showed a baying dog with a huge erection surrounded by more flames. "Marianna, we've been invited to attend Blackwood Abbey, and the next meeting of the Hell Hounds Club!"

"I do not like this," Lord Rogersme said, turning the collar of his cloak against the river's damp. "Not one blasted thing about it."

It was nearly ten o'clock, long past the hour when honest folk began journeys and junkets. The night was unusually dark, with low clouds to mask the moon and stars. Their lanterns' light seemed pale and insubstantial, and made weaker still by the low mists that rose from the water's surface.

"Oh, My Lord, please, don't grumble," Calliope said, slipping her hands inside his cloak to coax him into a better humor. "This is meant to be a lark, not a funeral."

"It's tempting Fate—that's what it is," he said uneasily, his gaze scanning the shadows around them. "You and Marianna should have stayed in the carriage until the boat was loaded."

"Oh, we shall be fine," Calliope said. "Won't we, Marianna?"

"Of course we shall," Marianna said, shivering with excitement and the chill of the river, too. She'd never done anything like this, *ever,* but still she shared Calliope's high spirits. They'd be on their way soon enough; the men were nearly finished loading their traveling trunks with their robes, masks, and other belongings into the boat. Most of the other guests bound for the Abbey would have already departed, taking the special scarlet-painted boat that Blackwood sent up to London, but Rogersme had insisted that they make the journey like this, on their own, claiming that there'd be far too much debauchery on board the scarlet boat for her and Calliope.

She and Calliope had giggled together over that—why fuss over decorum and propriety on one's way to what would surely be an orgy?—but perhaps the earl had reason to be so protective. He'd attended the Abbey's festivities before, and knew well what to expect, while Marianna and Calliope, as novice nuns, could only imagine. No wonder Marianna could not keep still, hopping up and down inside her cloak!

The boatman helped her step from the queue down into the boat, and she took her seat beside Calliope.

"I don't know what could be keeping Goodleigh," the earl said. "I know I told him the hour."

"Goodleigh!" exclaimed Calliope with dismay. "Oh, My Lord, you didn't tell me Colonel Goodleigh was traveling with us!"

"I don't tell you everything, Callie," the earl said testily. "Goodleigh's my friend as well as a favored guest of Blackwood, and besides, I'll welcome a brave gentleman like him on this black night."

"What is wrong with this Colonel Goodleigh?" whispered Marianna. "Why don't you wish him to join us?"

"There's nothing really *wrong* with him," Calliope said, grumbling a bit herself. "Colonel Goodleigh's just not very genteel, that is all. He's a hale old soldier who served in the colonies, slaughtering the savages and Frenchmen. Not that he had any choice. He's only the fourth son of a viscount, with no fortune at all. Mind you, you are under no obligation whatsoever to be agreeable to him. You're meant for a marquis this week, not the likes of Goodleigh, and I— Oh, hush, he's here."

Marianna looked up as the earl made hasty introductions. By the shifting lantern light, she had only a glimpse of the Colonel's face—broad, ruddy, and peppered across the cheeks with smallpox scars—and his bright red hair. But his smile was pleasantly cheerful and his manner not nearly as rough as Calliope had implied, and as he climbed into the boat with Lord Rogersme, she had to admit that it would not be so very bad to have an officer skilled at fighting savages and Frenchmen as a member of their party.

"I know this is Mrs. Wiles's first visit to the Abbey," the Colonel said once they were properly on their way. "What of you, Miss Wren? Have you attended the rites before?"

"No, sir," Marianna said. "This will be my first time as well."

"Oh, Marianna." Calliope giggled. "He's trying to figure out whether or not he's fucked you before."

"True enough," the Colonel admitted. "When the masks

are in place and the wine is running like water, it's no mean feat to tell one nun from the rest. Not that the robes stay on for long, eh? The rites are like that. I've heard that in the heat of the fray, brothers have ended up mounting their sisters. Or even worse, that some poor sots find themselves in the garden heaving away at their own wives."

"You never had Miss Wren," the earl said. "She's that's rarest of creatures, a *bona fide* virgin."

"A virgin?" The Colonel craned his neck to look at Marianna as if she were a genuine curiosity, a calf born with two heads. "Here?"

"Hold back there, Goodleigh," the earl warned. "Miss Wren's not one of those scattershot maidenheads imported for the entertainment. Once you see her in proper light, you'll understand. Calliope's taken her under her wing, trying to see who'll bid the most for the rights to her cunt. Rather like bringing the prize mare to market."

"Or like the proud mamas with their daughters searching for rich husbands at Court." The Colonel shrugged. "At least Miss Wren's being more honest about her pursuit, though I'll wager she'll have the devil of a time holding firm with this randy crowd."

"The randy crowd doesn't interest me, Colonel," Marianna said proudly. "I'm attending the rites by the express invitation of Lord Blackwood himself."

"Blackwood!" the Colonel exclaimed in patent amazement. "You've set your cap on a rare prize, missy, haven't you?"

"Aye, Blackwood," the earl said, passing the Colonel a small silver flask. "That's what comes from being rich as Croesus. If there's enough plunder, the ladies are willing to overlook everything else."

"Well, now, I wish you joy of that, Miss Wren," the Colonel said, solemnly raising the flask towards her in salute. "Luck, too. You might be going down to the Abbey as a virgin, but Blackwood will be doing his damnable best to make sure you don't return as one."

"If His Lordship pleases me," Marianna said quickly. "He must please me first."

The earl snorted. "Please *him*, Miss Wren. He's the one holding the purse strings. Please him, and he'll make you a queen."

Marianna nodded, adding his advice to all the rest she'd received. Being a queen was what she wanted, what she'd wanted ever since she'd left Worthington, and now perhaps the time had come. She and Calliope had discussed this endlessly, how, if the time and the offer seemed right, she'd succumb to the marquess.

She was prepared, too. She and Calliope had shaved each other again, to be sure that not a single downy imperfection marred their sleekly smooth cunnies. For the last few days, she'd been sitting in a bath of alum water, which had made her passage so tight that she could scarce slip her own finger inside. And in her trunk she'd also a small vial of pig's blood and a sponge to soak it in, to be able to present the proper gory display of deflowering.

Calliope had also demonstrated how best to play out her part—to the hilt, as it were. No matter how much desire Marianna might feel at the time, she must steadfastly resist showing any signs of her pleasure, and thrash her limbs about and weep and do everything she could to resist until the very last. According to Calliope, a hard-fought deflowering was considered the best by the men who valued such things, and the closer Marianna could make it seem like an out-and-out rape, the greater the reward she'd be able to expect for her troubles.

Yet the more Calliope had assured her that this was how such things were done, the more Marianna's uneasiness had grown. Calliope could advise her all she wished, but she'd only been with merry gentlemen like the earl. She'd never been confronted by the intensity of Lord Blackwood's pale blue eyes, or borne a bruise of his making, either.

But in the handful of times Marianna had seen Blackwood since then—in a shop, riding in the park, in the lobby of a playhouse—he'd been the model of a gentleman, his manners impeccable and his humor droll. In addition to sending the nun's habits, he'd written the most charming letter of invitation imaginable, promising her endless amusement. It had been as if he were inviting her to his house in the country to see the roses in bloom and stroll beside the mill pond, instead of taking part in decadent, blasphemous rituals fueled by wine and fornication and who knew whatever else?

Marianna hugged herself inside her cloak, and tried not to consider whatever that might be. Oh, yes, she'd need her wits this week, and every bit of the luck that Colonel Goodleigh had just offered.

"You'll have your first sight of the Abbey around the next crook of the river," the earl was saying. "You won't soon forget it, either. I'll grant that Blackwood does know how to do things up properly."

Eagerly Marianna leaned forward on the bench, seeking Calliope's hand for reassurance.

"Oh, my dear friend," she whispered, her voice trembling with excitement. "We're almost there."

The boat glided with the current, the oarsman feathering the blades to follow the river's bend, and past the last clump of shadowing trees. Marianna gasped, and her fingers tightened on Calliope's.

The Abbey stretched before them, a long, rambling building of severe gray stone, in the ancient style of buttresses and pointed windows. Parts had been permitted to fall into romantic decay, with porches tumbled down and columns slanting at nightmarish angles. Lanterns were hung in carefully chosen places, from tree branches and beneath windows, to cast more ominous shadows and increase the effect. The chapel was brightly lit from within, but the original windows had been replaced with bloodred glass, to make it glow like a giant, ominous ruby at the end of the Abbey. Snatches of solemn music drifted towards them over the water, beaten drums, and chanted choruses. A few figures could be seen passing beneath the lights; they were dressed in long robes like the ones Marianna and Calliope had been given, with their hoods pulled up and low over their faces.

Their boat drew closer to the Abbey's landing, where more hooded men waited to greet them. Two life-sized statues graced the end of the landing, each holding a flaming torch as a beacon: a naked nymph with hugely jutting breasts, and across from her a leering satyr with goatish ears and nether quarters and an enormous, rigid cock pointing towards the nymph.

"La," said Calliope whispered with enthusiastic awe. "I vow we're in for it now, aren't we?"

"Indeed," Marianna murmured, with not quite the same degree of cheerful enthusiasm generally expected of a Heroine. "Oh, indeed."

Chapter Fourteen

*In which Marianna learns more of the
curious practices & customs of Blackwood Abbey;
& Lord Blackwood demonstrates a stimulating
new jewel of Gold & Rubies*

"The robes are worn with nothing beneath, ma'am." The lady's maid, a member of the Abbey's staff (there having been certain problems in the past regarding the unfortunate coercion of unwilling servants brought by their masters and mistresses), was masked and dressed in a similar hooded robe, but sewn from common linen, not silk satin, to differentiate her from the guests. Though half of the maid's face was hidden behind a plain black mask, Marianna guessed the other woman to be not much older than herself, with a sweetly pretty mouth and full breasts beneath her robe, and Marianna wondered if the servants, too, were drawn into the sexual games.

"No jewels, or ornaments in the hair, either," the woman continued. "Nothing that sets you apart, or by which you could be identified by other guests. All that's permitted is white silk stockings, tied with plain white ribbons, and slippers, on account of how nicely they show the legs. That is the code for dressing for ladies at the Abbey, ma'am."

Marianna frowned down at the robe in the woman's hands. She hadn't realized she was to be naked beneath it, nor had she realized that everyone else would be in the same near-natural state as well.

"It won't take long to grow used to it, ma'am," the woman said, more gently. "At first it feels shameful, I know, but then the freedom's nice enough. If you wish, ma'am, I'll help you unlace your stays."

"Thank you, yes." Marianna turned her back. As the maid began to unknot the lacings, Marianna glanced curiously around her bedchamber. While Calliope and Lord Rogersme had fittingly been shown to a single room, she'd been given this room to herself. Not that she'd any reason to expect real privacy; Lord Rogersme had warned her that there were master keys to every lock. He'd also said that there were peepholes between every bedchamber, for guests to spy on one another for mutual titillations, though given the number of public couplings (and triplings, et cetera) that he expected would take place throughout the Abbey, she wondered why anyone would bother being so discreet.

Peepholes or not, the room didn't look any different from chambers for guests in any country house, with furnishing of a good quality. But there were several subtle differences. The looking glass was far larger than usual, and placed directly beside the bed, much to Marianna's amusement. The framed engravings on the walls were not the usual edifying scenes from history or plays, but the infamous *Postures* of Aretino, showing muscular, bearded men engaged in complicated, vig-orous sex with equally athletic women.

Marianna leaned forward to consider the nearest engrav-ing. Shamelessly her heart began to race as she studied the man's engorged prick stretched and pleasuring the woman's full-lipped cunt in glorious detail, with the woman's leg con-veniently raised over the man's shoulder to give an unob-structed view. Penetration and possession, beautifully drawn, and unconsciously she ran her tongue over her lips as she studied the picture.

It had been over a month now since she'd last fucked John, between the bars in the Worthington gaol, and while Calliope had offered her many thrilling substitutes, she was thoroughly weary of playing the virgin. She lusted for a man's cock, and a man's fucking. How would she ever survive this week of car-nal excess if she were doomed to remain only a spectator?

The maidservant behind her noticed her interest, and her quickened breath, too.

"Ahh, you'll enjoy yourself this night, ma'am, for certain," she said with approval. As she reached around to remove Mari-anna's stays, she dipped her hands into the front of Marianna's shift as if by accident, and cupped her breasts. With the gen-tlest of fingers, she rubbed Marianna's nipples into stiff but tender peaks, making her gasp with the unexpected pleasure of so familiar a caress.

"You've a warm temperament, ma'am," she said, with-drawing her hands and pulling the stays over Marianna's head. "That's a fine thing, especially in a lady of your few years. So many of the younger ones are too green for real pleasure."

She hung the stays in the clothespress along with Marianna's gown, as if tucking away Marianna's everyday self along with her clothes.

"Nearly all the guests are arrived, ma'am," she continued, "so pray listen for the bell. That's to call everyone below, to the great hall, where His Lordship will initiate this session's rites. Now your shift, ma'am, if you please."

She drew the fine linen up over Marianna's head, putting it away with the rest of her things, and returned with the hooded satin robe.

"What a shame to cover so fair a figure, ma'am," she said with a sigh as she slipped the robe's sleeves along Marianna's arms. "Though I don't expect you'll be dressed for long. The gentlemen will all be wild for that shaven quim of yours, and besides, they always look for the novices. That's what this embroidery means, here, the lightest stitching on the cuff: that this is your first time with the Hell Hounds. You'll see some folk tonight whose sleeves are nigh covered with red thread, they've been attending for so long."

Marianna nodded, smoothing the silk over her body. The robe was cut to fall straight to the floor, a mockery of a true Romish nun's habit, yet was open from the neck to the waist to reveal the curves of Marianna's breasts. The white slippery silk seemed to melt over Marianna's naked flesh like another caress, and when she looked at herself in the glass, she realized how the thin, shining fabric enhanced her nudity rather than masked it. The silk accentuated the full tremble of her breasts and displayed the hard arousal of her nipples, then slithered lower, clinging to the sweeping curve of her waist to her hips and the slight dip for her navel. It slid wantonly into the valley between her thighs and over her hairless mound, even hinting at the tempting pout of her nether lips. She turned, and the silk briefly spun away from her, then settled again, this time nestling into the furrow between her bottom cheeks, highlighting each globe as if by moonlight from above.

Watching, the maid clucked her tongue. "There now, ma'am, have you ever seen such a toothsome sight?"

Marianna stared at her reflection, transfixed by how seductive she looked in such a deceptively simple garment. Was this how she looked to gentlemen? she wondered. Did they see the eager desire that it took this white silk for her to see?

"I've never seen myself like this," she said softly. "Perhaps because I've never *been* like this."

The maid laughed knowingly. "Oh, aye, ma'am, most likely you haven't," she said. "If you wish to prime your honeypot a bit before the rites, there're playthings in the box on the sideboard."

"Playthings?" Curious, Marianna turned to the large box, fashioned of richly figured burl wood inlaid with silver wire inlay. She opened the lid, and her eyes widened.

Playthings, indeed. Snugged in a nest of red velvet was a set of a half dozen ivory dildos, the false cocks that Calliope had first described—and later demonstrated—to her. These were beautifully carved in lavish detail, from the flared crowns with dimpled glans, to the pair of large wrinkled ballocks at the bottom. The dildos were arranged from large to larger to one that seemed to Marianna to be more worthy of a stallion at stud than any mere mortal man.

"There's a vial of sweet oil in there, too, ma'am," the maid explained, as plainly as if she were speaking of starching linen or making tea. "It's useful for easing the way for the larger tools, or if either party wishes to test themselves with a bit of buggery. There are some ladies who wish to take two at a time as well, or a false lover in her ass with a fleshly one in her cunt. All's fair at the Abbey, ma'am, all's fair. Will there be anything else, ma'am?"

"You may go." Marianna waited until she heard the door shut behind her before she touched the neatly arranged dildos. It amused her to see them in a row like this, like well-ordered soldiers presenting their cocks for her review. She touched each one in turn, letting her fancy wander languorously from the handsome soldiers back to the bearded man in the Aretino engraving. She'd have no need of the sweet oil—that was certain—for her honeypot was already primed, her thighs already moist with her juices. She could make use of one of these before the meeting bell sounded, a quick spend to help her ease her anxieties about the night.

Her fingers went first to the cock whose size most resembled her Johnny's, not the most exuberant, but not the slightest, either. Then she recalled how in this place she was regarded as a virgin still, and how she'd taken such pains this week to make her cunny appear as she claimed. She wasn't sure if she could take this size, let alone enjoy it, and with a sigh of regret, she chose instead the smallest of the phalluses.

She once again stood before the glass, and began to trail the dildo along the deep-cut opening at the front of the robe, making it linger over her breasts and follow the heavy under-curve beneath. The ivory was warming from the heat of her skin, becoming more realistic in her hands, and she closed her eyes to focus more surely on the sensations.

She imagined her Johnny here with her, the two of them on this bed, in the same posture of the Aretino engraving. She'd tuck her ankle over Johnny's shoulder with the same agility, making her slit tighter around his cock, and he would hold her by her hips, tilting her towards his cock as he slowly pushed his way into her, letting her become aware of every pulsing inch as he opened her, stretched her, filled her until she—

"Why, Miss Wren," Lord Blackwood said in dry observation, "it would seem that I have arrived just in time to save your maidenhead from being ravaged by that scrap of elephant's tusk."

She whipped around to face him, her face crimson and the incriminating dildo still clutched tight in her fingers. She'd been warned that doors did not stay locked, and he was here as the proof.

He was dressed in a robe styled much like her own, but in black satin, his hood pushed carelessly back for now. Rich embroidery in both scarlet and gold thread formed a deep border on the sleeves, doubtless to signify his superior experience and rank, as the maidservant had explained.

"My Lord." She bowed her head with shame, and sank into a curtsy of contrition, the white silk puddling around her feet.

This time when he came to stand before her, he did not take her hand to raise her up, but to prize the dildo from her fingers, holding it up for consideration.

"You chose quite modestly, Miss Wren," he said, remarking on the dildo's size. "Or are your expectations simply that small?"

He passed the dildo beneath his nose, inhaling. "Why, it would seem that this poor phallus is as virginal as yourself. Clearly I arrived too soon. What a pity for you both!"

"Yes, My Lord." Slowly she rose, her hands clasped before her. He was a peer, not royalty; there was no need for her to remain bent on his account, except that he preferred it that way, and for that alone she would not oblige him. "It *was* a pity."

He raised a single brow, bemused by this small show of defiance. As he did, an elaborate necklace slipped free and swung forward, a gold pendant of a twisting, snarling dog with glittering ruby eyes and a ruby-tipped erection between its hind paws: the symbol of the Hell Hounds.

"Then I offer my apologies for interrupting you," he said. He tossed the dildo aside, and bent low before her in a mocking bow. "I must do my best to offer sufficient compensation."

"Yes, My Lord," she murmured, the breathy anticipation in the words shamelessly unmistakable.

He heard her eagerness, and smiled. "The novice's habit becomes you, my lamb," he said softly. His gaze made a leisurely journey over her white robes, his expression not changing but his pale eyes betraying a hungry desire that she'd not seen from him before. "I cannot recall any other woman on whom it looked so well."

"Thank you, My Lord." She liked that he would study her so carefully, and liked that he wanted her, and in response she felt a rush of arousal. Perhaps he was a man more given to passion than she'd first thought, flesh and blood after all.

And bone. She glanced down at the front of his robe, the silk across his body as revealing as it was on her own. His cock was long and narrow and fully erect, the head rising up against his belly, pushing against the spill of black satin like some budding stalk rising from the earth.

"Do you like what you see, my lamb?" he asked.

"I do." She wasn't sure what to make of him calling her his lamb. Was it simply an endearment, the sort of nonsensical name that gentlemen employed with women they fancied? Or did he intend it to have a more ominous ring, with hints of sacrifice to it? She did not mind being a lamb, but she'd no wish to be anyone's sacrifice. "As you say, you have much to offer me."

"You speak with surprising frankness for a maid."

"Forgive me, My Lord," she said. "But I'd been told that frankness was the order of the place."

He smiled again. "It is. Here you will find we are without the petty morality of the rest of the world. If you are able to free yourself, then I believe you shall find much enjoyment here at the Abbey."

"You make an agreeable host, My Lord," she said.

"You are a most agreeable guest." He reached out and slipped his hand inside the neck of her gown, his fingers tracing along her collarbone as he slowly pushed the silk from her shoulder, watching as it slithered down her arm and across her left breast, slowly, slowly, baring it to his gaze as at last her nipple slipped free. It was curious how much more wicked it felt to have one breast exposed while the other remained covered, and she felt her excitement glowing within her.

She knew this was the place where Calliope had advised her to play the outraged, fearful virgin, to protest and clutch her clothes back in place. If she didn't, she'd risk ruining the whole carefully contrived ruse, and her prospects with it. Yet instead she stood without flinching, her single breast exposed boldly, even proudly, to the marquess's salacious scrutiny.

Now it would be most admirable if Marianna had chosen this course from honorable intentions, if she had decided to throw aside the falsehood of her restored virginity for the sake of purest truth in her dealings with the marquess. Because she was a Heroine, such honorable behavior should be expected from her, even required.

But alas, as a Heroine, Marianna was flawed, as are all mortal women. She had her weaknesses, her flaws, and likewise she had the wildfire of passion raging in her blood. She put aside the role of the hapless, fearful virgin, yes, but she did it not from honor, but because she took more pleasure in boldness over false modesty, in pursuing the satisfaction of her desires over calculation.

So it was with Marianna. And to be equally honest, the marquess did not object.

"Beautiful," he said with genuine admiration as he regarded her single bared breast, creamy pale beside the white satin. "What if I ordered you to appear like this before the others, to share your beauty with them so brazenly? Would you obey?"

It was a most curious request, made more curious still by how it was framed. But Marianna knew that lust made men (and women) behave in peculiar ways, and engage in games that might seem preposterous to others, but offered the high-est fillip of pleasure to them. She'd only to recall how she'd relished being fucked on Lady Worthy's dining table to un-derstand that. Likely wealthy, titled, jaded gentlemen like Lord Blackwood were even more demanding. If he needed his rites and rituals and long satin robes to achieve that splendid cock stand of his, why, then who was she to question it?

And yet the true quirk of fate in our Heroine's story was not Lord Blackwood's request, but the randomness with which he had chosen which of Marianna's breasts to reveal. The one so honored was the left—the same one undistin-guished by her heart-sharped birthmark.

How Marianna's fate would have been altered had this mark been put on such public display that night! How differ-ently (and far more briefly) her story would have been told if His Lordship had pulled away the other sleeve, and asked her to appear in that way before the others!

But he did not, and she did not, and thus our Heroine's tale continues, with her standing before His Lordship with that single, lovely, unremarkable, and unmarked breast ex-posed to his regard.

"I would obey you, My Lord," Marianna said. She would, too, for her own amusement and arousal as much as for his. "Because you ordered it, I would show myself to the others."

"What an obedient lamb," he said. "No wonder I am loath to share you with the others tonight."

"Then don't, My Lord," she said, as if that were the only answer.

"You'd like that, wouldn't you?" He slipped his hand

beneath her breast, rubbing his thumb over her nipple. "Knowing you belong to me alone?"

"You are our host, My Lord," she said, looping her arms around his neck so she could rub her body against his. She liked the way the silk felt, the slightest, slippery presence between them, yet through it she could still feel the heat of his skin and the hard promise of his cock. This she could understand. She tipped her mouth to kiss him, coaxing his to open. She could feel the heavy pendant with the snarling dog around his neck, pressing into her chest as well as his. Oh, yes, she'd be a Hell Hound with him, if this was what it meant. As she slipped her tongue between his lips, she began to draw aside the silk that separated her cunny from his rampant cock.

"Tell me, My Lord," she said in a husky whisper as her fingers curled around the head of his cock. "How could I not be honored to be with you?"

"You are honored, my lamb," he said, "more honored than you realize."

Swiftly he pulled her robe to her waist, baring her, and slid his hand over her mound. "You're shaven," he said with a grunt of surprise. "That's neatly done."

"I thought you'd like it, My Lord." She separated her legs for him, sure now he'd fuck her. He'd promised her compensation for taking away the dildo, and she was eager to claim it. He slipped his hand between her legs and dipped into the cleft of her cunny, and she sighed her encouragement.

"You're wet," he said with approval as he found the swollen nub of her pleasure. He rubbed it gently with his thumb, making her shudder.

"You like that," he said, not a question.

"Oh, yes," she gasped. "Please!"

"Even your thighs are soaked," he continued. "You've an ardent nature."

"Oh, yes—yes," she said, swaying into his caress. "I am for you, My Lord."

He pushed a finger into her passage, stirring her further. "Wet but tight. Faith, you're small."

She writhed wantonly against him, eager for far more than this single, frustrating finger. She fought against the tension, the pleasure, not wanting to spend like this for him, but with him instead.

"I am yours, My Lord. If we could but repair to the bed, I shall show you the depth of my—"

"No, my lamb, no," he said, his voice tight with self-imposed restraint. "When I take you, it will be with the care and ceremony you deserve. I'd already determined you to be my priestess for this night. Now I believe you are worthy of even more glory. Every monk will worship you in turn, and I will make sure of it. You will truly be blessed among the nuns."

With no more explanation than that, he eased himself free of her and turned away, leaving her trembling with need, her cunny throbbing with unfulfilled (in every sense) desire. It didn't seem fair, abandoning her when clearly he wanted her, too, and it confused her. What manner of gentleman would walk away from such an offering as she'd just made?

She watched him cross the room to the table, and the flat, leather-covered box that he'd brought into the room with him. Jewels, thought Marianna at once, well schooled as she'd been by Calliope's happy avarice. Could that be the compensation he'd meant, the cold comfort of stones instead of the warm solace of a hard cock?

When he opened the box's hinged lid, she saw that she'd guessed right. There *were* jewels inside, the engaging glitter of cut stones and gold. They just were not a manner of jewels that she'd ever seen before.

"I want to mark you as our high priestess," he said, making his choice. "I want everyone who sees you tonight at once to know that you are mine by choice."

He held up the first piece for her to see, a matching design to the pendant she'd glimpsed around his own neck. Though she'd not Calliope's eye, she could imagine how valuable it must be, a cunningly wrought golden hound with ruby eyes, curled into a narrow ring by biting its own tail in its fangs, with a dangling cascade of smaller dogs and tear-shaped rubies falling from it. The hanging stones made it too long and pendulous for an ear bob, and would likely brush her shoulders, but so dramatic that of course she'd wear it if he wished. If he wished everyone to take notice of her, then this would do it.

"You wear this, my lamb," he promised, "and no other monk will dare touch you. You'll be reserved for me alone. Here, let me help you."

She turned her head, leaning forward to offer her ear. To her surprise, he reached for her breast instead, slipping the serpentine ring over her nipple. Then he bent and suckled hard, lashing at her gold-surrounded nipple with his tongue. She felt her nipple swell with excitement, making the fit of the ring tighten and stimulate her the more, and she gasped, startled by the rush of unfamiliar sensations. His artfully flicking tongue, the gold band pressing into her nipple, the weight of the other pieces swinging from it and tapping lightly against her ribs: who would have conceived of such myriad pleasures?

"There," he said at last, rising to survey his handiwork with satisfaction. "So long as you remain in a state of arousal, the ring shall hold its place. So long as you think of me, and my cock, and how this night I intend to make you scream with pleasure, then the ring will stay."

He turned her back to face the mirror, so she could see the provocative picture she presented: her creamy-pale breast crested with the tight little nipple, wine red with arousal and ringed snugly with gold, and the shimmering jewels and talismans spilling beneath it. Her eyes were heavy-lidded, her cheeks flushed with seductive wanting and blatant lust. The front of her robe was crumpled to her waist from where he'd pulled it high to test her cunny, but anyone else who saw the purposeful folds in the white satin would assume she'd already been hastily fucked at least once that evening.

It was a good thing that the other gentlemen would see the nipple ring as a warning to keep their distance, she thought, because when she looked as alluring as this, they'd be swarming round her as soon as she appeared among them, with their tongues hanging from their mouths and their cocks ready in their hands.

Blackwood flicked the dangling jewels to make them swing, and make her gasp, and he smiled at both reactions.

"You look like priestess and goddess combined, my lamb," he said, "your breasts overflowing and your luscious teat spraying the crystalline milk of excess, ready to give suck to your sinful progeny."

She looked so much like a pagan goddess that as inflamed as she was by his game, she was almost frightened by it as well. How far would he expect her to play this character, she wondered, and what else would he demand of his divine priestess?

She found herself listening for the summons bell that the maidservant had promised so she'd be free to join the others. As entertaining as all the marquess's gloomy hocus-pocus had been, she'd had enough of it for now. She wanted the merry companionship of Calliope and Lord Rogersme and the Colonel, for whom this trip down the river was no more than a happily debauched lark. She longed to be her own lighthearted self again, free to laugh and romp and tease, if she wanted, without having to act like some dark, moody priestess or a goddess or whatever else she was supposed to be. Most of all, she wanted to be free from the ominous intensity of Lord Blackwood's solitary company.

Perhaps he guessed her feelings then, for a shadow of concern clouded his eyes as he gazed at her in the glass.

"Yet as lubricious a creature as you are, my lamb, I worry for you," he said, touching the dangling jewels again. "You are so young, and this is a weighty burden for you to carry. If you should lose focus, or let your thoughts slip away from me and my cock, then I fear you'll falter, and the ring will slip free and fall from your body."

"It won't, My Lord," she said in perfect confidence. How could she not, when she felt like this? "I swear to you, it will remain exactly as you have placed it."

"No wonder you are my priestess." He smiled warmly, and for the first time Marianna thought he might be genuinely pleased. He brushed the backs of his fingers across her cheek— a gesture that seemed to Marianna to be reassuringly ordinary, such as any gentleman might make with a lady.

She smiled, too, and turned to face him, the jeweled ring on her nipple swinging in a quite enticing manner. "If you please, My Lord, I've a query about that. I know full well what's expected of a mistress, but what, pray, does a priestess do?"

"You do not know?" he asked, surprised. "No one has told you?"

"Nary a word." She slipped her hands inside the wide sleeves of his robe, and grinned up at him. "Most likely they don't know, either. It's not as if there's a priestess to greet you at every church door."

He laughed aloud, the first time, she realized, that he'd done so in her company.

"No, there is not," he agreed. "The church is hardly the place for a priestess, especially one garbed as you now are."

"Then what—"

"In time, lamb, in time," he said, laying his fingers over her mouth to silence her. As he did, the bell rang from the Abbey's tower, tolling to call and gather the visiting monks and nuns to the great hall. "There, now we must go. It wouldn't do for us to keep the others waiting."

He handed her a white satin half mask, then tied on his own in black. He pulled the pendant from his robe, making sure it would show, and drew his hood forward to shadow and disguise his face further.

Marianna tied the ribbons of her mask, weaving the ends into the pinned knot of her hair. She tried to pull her hood forward the way he had done, but still leaving her breast exposed as he'd wished, a seeming impossibility.

"You needn't do that," he said, watching her struggle. "It's more important that you display the rubies and the ring on your teat. I don't want any other monk to grow too bold, and try to claim what by rights belongs to me."

"Fair enough, My Lord," she said, glowing with anticipation. She proudly took his arm and let him lead her into the hall, the gold charms and rubies swinging from her nipple in a most provocative and invigorating fashion.

By the time he finally did take her later this night, they both would have been simmering for hours, and all that simmering was sure to make for a glorious, glorious fuck.

La, she could not wait.

Chapter Fifteen

❧

In which Marianna views enough Diverse &
Extraordinary Sights to last a Lifetime;
& to her joy discovers that a Younger Son
is not necessarily a Lesser Man

From the river, Marianna had thought that Blackwood Abbey resembled any other ecclesiastical building or church. England was full of such stone churches, parish halls, and abbeys in various states of tumbledown decay. But though the outside might have looked respectable enough, the interior, as refashioned by Lord Blackwood's orders, was far from respectable, and the activities that were already taking place within the stone walls were even less so.

The stained-glass windows that had shown so vividly from the river now, on nearer inspection, did not depict saints or other holy figures, but various scenes of fornication, in diverse combinations of naked men servicing equally naked women; pairs of women engaged with one another, with tongues and oversized dildos; and even several images of women on their hands and knees, being mounted by the huge ravening dogs that were the club's symbol. Every candlestick and chandelier, every door latch and hinge, had been replaced with cleverly wrought irons and brasses of writhing intertwined figures.

The ceiling overhead was painted to show gods and goddesses frolicking in the clouds, as was often done on ceilings, but again the deities were vividly engaged in every manner of perversion, with countless full-lipped quims and puckered anuses being penetrated by countless swelling cocks, all painted as if viewed from below, like skulking schoolboys beneath a staircase.

But the painted scene overhead was nothing compared to the live one being played out before Marianna's astonished eyes. Lord Blackwood had paused with her, here on the gallery, to look down at the festivities already under way in the great hall below them before he made his entrance and joined his guests.

Forty or so monks, dressed in their black satin robes and masks, were in attendance, many with goblets of wine that were constantly refilled by servants. Music played, a small group of fiddlers to one end of the hall, attempting to be heard over the din of voices, laughter, and shrieks and grunts of pleasure. There were far fewer nuns, their white satin robes standing out among the black, and in vain Marianna searched among them for Calliope. Perhaps at the last moment, the earl's possessiveness had made them keep to their chambers; Marianna was quite certain that if he hadn't, Calliope would now have been one of the most eager participants.

To make up for the shortage of satin-clad nuns, a larger group of women in off-white robes of a meaner quality were waiting in an enclosed area that most likely at one time had served as stalls for choirs or musicians. Now it was the domain of the novices provided for the monks, and each in turn was made to drop her robe, and stand up naked on a small riser for inspection and admiration. Some posed and postured to the crowd, while others stood with weary resignation.

A raucous monk whose booming voice on other days addressed the House of Lords was serving as a kind of auctioneer. He fondled ripe breasts, smacked plump bottoms to make them jiggle, and spread legs to display quims to the delight of the monks who were offering for the novices, and claiming the ones that took their fancy. The novice then gathered up her robe and went off with the monk, often only so far as to one of the cushioned settees that ringed the hall. There the monks set to using the novices however they pleased, while others watched and called out lewd suggestions and encouragement. Most monks showed no kindness or care, taking the women with no preliminaries. Others were determined to make a good showing before their audiences, bending the women into exotic positions or inviting their friends to share in the fleshly bounty, with one pumping into the woman from behind while another spent in her mouth.

But the satin-clad nuns were not to be outdone, either, having chosen their own partners from among the monks. On a nearby settee a nun had shed her robe to let one monk suck and pinch her enormous flaccid breasts, while another vigorously licked her quim, her wriggling thighs over his shoulder. Another had simply pulled her habit over her hips and bent over, bracing herself against a stone column against the driving thrusts of a monk with a huge crimson-crowned cock. Yet another woman lay on a settee while two men held her legs spread wide for an enormous dog to lick her cunny, his long purple tongue lapping over her buttocks and belly as she shrieked with delight.

"I love to watch the other monks disporting themselves so freely," the marquess said with the same satisfaction that a squire would display when surveying his prize breeding stock. "It's good for them to have a taste of debauchery in the beginning, to take the edge from their lust so as not to shame themselves later."

"If this is not shameful, My Lord," Marianna said, leaning over the railing to watch the woman with the dog, "then I cannot conceive of what your notion of shame must be."

He laughed. "Shame achieves nothing, my lamb," he said mildly. "Shame, like guilt, is a useless drain upon the human spirit, consuming as it does energies that would be more profitably disposed in other areas."

"You would tell me that that gentleman there is not being shameful, with the dildo waggling from his bottom while that gold-haired hussy nibbles—"

"She is a novice, my lamb, not a hussy," he interrupted mildly. "One of our virgins for the night."

She raised her brows with surprise. From the brazen manner of the women in the coarser habits, she'd have guessed they had been brought wholesale from some Covent Garden bawdy house, with virginities but a distant memory. Not, she thought wryly, that she herself was in any particular position to be so overnice.

The marquess's eyes were watching her closely from behind his mask.

"You've not turned suddenly shy, my lamb?" he asked with
a solicitude she'd never expected. "This is not the time to falter, you know, especially not with you as captivating as you
are tonight."

She smiled at his concern. Perhaps they were better suited
than she'd realized. "I'm not shy," she promised, "nor will I
falter. You'll see. I won't disappoint you."

"I never thought you would," he said. "And once I saw
you'd discovered that pretty arsenal of dildos, and were preparing to make use of it without any encouragement—when
I touched you, and found your juices already flowing on your
thighs, and with so little provocation—why, I knew you must
be my priestess."

"I'm glad, My Lord," she said softly, her gaze drawn once
again to the excesses taking place in the great hall. "I am most
glad."

She wasn't feeling exactly shy, but her head did spin at the
sheer quantity of debauchery before her. To realize that so
many gentlemen (and not a few ladies) were so eager to behave with such freedom amazed her, and also aroused her.
Would Blackwood expect her to copulate with him before the
others? As his priestess, his goddess, would she be the centerpiece of the night, there on one of the settees?

She could imagine it in shocking detail, how she'd shed her
robes, and present her naked body dripping with chained rubies for the lustful scrutiny of all those masked gentlemen.

She'd hear their lewd commentary as Blackwood opened her pale thighs, and feel him taking her so-called virginity with that elegant long cock of his. On her back, she'd gaze up over his shoulder at the wanton play of the painted gods and goddesses, and she'd curl her long-stockinged legs over his back and take him deep and deeper still. She'd moan, and she'd feel the unstoppable force of her spending as her cunny tightened around his cock, and scream her release as she came with an audience of gaping, envious men, came and came and—

"Shall we join them, my lamb?" His Lordship smiled, tucking her hand into the crook of his arm, as if they were going in to dinner. Then he bent to flick her gold-ringed nipple with his tongue, grazing his teeth over the tender flesh to make it redden and swell anew, and make her gasp as pleasure streaked through her veins.

"Yes, My Lord," she said breathlessly, agreeing to everything. "Let's not keep the others waiting."

He led her down a winding staircase, through an arched passageway, and into the crowd. Not quite certain how a priestess was to behave, Marianna smiled, but left the greetings to His Lordship. From all sides, gentlemen bowed and called to him, even those furiously engaged with partners, while the women curtsied, a curious sight indeed for the ones who'd already been divested of their robes, yet dipped low regardless, holding their empty hands out at their sides as if displaying phantom skirts. Putting aside titles for the sake of anonymity might be the ordered rule of the night, but in practice it clearly carried little weight; everyone knew who was deserving of a bow or curtsy and who was not.

But for Marianna, who'd never been graced with any rank or title beyond her given name, there was far more. For the first time in our Heroine's short life, she found herself treated with a rare degree of admiration, desire, and regard. As His Lordship had promised her, the rubies that ornamented her breast carried a rare power, and with them (and with the marquess himself on her arm) no other man dared reach for her, or ventured so much as a single murmured endearment or licentious suggestion. For this night, she was the High Priestess, the mate of the High Priest, a position she'd earned entirely not by birth, but by her beauty and concupiscence.

As she and Lord Blackwood crossed the room, she had the eye of every man they passed upon her. The very air seemed to vibrate with lust and raw hunger. Her provocatively altered robe, with the single jeweled breast revealed, was infinitely more erotic than the women who were more thoroughly naked. Every man, old and young and in between, admired her, desired her, would have given away his soul to be able to fuck her there, before all the others in the middle of the great hall. She felt like a goddess, and it was a heady feeling indeed.

"Marianna!" Calliope ducked through the crowd towards her, her robe in tumultuous disarray and her hair trailing down her back, and the earl in tow not far behind. Her cheeks were overly rosy, her eyes too bright, and Marianna was certain her friend had already indulged in the delights of the night. As she'd predicted herself, her famous silvery hair gave her away even with the mask in place, even as she seized Marianna's arm. "It's me, my dear, your Calliope. Oh, I have never seen you so fantastically arrayed!"

"She does have a certain glory, doesn't she, Mrs. Wiles?" Lord Blackwood asked, and belatedly Calliope remembered to curtsy to him.

"My Lord," she said, favoring him with her most winning smile. "My Lord, I cannot begin to tell you how vastly delighted I am to see my dear cousin in your company here tonight, and the rare fine joy you would seem to have both found in each other's company."

"Rather I should be thanking you, for bringing your divine cousin to my notice," he said. He kissed Calliope's hand, then pulled her closer until he kissed her on the mouth, and with such intensity that it reminded Marianna more of a man diving headfirst into a well than of a genteel kiss. From the way that Calliope's eyes widened and her arms flailed, it was likely she felt that way, too.

"Here now, Blackwood, that's enough," Lord Rogersme said, glowering as he pulled Calliope free and tucked her safely behind his back. "I know we're all supposed to be free and common here, but show a bit of regard for a friend's property."

"But I am showing your property exactly the regard I feel for it, Rogersme," he said, his smile without any humor beneath the edge of his black mask. "The very highest regard possible."

But clearly the vision of Marianna's jewel-bedecked breast had driven all thoughts of regard from Rogersme's head.

"You've chosen Marianna, then?" he asked, staring down at her fiercely aroused nipple with the same rapt fascination as had every other man. "She's a young lass to be your, ah, priestess for tonight?"

"We have done each other that mutual honor and favor, yes," the marquess said, smiling indulgently at Marianna. "She understands that she will be well rewarded."

"Of course I agreed when His Lordship asked me," Marianna said proudly, sliding her hip against the marquess's side and sending the hanging rubies to swing and tug at her nipple with delicious torment. As for the reward beyond that, why, the very skies could be the limit with a gentleman as rich and generous as Lord Blackwood. A carriage like Calliope's, a house of her own, clothes and jewels and ready money, and even a small place in the country were not beyond expectation. "What greater—or more pleasurable—position can there be than to please Lord Blackwood?"

"Does that content you, Rogersme?" Blackwood cupped his hand beneath Marianna's bared breast, raising it slightly in his hand so the soft white flesh spilled over his fingers. "She's of age, old enough to decide for herself. Or didn't you stop to ask before you and Mrs. Wiles tongue-fucked her?"

Marianna gasped, not from shock, but from the audacity of his words. She'd never had two men, let alone gentlemen, quarrel over her like this. They both wanted her in their beds. Neither wished to give her up. Other men had gathered in a ring around them, drawn together now by bloodlust, and eager to see the woman who'd caused this furor. It was the sort of foolishness that resulted in fights or even a duel, and in gentlemen killing one another.

And, as Marianna realized with a start, it was also the sort of foolishness that was fantastically, gloriously arousing. Who would ever have guessed her cunny would inspire such passion?

Who would have predicted two peers of the realm would be scrapping over our humble Heroine?

Rogersme's face went livid, his barrel chest swelling with belligerence beneath the black satin. "Damn you, Blackwood, you've no right to—"

"But I have, Rogersme," Blackwood said. "She's mine for tonight, to do with whatever I please, and after that as long as I wish it. You can't have them both, you know. Your pockets aren't deep enough for that."

"Nor would he wish us both, Lord Blackwood," Calliope said firmly, squeezing back between them. "He has me, and you shall have my cousin, and there shall be an end to it. My own darling Rogersme, I feel a perilous thirst. Pray, be my savior, and find one of those footmen with the wine, else I shall perish where I stand."

Rogersme glared, unwilling to back down. If he were indeed a Hell Hound, he would have been growling still, but at last he turned away on Calliope's errand, pushing his way through the others.

Blackwood chuckled with disgust. "What a fearsome grip you keep on that poor sot's balls."

"What I keep, My Lord, is Lord Rogersme alive, and safe from his charmingly impulsive nature." Calliope smiled sweetly, and slipped her arm into Marianna's to draw her away. "If you please, I must borrow my dear cousin from you."

Before Blackwood could protest, Calliope pulled Marianna away, hurrying her to a small alcove to one side of the hall.

"Oh, Calliope," Marianna began, eager to tell her friend

everything that had happened since they'd parted. "You will not guess—"

But Calliope would have none of it. "What manner of folly was that?" she demanded hotly. "To pit those two against each other for your amusement, to see them spark and fight over *you* for sport!"

"No one has before," Marianna confessed. "I found it … exciting."

"It would have been vastly exciting if they'd met with pistols tomorrow at dawn on the riverbank, and killed each other, leaving us with nothing," Calliope said sharply. "If you are to be a success at this life, you must never make a gentleman jealous, or envious, or make it so he must act rashly for the sake of his cursed honor. They must always, always, *always* be placed first in your thoughts, for they are most necessary to your very survival. What you did was every bit as bad as casting off one gentleman before you've found the next."

"I am sorry," Marianna said contritely, though this notion of always placing the gentlemen first, whether he deserved to be there or not, was a rankling one to her. "I meant no harm."

"You very nearly caused it." Calliope sighed, and glanced down to Marianna's gold-ringed nipple. "I wonder if Rogersme will buy one of those for me, considering the way he ogled yours, and I—"

"Your wine, Callie." Rogersme handed her the goblet, shoving his mask up to sit on his forehead. "We're leaving now. I've had enough of this damned place, and Blackwood with it."

"But you must stay for the rites, My Lord," Marianna protested. "You must see me as the priestess."

"I'd sooner see us all in Hell," he said bluntly. "Callie, now. Miss Wren, Colonel Goodleigh will see to you."

The officer was suddenly there before Marianna, with his red hair as unmistakable as Calliope's pale blond had been.

"Forgive me for speaking plainly, Miss Wren, but we must leave directly," he said, his voice low and urgent. When they'd all been together earlier in the boat, she hadn't been as aware of his military air and manly confidence as she was now, more glaringly outstanding in this crowd of debauchees than his carroty hair, and if he'd suddenly thrown aside his satin robes to reveal and draw a terrible sword, she should not now be surprised (well, perhaps a little).

Brusquely he glanced over her head, back at the others, his gaze never ceasing in its vigilance. "We haven't much time before Blackwood will come hunting for you."

"Forgive me, sir, but you are mistaken," Marianna protested. "I've no wish to leave."

He shook his head with disbelief. "Miss Wren, I must insist," he said. "Your situation here is far more perilous than you realize, and—"

"Here you are." Lord Blackwood appeared suddenly beside them. With him were two large attendants or guards, and an equally imposing maidservant. "I'd wondered if you'd abandoned me."

"No, My Lord," she said with a meaningful glance to the colonel, as if to snub her nose at him and his meddling. "A priestess can't be so cowardly as that."

"No, she can't," he agreed, smiling warmly, and ignoring the Colonel as if he were not there. He kissed Marianna on each cheek, and full on the lips, and as he did, he pushed the thin satin between her legs to briefly, possessively, cover her mound with his hand. He pressed the satin farther between the lips of her quim, and rubbed across her nub. The unexpected intensity of his caress made her fair swoon with delight, the pleasure of it scorching hot, and she caught his shoulders to keep from toppling over.

"It's time to prepare for the rites, my lamb," he whispered in her ear. "I must give you over to your handmaiden, as befits a priestess, and then, at last, I'll make you mine."

"Oh, yes," she murmured fervently, but as she began to embrace him, he stepped away from her. At the same time, the satin pulled free of where he'd thrust it, there between her legs, leaving her achingly bereft, with only a humiliating damp blotch on the front of her robe left to prove his caress.

Now it was the maidservant who supported her, clasping her tightly by her arm with the burly strength that Marianna remembered from women who'd worked in the fields at Worthy Hall, a strength that was a match for the men they'd toiled beside.

"You're to come to the chapel with me, miss," she said. "This way, now."

Marianna looked back over her shoulder, one final glimpse of the Colonel. He'd shoved his mask up, his expression full of alarm and concern as he watched her led away—an alarm that, at last and too late, our Heroine now shared.

"Where are we going?" she demanded, her trepidation

growing. The bell had begun to toll overhead again, calling the monks and nuns to gather, but this time Marianna couldn't help feel as if the bell were tolling for her as well. "Where are you taking me?"

"I told you, miss, to the chapel." The woman's haste made Marianna tangle her feet in her robes and stumble, only to be dragged back to her feet. "First you must go to the tiring room, to be made ready for His Lordship, and your part in the rites."

At last they reached a small candlelit chamber, scarce more than a closet, with a looking glass, a few items of toiletry and refreshment, and extra black robes of coarse linen from pegs along the wall like so many sleeping bats with folded wings. The maidservant led her inside, then nodded to the two men, who closed the door and left.

"There now, miss, sit," the woman said, pushing Marianna down on the rough stool. She filled a goblet from a pitcher on the table and handed it to Marianna. "You must be thirsty, miss. His Lordship said he didn't believe you'd dined yet."

"I haven't." Marianna took the goblet and drank deeply. With Calliope, she'd learned a taste for wine, and this was fine indeed, if sweet. But what she'd not learned, in her trusting innocence, was that gentlemen who wish ill to the weaker sex will often weaken them further by lacing their drink with various drugs and potions.

So it was with this wine, and Lord Blackwood. The wine had barely coursed down Marianna's throat before she began to feel its effects. A curious lassitude filled her body, and a heaviness settled in her limbs, while at the same time she felt the itch of desire growing ever stronger in her cunny, making her wriggle against the hard stool and sigh and press her thighs together in search of relief.

"Ah, there, so you're feeling better now, miss, aren't you?" The woman brought out paint and brushes such as were to be found on any lady's dressing table, and with it darkened Marianna's eyelids and brightened her lips and cheeks. Made docile by the wine, Marianna sat still for her, even turning her face upwards to ease her task and giggling as the brushes tickled her cheeks.

"What is that smell?" she asked, her voice sounding mumbled and thick to her own ears.

"That's the incense," the woman said, as if the heavy, cloying fragrance that had even permeated the tiring room was commonplace, and unworthy of notice. "His Lordship always burns it for the rites. You can hear the chanting now, too, can't you? He hires the men who sing, for of course the monks are too far in their cups for music, but it does make the rites more solemn. They'll be sending for you soon."

She set down the brush, looking closely at Marianna's eyes. "How are your feeling now, lass?" she asked softly. "Are you feeling easy and calm?"

Marianna nodded, for so she did feel.

"That is good." The woman sighed, putting away the paints. "You're very young to play the priestess. Usually the ladies are older."

"I am of *age*," Marianna insisted thickly, just remembering the discussion between Lord Blackwood and Lord Rogersme earlier. "I—I agreed."

"Yes, miss, I'm sure you did," the woman said. "His Lordship could coax the sun from the sky if he wished it. I pray he'll use you kindly, you being a maid, and afterwards they'll pour an oil on you. Anointing you, they'll call it, but it's mostly to make it easier for you to bear all the others."

"The others?" Marianna asked through the clouds in her thoughts—clouds that were, mercifully, not quite so thick as her handmaiden believed.

The woman nodded. "I know His Lordship must have explained it to you, what a priestess does and all. More proper, it's what's done to her. You'll be led to the alter and laid upon it, and you'll be bound there by velvet cords, with your legs spread open. They'll say all manner of oddities over you, in Latin and French and I know not what else, before His Lordship will fuck you. After that, all the full monks will have their turn, leastways those that can raise a cock stand after the drink. There's not so many monks here tonight, too, only twenty or so."

Twenty or so. That was enough to part any clouds, and smartly, too. Marianna had expected to be taken by Lord Blackwood before the others, and had even anticipated it. But to be tied down with her cunny gaping like a reluctant mare at her first breeding was not exciting, nor was the dreadful prospect of lying there whilst twenty others came afterwards, huffing and pounding and spilling their seed into her poor little cunny.

She remembered the raw hunger she'd seen on the faces of the men in the hall, the way they'd slavered with anticipation for *her*. No wonder Blackwood had called her his lamb: was there any other foolish creature so willingly going to her own fearful slaughter? She felt her stomach twist and knot at the very prospect, her whole body tremble with sick dread.

What was it that Calliope had told her, that the gentleman's wishes must always come before hers? Well, she'd not do that tonight, nor ever with Lord Blackwood, not if he'd meant to treat her like this. There was no carriage or house in the world worth such a terrible price.

"Might I fill your glass for you again, miss?" the woman asked, reaching for the pitcher.

Marianna shook her head. She must get clear of this room now, before they came for her, and leave the Abbey as fast as she could after that. Too late she remembered Colonel Goodleigh, and how she'd imprudently shunned his offer to help. Or perhaps it was not too late: if she could but reach him and cast herself on his mercy, he might still help her escape.

"Are you certain you've no thirst, miss?" The woman's face betrayed her own discomfort with what had been asked of her. "They say the wine's the one sure way to make it bearable, and once the monks have begun to take their pleasure, there's no stopping for more drink until they're done."

Again Marianna shook her head. "It's not drink I wish," she said plaintively. "I've need of the chamber pot."

The woman frowned, glancing about the tiring room. "Most days there's one here," she said. "Will you be well enough if I leave you here to fetch another?"

Pretending to be more affected than she was, Marianna yawned hugely. She leaned against the wall behind her and closing her eyes. "Perhaps I'll nap until you return."

"I'll be back directly," the woman promised, leaving the tiring room and, better yet, leaving the door ajar as well.

At once Marianna was on her feet, albeit wobbly feet at that. Groggy or not, she'd no time to squander, and at once she tore her white satin gown over her head and traded it for one of the coarse black ones, stuffing hers beneath the others to hide it. She tied on a black half mask, thankful that it would cover most of her newly applied rouge, and pulled the hood low over her face to hide it further. She began to unfasten the now-odious ring from her nipple, then thought the better of it. As dreadful and shameful as it had come to be to her, the thing was a costly piece, heavy with gold and rubies, and any jeweler would be happy to buy it from her.

She peered from the half-open door, checking to see if the woman was returning. The passage was empty, though she could hear the chanting voices that signified that the rites had begun. As quietly as she could, she slipped from the door, and headed back towards the great hall. She kept her head bent and her hands tucked inside her sleeves, the black linen rough across her skin. Inside the rubies and chains swung against her ribs, still tormenting her, but this time as a mocking reminder of how close she'd come to ruin. She took care not to give in to her panic, and run: a running servant was sure to be noticed. At least now that she was moving, her head was clearing, too. She could *think*, and when she saw two empty bottles, left behind on the floor beside the wall, she gathered those up in her arms to give the semblance of an errand.

The monks and nuns were slowly making their way back to the chapel, most in no hurry nor capable of moving faster. Trying hard not to seem too attentive, Marianna searched vainly for the Colonel's red hair. He might already have left the Abbey in disgust. He might have joined Lord Rogersme and Calliope, wherever they had gone, or some other acquaintance unknown to her, or perhaps he'd joined the others already in the chapel anyway.

"Boy, here!" a drunken monk called, barely supported by the giggling nun staggering beneath the weight of his arm. He waved an empty glass in his hand, waving his wrist back and forth as if threatening to toss it crashing to the stone floor. "Take this, won't you? Wouldn't be proper going in t'church with a glass in m'hand."

Marianna darted forward, barely remembering not to curtsy, but to bow. As she reached up to take the glass, she glimpsed a monk's hood fall back to reveal the unmistakable red hair of Colonel Goodleigh, bright as any beacon promising salvation to the lost. She took the glass, and hurried towards him, falling into step beside him.

"What of you, sir?" she asked, trying to deepen her voice to a boy's range. "Might I fetch you something, sir?"

"Away with you, you scamp," he said curtly. "I've no need of anything further from this place."

"But, sir," Marianna said, desperation creeping into her attempt at a boyish voice. "If you please, sir."

"I told you, boy, I don't—" He broke off abruptly as he turned and realized her identity. He nodded, his expression grim. "Some poor bastard puked in the hallway back there. Come, I'll show you so you can clean it directly."

She followed, trying to match her unsteady legs to keep pace with his stride. As soon as they were out of sight of the others, he paused, taking her by the arms.

"I can't tell you how thankful I am to see you again, Miss Wren," he whispered fervently. "How did you come to be here?"

"Oh, dear, dear sir!" she cried softly, falling into his arms with joy and relief. "It doesn't matter how I came here. All that matters now is that I must leave, and that you—*you*, dear Colonel!—will agree to be the hero my pitiful and undeserving self needs."

He gathered her up against his chest, and held her close, and smiled fiercely down on her.

"Consider it done, Miss Wren," he said, resolve and determination and bravery, too, reverberating through him in a bluff and hearty way that was most comforting to Marianna. "Consider it done."

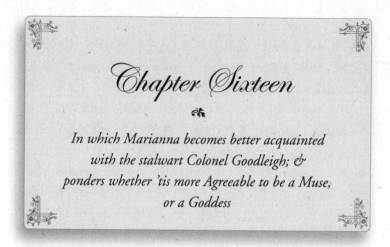

Chapter Sixteen

*In which Marianna becomes better acquainted
with the stalwart Colonel Goodleigh; &
ponders whether 'tis more Agreeable to be a Muse,
or a Goddess*

How exactly Marianna and Colonel Goodleigh left Blackwood Abbey should have made for a wondrous adventure, filled with swordplay, gallantry, and leaping boldly from windows onto galloping steeds. Marianna is our Heroine, and having just declared the Colonel to be her hero (but not the Hero, a fine but important distinction that attentive readers will already have noted), it should be guessed that their escape should be equal to their roles.

But just as Marianna has often demonstrated qualities more fitting for an ordinary woman of mortal clay rather than a shining celestial Heroine, so it was with her flight from the Abbey with the Colonel. No swords were crossed and parried, no pistols drawn, no blood spilled, nor did Marianna at any time toss her arms over her head and swoon in a becoming manner.

No, in short, their entire departure was lacking in adventure. Being already familiar with the Abbey's plan, the Colonel hurriedly guided Marianna down the back stairs to the kitchen, and thence through the backyard, the stable, and other dependencies, and the gardens, until, finally, they had reached the London road. They walked only half a mile or so along this, until they came to a large tavern, where they were warmly welcomed. Their unusual dress was not remarked, beyond being from the Abbey, for it seemed that they were far from the first visitors to that place who had suffered a change of heart in the middle of the night.

Even when clad in a black silk monk's habit, a colonel in His Majesty's army and a viscount's son (albeit a fourth son, but no matter) will always impress a tavern keep, and such a gentleman can expect to have food, drink, and a change of clothes promptly produced, and a carriage swiftly hired. Thus before the first gray light of dawn had begun to shine, the pair were on their way back to London.

"Where are your lodgings?" the Colonel asked with the same gentleness he'd shown her since they'd left the Abbey. "I must tell the driver."

Marianna sighed, resting her head back against the squabs. She was wearing humble dress, a plain linen gown, shift, and kerchief brought from one of the serving girls at the tavern. In a sad, strange way, she'd felt as if she'd been tossed back to where she'd begun her journey, with these last merry weeks nothing more than a dream from which she'd been roughly awakened. Yet at least if she'd been awakened at Worthy Hall, she would still have had a slated roof over her head and break-fast waiting for her in the kitchen.

Now, it seemed, she'd less than nothing—nothing, that is, beyond the rare kindness of the gentleman sitting across from her. For a Heroine as resourceful as Marianna, this offered no inconsiderable possibility.

Colonel Goodleigh had not been blessed by nature with manly beauty. His nose was large and crooked, having been broken in long-ago combat, his complexion rough with small-pox scars and the effects of years of harsh living in the colonial wilderness, his chin blended too softly into his neck, and there was of course his unfortunately colored hair. Yet there was both good humor and common sense also to be found in his face, qualities that were (as Marianna had already discovered) too often rare in men of his breeding and rank. Though he was not young, being more than twice Marianna's sixteen years, he still stood lean and tall, his belly flat and his move-ments full of purpose and grace. Most of all, he'd proved him-self to be a gentleman of honor, and he had saved her last night when she'd been unable to save herself. On this morn-ing, that held much charm for Marianna, much more than a straight nose and a firm jaw ever could.

"I have no lodgings of my own, sir," she confessed. "I came to London as the guest of Mrs. Wiles, and have stayed with her ever since."

"She is your cousin, yes?"

Marianna hesitated, wondering whether she'd a right to continue that relationship.

"Yes," she said finally. "But Mrs. Wiles depends on the generosity of Lord Rogersme, and since I am uncertain about His Lordship's feelings towards me after last night, I don't think it would be wise to return there. I've no wish to cause my cousin sorrow."

"Rogersme's generosity," Goodleigh said wryly. "That's a neat way to put it."

"You cannot deny he's been generous to her," Marianna said, her eyes wide with wonder. "*Most* generous."

"A good deal more generous than he's been to the countess."

"From what I've heard, sir, Mrs. Wiles is a good deal more agreeable to His Lordship than Her Ladyship, and a good deal more beautiful as well."

"Now that *is* true." The Colonel laughed, a pleasing sound to Marianna's ears. "You're very honest, Miss Wren."

"I try to be, sir," she said, tipping her head to one side as she smiled sweetly. Of course she had just spoken an out-and-out lie, in regards to being Calliope's cousin, but then honesty and truthfulness were not necessarily the same. "That was how I was raised, sir."

He nodded, pleased. "It's only in London that there's any shame to it."

"Yes, sir," she said, letting a note of melancholy creep into her expression. "I've learned that."

He leaned forward, closer to her. "What exactly did Lord Blackwood tell you of his entertainments at the Abbey? I know you agreed to take part, but did you realize what would be expected of you?"

"Oh, sir." She didn't have to feign her distress, not over that. "Surely there was no greater fool in that regard than I."

"Not a fool, Miss Wren, but an innocent wronged," he said firmly. "I thought as much."

She looked down at her lap. "I believed it would be a sort of masquerade, where His Lordship would—would favor me. I never thought he'd give me a potion to make me forget—"

"Blackwood drugged you?" he asked, appalled.

She nodded. She'd already guessed he liked playing the gallant protector, and here was further proof. "I was not myself, sir. I never realized he meant me to—to serve all the other gentlemen as well. To be tied down so barbarously and used—"

"You needn't continue," he said swiftly, coming to sit beside her, putting his arm around her shoulders to comfort her. "I don't wish to cause you more pain. It was exactly as I'd guessed."

Snuffling back tears, she drew herself upright, away from his arm in a show of being brave. She reached down to her bodice, to where she'd left the ruby jewel still ringed to her breast for safekeeping.

"Here, sir, here," she said, pulling the bodice open to reveal not only the jewel, but her full creamy breast, crowned with the rosy, distended nipple, as ripe and tempting as a berry. "His Lordship put this on me himself to mark me as his, and now I cannot wrest the shameful thing from my person."

"Please permit me." Brusquely he took charge as she suspected he would, and took possession, too, of her breast in the process, cradling the soft flesh in his palm and stroking it lightly with his thumb. With the greatest care, he began to remove the ring, and she winced.

"I don't mean to hurt you," he said gravely. "I'd never wish to do that. It's only that—"

"I must be brave," she said, letting her voice waver. In truth his ministrations were anything but painful, and the reason the ring was so snugly in place was her near-constant arousal over the last twelve hours. "Perhaps if you were to—to moisten it in some fashion, the ring would slip free."

"Aye, now, that's an idea." With great reverence he bent over her and began to lick her nipple, making his tongue purposely flat and wet to cover not only the aching tip, but also the entire areola around it in the most delightful way imaginable. Was it any wonder that she closed her eyes and sighed, the better to relish it?

"I think I've almost loosened it," he whispered, more to her breast than to her.

"Yes," she breathed. "Oh, yes, sir, that's exactly what was needed."

To her amusement (but also her regret), he worked the ring free with his mouth alone, finally drawing it off with his teeth.

"There, lass," he said, holding the dangling jewel up in his hand like a trophy. "Now you're free at last of that bastard's thrall. Here, let's cast it away, and with it banish the memory of his heathen practices."

He opened the carriage's window, and drew back his arm to hurl the jewel away.

"No!" she cried, lunging across him to grab his arm. No matter what the association, the thing was worth money to her, certainly more money than she possessed at the present. "That is, sir, I'd rather keep it, and put it aside as a warning, a talisman, to remind myself against such folly again."

He looked at her with thoughtful surprise, and lowered his hand. In her haste to stop his hand, she'd ended up upon him with her arms braced upon his shoulders, her legs straddling his, and her bared breasts (for the other had likewise slipped from her loosened bodice) thrusting against his chest. His face was so near beneath hers that, if she'd wished, she could have counted the coppery sprouts of the beard on his jaw.

"That's an interesting notion," he said, his gaze fixed on her breasts, so temptingly near to his mouth. For the first time, he glimpsed her new-revealed birthmark, and frowned. "Did Blackwood do that to you, too?"

"Oh, no, sir," she said. "I was born with that, a gift from Venus herself, they say, as a mark of an affectionate nature."

"An affectionate nature, and now talk of Venus, too," he said. "You would seem wise beyond your tender years, Miss Wren."

She giggled charmingly, to prove she wasn't so vastly old after all.

"Oh, sir, that's not so." She shifted as if to return to her place, but lost her balance with the carriage's rocking motion. Instantly he put his hands around her waist to steady her, and kept them there, to be certain. She slid her hands lower, from his shoulders to his chest, and felt the rapid thumping of his heart, readying to begin the race with her. "I should doubt I'll ever be wise. Clever, perhaps, but not wise."

He smiled up at her, his voice low. "Are you being clever now, lass?"

"Perhaps." Her whisper was husky with invitation, and she sank a little lower on her knees, so that she was sitting directly over the front of his breeches. Ah, so there it was, she thought happily, a sturdy invitation of his own, and gave a small slide of acceptance along the thick ridge of it. "Perhaps you should tell me, sir."

"Oh, I'd say you're being clever indeed." He slid his hands from her back to her bottom, filling each palm. "Especially for a country girl."

"I do know my country ways," she said, arching her back to rub her bottom against his hands. She reached between them to unfasten the buttons on his fall, one by one, to tease him with an agonizing lack of haste. "And in the country, we believe in doing things plainly, without those fancy gewgaws like that."

"Don't judge all men by Blackwood," he said, pushing up her petticoats to slip beneath. His hands were warm on the backs of her thighs, warmer still on her bare bottom. "Most of us don't need anything to trick out a comely young woman like you to raise a cock stand. Your country ways suit me most admirably."

"I am glad of that, sir," she murmured, shifting her legs to encourage him to more daring. He slipped through her legs to find her cleft, his brows rising as he touched her clean-shaven mound.

"A London-style barbering," she explained, and winked. "I suppose I could let it grow back in time, like any other parsley bed."

"Don't," he said with a low grunt: all, in truth, that she needed to hear to know that he was righteously aroused by her naked cunny.

Fascinated, he stroked her gently to savor her moisture, and she circled her hips, yielding to the insistent pressure of his touch. The contraction wrought by the alum bath to make her false virginity had finally melted away, leaving her sleekly open for him, the lips of her cunny swelling plump and ready.

With the last button of his breeches undone, they both were rewarded with his cock springing free: a thick, handsome truncheon that filled her hand. She gripped it, relishing its feel of velvet over steel, with a tiny tear of admiration for her gleaming on the tip. "Ah, look here, squire. The bull's broke free from the stable."

He chuckled, the head of his cock bobbing against her hand. "If you ask me, the bull's bound for the meadow with the cows."

"And here I've scare begun my milking," she said, grinning wickedly as she stroked him from the nest of wiry red curls to his tip. Faith, but it had been a long while since she'd felt a prick as fine as this one! "That's a gladsome sort o' pintle you have there, sir. 'Twould be a shame to let it go to waste."

He caught her hand, his smile fading, and his playfulness with it.

"Do not believe you must do this, lass," he said gruffly. "I did not expect any such reward for helping you as I did."

She smiled, and rocked forward to kiss him, her tongue dipping deep into his mouth.

"I never meant it as a reward for you, sir," she said, her voice husky with desire. "Think of it rather as a—*ahh!*—prize for me."

She shoved aside her petticoats and reached down to part her lips, white linen billowing like a cloud around their bodies. With her thighs spread wide, she slid slowly downward on his cock, relishing the agonizing bliss of being opened and filled, inch by tantalizing inch. He grasped her hips hard in his hands, his fingers digging into her flesh as he pulled her down farther to make his possession complete.

She threw her head back and rode him then, her thighs flexing and her breasts bouncing and her hair flopping in half-pinned pieces down her pack. He bucked up from the seat, driving into her hard. The rhythm was not quite right, not with the rocking of the carriage, but Marianna didn't care, and neither did the Colonel. He groaned abruptly and spent first, grinding into her and lifting her from the seat with the force of it. That was enough to finish her as well, and with a ragged cry she felt her quim convulse around his cock, sucking him deeper, before she shuddered and tumbled forward onto him.

Thus began a most pleasant, and pleasing, arrangement between Marianna and Colonel Goodleigh. By Calliope's standards, he was not rich, but by the measure of most every other Englishman, he was wealthy and, further, happily without the draining encumbrances of a wife, family, or vast estate. He could easily afford a mistress, and within a week he had set Marianna up in keeping, in well-appointed lodgings in a town house on the edges of the West End. In short order, she became Mrs. Wren.

Calliope was horrified, convinced that Marianna had tossed herself away on a fourth son when she could have claimed a duke. But Marianna was perfectly pleased. The colonel suited her, both in bed and out of it. He was endlessly kind to her and direct in his wishes, which, after the complicated expectations that Blackwood had placed upon her, was welcome indeed.

Best of all, the Colonel never once spoke to her of love, or marriage, for which she was endlessly grateful. She loved to lie with him, and to have him wring endless pleasure from her eager, quaking body, but she did not love him. She couldn't. Her heart still belonged to John Lyon, and in that curious way of given hearts, it always would.

Which is not to say that all was peace and quietude in Marianna's life. Her hasty departure from Blackwood Abbey had attached a banner of scandal and notoriety to her name and person. Lord Blackwood was said to have been so furious that, when he'd learned she'd fled, he'd fallen to the floor of the chapel in a mindless rage, his eyes rolling back in his head and flecks of froth spitting from his lips.

It was, in short, such a spectacular display that many of his guests applauded, believing it was a performance for their entertainment. Their amusement was short-lived when they learned the virgin they'd meant to share in a ritual deflowering had vanished before they'd had their sport. The next day, the marquess was carried, pale and lifeless, on a pallet to France, with two physicians and his solicitor in fluttering attendance. It was said His Lordship had left the country to recover his broken health and wits, though others whispered that his hasty departure was to avoid pointed questions about his activities at the Abbey.

It seemed almost as if the scandal had reached London before Marianna had arrived in the hired carriage with the Colonel. Titillated beyond reason, the town spoke of nothing else. Why shouldn't they, when the tale featured a peer famous for perversions, and our Heroine, growing ever more known for her beauty, and now the boldness of her escape from a hideous ravishment?

If the new pair of Marianna and Goodleigh had not been engaged in their lovers' honeymoon, content to amuse themselves in the Colonel's bed, then surely Marianna would not have been able to be seen without a clamor and jostle following her. But even the most luscious gossip has its day, and by the time she and the Colonel did reemerge, the idle tongues had subsided, and moved along to other indiscretions and misdeeds. The Colonel was not a man of fashion or excess, but an officer of considerable reputation, who now took pride in serving his king not on the field of honor, but in the dull offices of Whitehall, and where, really, was the tattle in that?

"You cannot simply vanish from company, my dear," Calliope insisted as soon as Marianna was receiving in her new lodgings, a month after their visit to Blackwood Abbey. Though gradually relenting, Lord Rogersme remained cross over the mischief (for, being a nobleman who'd always had whatever he'd wished, that was what he'd deemed her near-rape by his friends: mischief, and nothing worse, with Marianna being the spoilsport), and Calliope was forced to take pains that they not meet.

She leaned forward on the edge of her chair. "I've explained this to you before, my dear, over and over. You must begin to search for Colonel Goodleigh's replacement now, while he is still infatuated by you."

"Oh, bother," Marianna said, licking the hot chocolate from the back of her spoon and feeling far too indolent so much as to consider anything she must or must not do. The Colonel had spent the night, and they'd both spent often, and that, for her, was likewise the lazy end of the following day. "So long as I keep him happy, then he is content, and so am I."

"It won't always be so," Calliope predicted grimly. "You'll see. He'll tire of you, or you shall weary of him, or—or he'll *marry*, and be forced to put you aside."

"He'll never do that," Marianna said with perfect, languid confidence. "He is nearly forty, Calliope. If he's stayed a bachelor to such a vast age, I should wager he'll now remain one until his grave."

"Then you must prepare now for the moment he's claimed," Calliope said. "You can't wait, dearest. There is nothing less appealing to a gentleman than the taint of desperation that comes from being left without a protector."

Absently Marianna twirled a lock of her hair between her fingers. "What would you have me do? Walk about St. James's Park with a signboard strapped to my back?"

"You must show yourself!" Calliope said, waving her hand

through the air for emphasis. "Ride through the park in an open carriage, or sit to the front of a theater box, or simply be seen with me! You must do as we did when you first came to London, and make gentlemen notice you, and speak of you."

Marianna wrinkled her nose. "That worked out vastly well, didn't it?"

"Perhaps not with Lord Blackwood, no," Calliope admitted. "But if you hadn't gone about, then you wouldn't have met your darling Colonel, either."

Marianna sighed wistfully. "What I wish most is for Johnny to return, and then I'll not have to consider any of this."

"But didn't you promise Mr. Lyon that you would become a goddess in London?" Calliope said. "While he is off making his fortune among the heathens, you must do your part, and make your way as best you can here. Tending your future or becoming a goddess for Mr. Lyon—it's one in the same, you know."

Yet while Marianna might lack Calliope's raging ambition for improvement, she did have her own extraordinary degree of luck, as befits a Heroine.

There were two other inhabitants of her town house, the first being her landlady, an agreeable older woman who wrote poetry and kept cats, and the second an Italian gentleman named Signor Amoroso, from the faraway city of Venice. Marianna had not been long in the house before she met this gentleman upon the stairs, and learned to her delight that he was by trade a painter. Swiftly she contrived to receive an initiation to his painting chambers, which he called his studio.

One autumn afternoon she climbed the next flight of stairs, and discovered Art.

Or rather, more accurately, Art (in the mortal form of Signor Amoroso) discovered Marianna.

It was hard for her to believe that the Signor's studio could be in the same house, for his chambers were so very different from her own. Everything was given over to his art. The windows were bare of curtains, the better to admit the sunlight so necessary to his work. His easel stood prominently in the center of the largest room, his palette, brushes, and paints on a paint-daubed table nearby. Opposite this was a small stage, on which, he explained, his models took their poses for him. Because he specialized not only in portraits but in allegorical scenes of ancient times as well, he also kept trunks of fanciful costumes—robes of velvet, plumes, tin-bladed swords, and pinchbeck crowns—for garbing his models.

But what drew Marianna's interest the most was the paintings, examples of Amoroso's work, that were everywhere about his rooms, hung on the walls and leaning on the floor. Untutored though Marianna's eye might be to the finer points of these paintings, at once she appreciated his skill and his talent. Perhaps because he had learned his craft in sunny, sensual Italy, he had a rare affinity for painting the womanly form, and his pictures were filled with women wonderfully depicted in the same state as Mother Eve.

To one side, there was also a number of pictures portraying mortal women being seduced by the god Jupiter. No matter what manifestation the whimsical god had assumed for his conquest, the woman was always delectably naked, and captured at the apex of her ecstasy. Because these pictures reminded Marianna of her first brush with Art under the guidance of Mr. Lyon, she was very taken with them in particular, and understood perfectly the Signor's success, as well as the flocks of wealthy patrons she had observed climbing the stairs to the painter's chambers.

She also understood the beautiful young women likewise climbing upwards, albeit with more nimble anticipation, who served as his models. Doubtless they served the charming Signor in other ways, too, for his tumbled, unmade bedstead was only a few steps from his easel.

"No matter how much an Englishman may delight in the picture of a nude woman, Mrs. Wren," he explained as he poured her tea from a Turkish pot, "he cannot give himself leave to enjoy it in company. Instead he must call her a goddess or a saint, and then he has provided a reason, an excuse, to study her. It is the most curious thing, yes?"

"Oh, yes," Marianna quickly agreed, not quite understanding his theory, but liking his company sufficiently to pretend that she did. The Signor was a slight man, perhaps forty or so years, but the feverish fire of his inspiration seemed to make him glow as if he were lit from within, his large dark eyes sparkling and his every gesture animated. Even his thick black hair held the unpredictable nature of a flame, curling wildly around his head like a dark nimbus of creativity.

"Surely you have seen the phenomenon yourself," he continued. "In England a woman with a passionate nature is viewed with nothing but suspicion. Yet as soon as I paint her as Aphrodite, rising moistly from the wave, she becomes a deity, fit for worship."

She nodded eagerly. "I understand perfectly, Signor. My friend Calliope and I are often treated with the most shameful disregard because we are beautiful, and admired by gentlemen."

"I could transform you, too, Mrs. Wren." He leaned closer, studying her through narrowed eyes. "I could paint you as Aphrodite, with not a single stitch to hide your charms, and hang you in the Academy, for all the world to admire."

"Aphrodite!" she exclaimed, dazzled by the possibility. "Oh, Signor!"

He folded his arms over his chest and tipped his head, turning crafty. "You are too shy to pose for me, Mrs. Wren? So burdened with the empty modesty of the English? Or are you too unsure of your beauty to wish to reveal it to me and the world?"

"Not at all," she said swiftly. "It is only that I have always wished to be a goddess, and to be painted by you as one—oh, Signor, I will be most honored."

"Very well, then. We can begin this day, this minute!" He smacked his palm on the edge of the table with enthusiasm, then paused, and frowned. "Your lover, the red-haired officer who carries the large sword at his waist. He will not object if I do this? He will not come after me with his sword for seeing his woman with an artist's eye?"

"So long as you employ only your artist's eye," she said, "and not your artist's hands or lips, then I don't believe Colonel Goodleigh would mind, no."

He pressed his palms together with gratitude and relief.

She raised a single finger, to show she wasn't done. "But you should know the rest, Signor. Lately there have been certain scandals attached to me that might make it unwise for me to be painted with such, ah, such freedom."

"What if I fashioned a pose that masked your face, and your identity?" He jumped to his feet and posed himself to demonstrate, standing with his back to her and his head coyly turned away, his bottom thrust outward and his face shadowed by his upraised arm. "If I showed you like this, then I'd wager ten guineas no one will be studying your face."

She nodded eagerly. "But when you show the picture, you must be sure not to attach my real name."

"Oh, no," he said, already gathering a sheaf of paper for sketching. "We'll invent another name for you. That's commonly done. What shall we call you? Madame Passion, Madame Wanton, Madame Bliss? Madame Bliss. That sounds the best, doesn't it? *Madame Bliss as Aphrodite, Goddess of Love*."

"Madame Bliss," Marianna repeated thoughtfully, already imagining the crowds who would gather around *her* painting. Calliope wanted gentlemen to speak of her; what better way could there be than this? "I do like that."

"It suits you, ma'am." He looked at her expectantly, chalk in hand. "Are you game to begin?"

"Of course I am ready." Marianna grinned. Most days she did little else than wait for the Colonel to join her for dinner, anyway. She rose and headed for the model's stand, briskly shedding clothes along the way.

"Would you like me to keep my hair pinned up, or down?" she asked when all that remained were her pearl ear bobs and the pins in her hair. "Which is more in the style of Aphrodite? If I truly were the goddess of love, I'd have it up. Gentlemen always want it down, but it does become tangled around one's limbs in any sort of vigorous encounter, particularly if the gentleman sweats a great deal."

Amoroso laughed, delighted by her candor. "Then by all means, keep it pinned," he said, taking his place behind the easel. "There now, raise your arm, and turn just a fraction. That's exactly it. *Madre di Dio,* but you're a lovely creature. And your ass—I vow you must make grown men weep. I prayed for a new muse for inspiration, and here you are, living beneath me, muse and goddess made one."

"Thank you," she said shyly, the only real shyness she felt. It was strange to recall how she'd never been completely without clothing before Johnny; it seemed very long ago now. How much he'd like to see her here now, standing here in the streaming sunlight for a painter! Perhaps when he returned from India all sleek and wealthy, as he'd promised, he could buy this painting from Signor Amoroso, and they could hang it over their drawing room fireplace, the way that Lady Worthy had done with the dour portrait of her grandmother.

The Signor was squinting at her fiercely now, concentrating with all his artistic might. "What a curious freckle you have on that pretty breast of yours, Mrs. Wren," he said. "It's a perfect little heart, isn't it?"

"And quite perfect for the Goddess of Love, too." She laughed, taking care as best she could not to move. "I've always had it. But I suppose if we're not going to keep my rightful name, you shouldn't put my birthmark on your painting, either. There's enough who've seen it who might recognize me by it."

"And the rest would say I'd used too heavy a hand, painting a heart on Aphrodite's tit," he said wisely. "I'll leave it off. When I'm done, you'll be goddess enough without it."

"Madame Bliss, the goddess of love," she said again, marveling at the curious path her Fate had once again taken. "Truly, who would have thought it?"

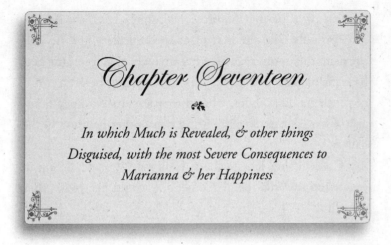

Chapter Seventeen

⌘

In which Much is Revealed, & other things
Disguised, with the most Severe Consequences to
Marianna & her Happiness

"Can you see the painting, Calliope?" Marianna whispered, so swathed in black veiling as part of her widowly disguise that she could scarce see three feet before her, let alone distinguish among the vast number of paintings hung together on the gallery's walls. It was the first day of the Academy's new season, and the rooms themselves were nearly as crowded with viewers as the walls were with pictures. "It must be here. It must! The Signor told me it was to be given one of the best spots, the acceptance committee did admire it so."

"I've found it," Calliope said, steering Marianna through the crowd, "though I doubt we'll be able to get near enough to see it. There are more gentlemen gathered before your pearl white bottom than ever clogged the betting stalls at Epsom."

"You jest!" Marianna exclaimed, raising the edge of her veil to look for herself. What Calliope had told her was true:

the first painting that Amoroso had done of her, the Aphrodite, proudly held the best place in the gallery, on the wall
opposite the doorway. There her divinely naked self (or perhaps her nakedly divine self) was holding court before a crowd
of gentlemanly acolytes, who in their eagerness to pay hom-
age to her charms, were ignoring every other painting in the
gallery.

"Come, come, let's go closer, Calliope," she said, taking an
eager step towards the gentlemen. "I would hear what they
say of me."

But Calliope caught her arm and held her back. "What,
and have them decipher everything at once? It's hazardous
enough that you're here with me, let alone if you go charging
into their midst like a bitch in heat. Besides, you know what
they're saying. They're saying your ass is spectacular."

Marianna laughed, and dropped the veil. The pose that
Amoroso had finally decided for her did concentrate on her
splendid posterior, her plump cheeks and the enticing cleft
between as well as the long, elegant length of her back and
seemingly acres of creamy pale skin. There was, in short, so
much to delight and amuse in this view that few of her newfound admirers had yet noticed that her face was turned into
the shadow so as to be nearly completely obscured. They were
men, and could not help themselves. "Signor did a handsome
job with that, didn't he?"

Calliope sniffed. "Oh, yes, and so did the mother who
birthed you. That ass is yours, my dearest, all yours, and that's
why you'll have your choice of admirers whenever you choose
to improve yourself."

"I've told you, I've no plans to leave the Colonel." In fact the painting had inspired the Colonel to new heights of desire. Far from being angry with her for posing in such a provocative way, he'd instead delighted in it, coming to the Signor's studio with her to watch and drink red wine, and then hustle her back to her bedchamber to fuck her most royally. The Colonel had even encouraged Amoroso to continue painting her, and there were three more feverishly in progress in his studio beyond the Aphrodite, with others being sketched each day. "I am perfectly, perfectly content with him."

"And I have told *you*, that in time that will change." Just as the gentlemen were studying the painting, so did Calliope study them. "There are Sir Thomas Stark, and Lord Richardson, and the stout one with the spectacles is one of the most prosperous of men in the City."

"I see," Marianna said, unimpressed.

But Calliope would not be discouraged. "Look, Marianna, mark that tall fellow to the front. That's the Duke of Morrich, new returned from a tour of the Continent. Very proper, that one. They say every mama in London is after him for their daughters, and la, who can blame them? Have you ever seen a more handsome gentleman?"

Marianna had, in the face of her darling Mr. Lyon. But Mr. Lyon was on the other side of the world, and the duke was here, and so she studied him: a tall, well-favored gentleman with waving dark hair and extraordinary blue eyes, as handsome as her bluff colonel was not. He stood close to the painting, observing it (or her bottom) with great concentration, which was most pleasing and flattering to Marianna. If the painted version of her could so thoroughly lay claim to his attention, how delighted he'd be with the ripe and warm-blooded reality—or he would be, after she coaxed and flattered him. There were few experiences more enjoyable to be had than warming the blood of a too-proper gentleman.

"Oh, yes, *you're* not interested," Calliope said slyly. "How delicious that His Grace appears intrigued as well! I vow the Signor may have an offer for the picture before the day is done."

"Perhaps," Marianna murmured, only half listening as she watched the duke laugh at something his friend had said. "Perhaps."

"Oh, perhaps nothing," Calliope scoffed. "You haven't heard a word I've said."

"I have," Marianna insisted, though she still could not make herself look away from the duke.

"You haven't, my dear, but no matter." Calliope looped her hand familiarly into Marianna's, and leaned close to whisper in confidence. "All you must do now is coax Signor Amoroso to put you in more of his pictures. If he does that, then I do believe your future is secured."

But as Marianna had already learned, there was no need to coax the painter. Amoroso had longed for a muse, and now that he'd discovered Marianna, he'd become as a man possessed, as if no other woman existed in the world. During the next eighteen months, he drew and painted her as every conceivable ancient goddess and a few of his own invention. He showed her as a bacchante, a nymph, a fairy, a wanton: any wild creature that let him paint her beauty, and with little clothing besides.

Painting after painting came from his studio, yet the public, too, could not get enough of Marianna. Engravings were made of the paintings, and hung on a line for sale in every shop along the Strand. Soon her face and form graced not only the walls of galleries and elegant drawing rooms, but of rum shops and public houses, army barracks and navy ships as well: art lovers were everywhere, it seemed, and anyone with a soul (and a cock) could appreciate the special genius of Signor Amoroso's art.

With so many admirers, it was not surprising that the mystery of Marianna's identity was soon uncovered. After Aphrodite's success, she had given the painter leave to show her face as well as her body, a face that had never been easily forgotten by any who saw it.

A breathless writer in a weekly gossip sheet was the first to reveal that Madame Bliss was none other than the sacrificial virgin who'd escaped Blackwood Abbey, fanning the flames of notoriety anew. Other tales arose, each more fanciful than the last, of how she was a Russian princess or a Gypsy's daughter, how she'd fled the advance of the King of Prussia as well as Lord Blackwood, and how Colonel Goodleigh was her protector in every sense of the word, assigned to watch over her after she'd served as a highly placed spy for the government.

It all amused Marianna to no end. But then, to her sorrow, the end did come, exactly as Calliope had predicted.

She had fallen asleep waiting for the Colonel's arrival, the candles guttering out around her. It was late, very late, when he finally appeared and woke her, still wearing his scarlet uniform coat, and a face so long that she instantly guessed.

"My darling!" she cried softly, her voice still muddled with sleep. "What has happened? What is wrong?"

"The French and the Mohawks are what is wrong, sweetheart," he said, full of regret. "The generals have decided I am of more use to them in New England than I am at a desk in London. I sail for Boston within the week to fight the savages, and I fear I must set you free when I go."

She wept more than she'd ever thought she would, both for the good man she was losing, and for herself as well. Twice now she'd been left behind by lovers who'd sailed away, and the sorrow of farewells had not grown any easier to bear.

Then she dried her tears, as Heroines must do, and repaired at once to Calliope for advice.

"We must do something grand for you," Calliope said as they sat together in the small garden behind her house. "You are Madame Bliss, my dear, and the news that you are finally ... *disengaged* from the Colonel will fair fly among the gentlemen's clubs."

"I have my lodgings until the end of the year," Marianna said, pulling her fox-fur scarf a little higher over her shoulders. It was not that the air in the garden was chill, for it wasn't, being September, but that the practical nature of their discussion, however necessary, chilled her more surely than any breeze. "The Colonel saw that I was generously provided for. He paid my bills, and left a pretty farewell for me with my banker."

"*Ppfft,* a pittance," Calliope said with a little wave of dismissal. "He was as generous to you as he could afford to be, yes, but now it's time you found a gentleman more worthy of you. When will the Signor's new picture be hung?"

"*The Judgment of Paris?*" Marianna said. "The Signor says next week."

This new canvas was the largest and most ambitious of Amoroso's pictures. *The Judgment of Paris* featured two of his other, lesser models as Hera and Athena, while Marianna reprised her role as Aphrodite. All three young women were gloriously unclothed, save for the diadems in their hair and the jewels hanging from their ears. As comely as the other two women were (the one with chestnut hair being a dancer at the playhouse when she wasn't playing Hera, and the fair-haired Athena more usually a milliner's assistant), Marianna shone far the brightest between them, like the clearest diamond set between two lesser gems, making the task of judging by Alexander (Amoroso's handsome nephew), with Hermes (the painter's apprentice) advising him, an easy one indeed.

But more lay behind the painting's breathtaking beauty than any gallerygoer would realize. Marianna smiled to herself, recalling a certain afternoon earlier this summer. The sun had filled the studio, making it warm even for the unclad models. Magnanimously Amoroso had let his favorite red wine run freely for them all, and soon the combination of the wine, the indolent heat, the trial of posing in the nude, and the vigorous youth and beauty of the five models proved a heady, irresistible brew.

What began as bantering flirtation soon progressed into

kissing, and toying, and fingering of cunnies and sucking of pricks, until all were soon tangled together on the studio floor in a writhing, fucking mass of well-muscled arms and legs, juicy quims and eager cocks, ardent sighs and passionate groans. All through it Signor Amoroso had sketched furiously, capturing as much as he could with his crayon and chalks, and the bawdy amusement of that day showed in the finished painting, a provocative undertone that was unmistakable.

It had been a frolic and no more, with all of them still playing their roles of gods and goddesses. For Marianna, it had also marked the first time in nearly two years that she'd dallied with a man other than the Colonel, a younger and far more handsome man, and the effect on her senses had been dazzling. Like a fruited ice will cleanse a gourmet's palate for richer dishes to come, so did this delightsome romp with four others seem to help Marianna put a fitting end to her time in the Colonel's keeping, and whet her appetite once again for others.

"It's a most beguiling painting," she said now to Calliope. "You'll see for yourself."

Calliope narrowed her eyes. "This is the picture that led to the orgy, wasn't it? You and two other ladies, and those delicious Venetian boys of Amoroso's?"

Marianna smiled slyly, and shrugged. "I told you, my dear, that you and everyone else will see for yourselves soon enough."

"What I *see*, Marianna, is what we are going to do," Calliope said, rapping her knuckles resolutely on the table's edge. "We shall give everyone a week to see the picture. Then I'll

invite all the most interesting gentlemen to my house to celebrate the Signor's achievement, and as our entertainment,
I propose a *tableau vivant,* in which you and the others re-
create the painting."

"Garbed as we were for posing?" Marianna's grin spread
slowly across her face. What sport it would be to stand serenely naked before a crowd of gaping gentlemen as Aphrodite! Not as a gentleman's plaything, as she'd been with
Blackwood at the Abbey, but as Madame Bliss, the goddess of
her own beauty. She'd gaze out among them, and she alone
would choose who would be her next lover, a wondrous power
indeed. Just the possibility of it was enough for the excitement to grow warm in her belly, as if that unknown lover were
already kissing her, stroking her, filling her with his cock to
make her moan with the sweetest delight. "*Exactly* as we were
in the painting?"

"Oh, yes, if you and the others will agree to it." Calliope
nodded solemnly, but her eyes were bright with giddy anticipation that was much like Marianna's own. "I might even
choose to dress as a nymph myself, in some cunning little
chiton that bares my breasts, to keep to the spirit of the night.
I'm sure Signor Amoroso will be delighted to help us, too."

"I'll tell you what you must ask him." Marianna leaned closer
to whisper, so delicious was her notion that she'd dared not
speak it aloud. "While we goddesses were, ah, engaged with
our gods that afternoon, he sketched everything. *Everything.*
There are at least three portfolios of these sheets that he
keeps for himself, the old satyr, and to share with his favorite
patrons."

Calliope gasped. "Have you seen them? Are they vastly wicked?"

"They are, my dear, precisely what you are imagining with two men and three women," Marianna said, laughing. "You must ask the Signor to show them to you, and then to make an invitation illustrated with ribaldry proper for the occasion. He shall be endlessly happy to oblige, I am sure. A sketch or two in the classical tradition always adds the correct solemnity to such occasions."

Calliope laughed, too, pealing merrily beside her. "Oh, my dear Madame Bliss, haven't you become the very veriest goddess?"

"Indeed," Marianna said, raising her arm and flaring her fingers over her head in a goddess-like pose. "But I promise you, Calliope, 'tis only the beginning of what I shall become."

It was a brave, bold declaration from our Heroine, though one made with more bravado and humor than with any real basis for such a prediction. But even Heroines can on occasion stumble across the truth, whether by design or wholly by accident, and that was now the case with Marianna.

For how, really, could she ever have predicted what Fate had next planned for her, or whom in fact she would become?

"There's the first carriage," Marianna said, peeking through the curtains of Calliope's bedchamber to look down into the street. She'd come to her friend's house early to dress for the party, and to see the last of Signor Amoroso's preparations for the *tableau vivant*. "Who would ever have guessed any of them would arrive at the time on the invitation?"

"They would have come early if they'd dared." Calliope studied herself one last time in the looking glass, smoothing her skirts and patting at her hair. "Well, now, what do you make of me, friend? I know most eyes will be on you tonight, but I'll steal a few stray glances, yes?"

"More than a few, I should think!" Marianna turned away from the window to come stand beside Calliope at the glass. Amoroso had designed their dress for the evening, assuring them (though with the sliest of winks) that they were garbed exactly in the manner of the ladies of ancient Athens.

Marianna didn't believe him for an instant, but she didn't care, either, not when their gowns were so wildly becoming. Hers was pink linen so fine that, when she moved, it revealed far more of her charms than it hid, banded around the waist and between her breasts with thin red silk ribbons. Beneath this gauzy wisp she wore neither shift nor stays nor stockings, and only silver leather sandals on her feet. If being as good as transparent weren't scandalous enough, the gown was without sleeves entirely, the bodice gathered over a single shoulder and the other left bare. Calliope's gown was much the same, save in blue linen.

"There now, we're a fine pair of classical hussies, aren't we?" Calliope said, spinning lightly on her toes to make her sheer skirts float away from her bare legs. "Ravishing *and* ravish-able. I can only pray that Rogersme doesn't suffer an apoplexy when he sees me in this."

"His Lordship will suffer, yes," Marianna said, smoothing the front of her bodice, her nipples showing rosy dark and pointed through the linen, "but only because he won't be able to take you away from your guests and upstairs to bed directly."

"Who waits for a bed?" Calliope said. "I'll wager a guinea that the only time I'll see one tonight with Rogersme will be to sleep. Now come. I want you to see the flowers they've put around the stage for the tableau."

They hurried down the backstairs to avoid the first guests already gathering in the front hall, and Marianna felt the excitement ripple through her at the sound of their rumbling male voices. It had been a month since Colonel Goodleigh had sailed from her life, and two years since she'd last been in so much male company, with such purpose. To know that she'd be standing before them all as Aphrodite made her blood warm and her body glow with anticipation. She felt wanton and ready for a new gentleman, as if she truly were the goddess of love, and beneath her fluttering short gown her breasts were already heavy and yearning for a lover's caress, her cunny plump and eager for dalliance.

"Ahh, Aphrodite, my darling cousin!"

She turned, and nearly collided with Billy Hodges, her fellow model, dressed not like Amoroso's apprentice, but once again as Hermes, in a short tunic, cloak, and winged helmet. He'd come from the country like Marianna herself, and because of it he more resembled the farmer's son that he was, with outsized hands and feet, than any god's offspring, but Marianna forgave everything because he laughed easily and often. He caught her hand and drew her back into the comfortable shadows of the passageway, keeping her there while Calliope continued onward.

"Won't you spare a kiss for your cousin, new arrived from Mount Olympus?" he teased, trying to duck and kiss her without knocking his helmet askew. "For me, darling 'Dite?"

"Not now, Billy," she said, bracing her palms on his chest to keep him at bay. Yet, in her present excellent humor, she couldn't help laughing at the foolishness of their situation, the two of them fumbling about in their ridiculous costumes while, just beyond them, was a rich cream of English peers and lordlings in their best evening dress. "Besides, you're not a god like me. Hermes was only the messenger to the gods. Amoroso says so."

"Hang Amoroso," he whispered cheerfully, pushing her back against the wall as he bent to nuzzle the side of her throat. "I know things about the goddess o' love that the old fellow never will."

"You don't," she said, laughing still. She knew she was risking much, lingering here with him like this, and if they were discovered, she could put aside all notions of being mistress to any of the gentlemen waiting in the front hall. She was supposed to appear as a goddess tonight, and goddesses weren't supposed to dally with apprentices in dark hallways. But she'd always rather liked Billy, and she most definitely liked the feel of him pressing his large, rough-hewn body against her, reminding her of that overheated afternoon on the studio floor. "What could you know of the goddess of love?"

"I know she likes this." He covered her entire breast with

his hand and gently began rubbing his palm in a circle, tugging and teasing her nipple into a hard nub.

"Don't do that," she whispered, but he was right. She *did* like it, and she liked the way he was pushing his hips against hers, making her feel the hard ridge of his cock through his tunic. She remembered that from their dalliance, too, for the length of his cock was as generous and glorious as the size of his feet or hands, and that as a country lad, he knew full well how best to plant his seed.

"Are you daft, Billy?" she said, imagining (yet relishing, too, truth to tell) if any of the gentlemen guests were to come across her with her gown pulled high and her legs around Billy's waist as she rode his cock in blissful abandon. "We can't do that here, not now."

"I remember other things about this goddess, too," he said, ignoring her weakling protests. "I remember how she likes two fingers on her cunny to make her juices run before she takes my cock, and how she—"

"Oh, pray excuse me," a gentleman said, backing away. "I didn't realize—"

"Your Grace!" Looking over Billy's shoulder, Marianna recognized the startled face of the Duke of Morrich, the very last gentleman she'd wished to find her thus. As swiftly as she could, she shoved Billy to one side and curtsied as gracefully as she could, under the circumstances. "Please forgive us, Your Grace. Hermes is just departing."

The duke's half smile betrayed his discomfort. "Flying back to Mount Olympus, eh?"

"Aye, Your Grace." Glumly Billy touched the front of his helmet. "Taking my letters and such to old Jupiter himself."

"You may go," the duke said to him, his gaze never leaving Marianna, and reluctantly the dismissed Billy left them. "It's Mrs. Bliss, isn't it?"

"It is," she said, moving from the shadows to see him, but really so he could see her more clearly, for she'd gain nothing by hiding. "I am most honored, Your Grace, most honored."

His eyes widened as he looked down at her gown, and at her breasts, now charmingly aroused thanks to Billy, thrusting through the insubstantial fabric. She'd forgotten how blue his eyes were, as blue, really, as her own, and her hopes rose as she wondered if that could be a sign of their compatibility.

"I don't believe we have met, Mrs. Bliss," he said, forcing himself to return his blue-eyed gaze to her face. "Not properly, that is. Yet I feel as if in some way we surely have met before."

"No doubt that is because of Signor Amoroso's paintings of me," she said. "He has told me you're a great admirer of his work, and have bought several of his paintings."

"I am an admirer, yes," he said. He'd kept his hands clasped behind his waist the entire time he'd been speaking, as if to make sure they wouldn't be tempted to wander over her person. "I would place Amoroso's pictures with mythological themes beside that of the other masters I purchased while I was abroad. The pictures of you are particularly, ah, fine."

"I'm glad you like them." Marianna smiled, striving to make that smile more angelic than Aphrodite-ish. She could have sworn the duke was blushing—*blushing!*—and now she could recall how Calliope had described him as being a proper and modest gentleman who took his responsibilities to his family and his estate very gravely; not exactly priggish, for no one who liked Amoroso's art could be called that, but still rather righteous, and so ill at ease in bawdy company that Calliope hadn't expected him to come tonight. "The Signor's talent is rare indeed."

"I didn't buy the pictures because of his talent, Mrs. Bliss," he said quickly. "I bought them because they're of you."

"Oh, Your Grace," she said softly, and it took no effort at all to make her voice melting soft over so pretty a compliment from so high a lord. "I'm honored."

"It's the truth, Mrs. Bliss," he confided. "Pictures of you please me above all other things. I would not have come here tonight if not for your presence."

"Now I'm truly honored, Your Grace," she said, wondering if it was the salacious drawing of her printed on the invitation that had drawn him.

"Not at all, Mrs. Bliss." He bowed to her—to *her*, a duke!—then glanced down the hallway, where Billy had wandered off, straightening his cockeyed helmet. "Will you, ah, would you care to join the others?"

She slipped her hand into the crook of his arm by way of an answer, taking care to press her breast into his arm as well, as if by complete unknowing accident.

Taking no offense at her boldness (not that she'd expected him to), he grinned down at her, as happy and pleased as a man could look, and settled his hand over hers. "That other fellow, then. He won't be back for you?"

"That's only Hermes," she said wryly. "Likely he's gone off with one of the nymphs by now. Did you know that though he lodges on Mount Olympus with the other gods and goddesses, he's not even a god at all, but a kind of messenger."

"I had heard that, yes," he said, squeezing her hand, and thereby brushing his knuckles over her breast as if by the same fortuitous accident that she herself had conveniently placed herself within range. "But then, I'd venture even goddesses have need of messengers once in a while, don't they?"

She smiled, teasing him with great gentleness and looked up at him through the veil of her lashes.

"I do need a messenger on occasion, yes, but there's one thing I need even more," she said. "And that, Your Grace, is a duke."

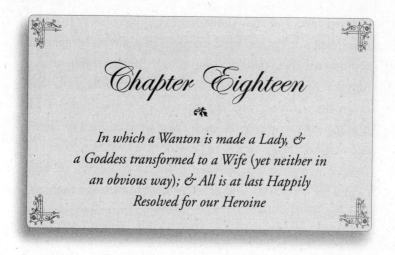

Chapter Eighteen

❧

In which a Wanton is made a Lady, &
a Goddess transformed to a Wife (yet neither in
an obvious way); & All is at last Happily
Resolved for our Heroine

The *tableau vivant* was set to take place in Calliope's drawing room. Screens had been used to close off the far end of the room during the earlier part of the evening, so as to preserve the surprise, and increase the guests' anticipation. Signor Amoroso had been put in full command of arranging the tableau, and because this was the first time that one of his paintings had been brought to life in this way, he had become not so much a commanding officer, as a bullying tyrant. He became determined to dictate every last detail to such an excruciating degree that two different men supplying flowers and plants in pots quit rather than work with him, half of Calliope's staff threatened to do the same, and if his apprentice Billy Hodges could have torn up his papers of indenture, then, he, too, would have gladly fled his master's employ.

Yet all who saw the final preparations agreed that Amoroso's fastidiousness had crafted another masterpiece, away from his usual paper or canvas. He'd managed to replicate his fanciful setting entirely in the drawing room, Paris's Troy here in a Mayfair drawing room. Now, finally, his participants had taken their places, standing exactly where they'd posed for him for the picture. To be sure, there were no lines to speak, no songs to sing or dances to be danced. The entire point of a *tableau vivant* was to freeze a moment of history or high drama for edification and admiration, and with the three naked beauties to the forefront, there would be much for the gentlemen to admire.

Marianna had the best place in the composition, of course, standing directly in the center with the other goddesses behind her. She was captured at the exact moment after Paris had awarded Aphrodite the golden apple that proclaimed her the most beautiful and desirable of the three. She stood with her arm gracefully raised, the apple glinting triumphantly in her hand, and a scarlet silk cloak drifting back from her other arm, a pose that displayed her figure to luscious advantage. Her breasts in particular were shown to perfection, and if the golden apple in her hand was the prize fruit, then her full, rounded flesh, trembling there beneath her upraised arm, was surely another kind of orb to be coveted.

"Signor, here," she whispered, calling him to her side behind the curtain as she took her final place. She pointed to her side that would face out to the audience. "I forgot my birthmark. You've never painted it into any of your pictures, and now—now here it is. I meant to powder over it, and I forgot."

"It's too late for that now, isn't it?" the harried artist said. "Well, no matter. The worst that will happen is that I'll be damned for having neglected the blasted thing, and forced to add it to every other picture as well. Are you ready, my cherubs? Everyone take a good, long breath, and when I signal, the curtain will be dropped."

Marianna raised her hand with the apple again, stretching upward for the most elegant line, as the painter had taught her. Her heart was racing, and she was surprised by how excited she was. That was likely Morrich's fault, sitting there as close as he could on the other side of the curtain, doubtless on the very edge of his seat. Such a charming, handsome gentleman, though a bit reserved in the way she guessed dukes were required to be, and with him in her thoughts, she was certain her expression must be beautiful indeed.

"Halloo, 'Dite!" whispered Billy, sitting across from her. He puckered his lips in a lewd, wet kiss and smacked it towards her, making the other two goddesses giggle. Marianna struggled not to laugh as well, and then suddenly the curtain was falling, and she had to concentrate instead on holding the brass golden apple properly aloft.

In unison the audience seemed to sigh with delight, followed by diverse exclamations and shouts of praise and wonder, and a rush of loud applause. To Marianna it was a glorious moment, a delicious moment, as she felt so much approval and admiration wash over her like a wave.

Then, as sweetly as it had began, the moment turned improbably, impossibly bitter and wrong.

Suddenly the Duke of Morrich was climbing on the stage,

his chair upturned behind him and urns of flowers tumbling and crashing to the floor. The other goddesses shrieked and scattered, while three more gentlemen from the audience lunged forward to try to grab him.

But the duke fought his way free, joining Marianna on the stage. His eyes were wild, his cheeks pale, his whole being that of a man in extreme distress.

"Madam," he asked, his chest heaving. "Madam, for the love of God, I must know this: when is your birthday?"

"My *birthday?*" she repeated, incredulous. Of all the things she thought he might say, she'd never expected that. Surely he'd lost his wits, and was bound for Bedlam in a winding jacket. "My birthday?"

"I tell you, madam, this is no idle whim," he insisted. "I must know."

"I cannot tell it, Your Grace." She took a step back from him, fearing for her safety. She realized now how quiet the spellbound room had become as everyone strained to hear what was said, as if this horrible scene were no more than a fascinating bit of playacting.

"I was an orphan, Your Grace," she continued, "a foundling abandoned by the side of a Devonshire road, not far from the village of Worthington. I was gathered up and saved by the charity of a Christian lady there, and raised in her household."

"Do you know the season of your rescue?"

"Summer," she said, "else I would not have survived as I did. It was July when I was found, so most likely that was my birth month as well."

"July," he said, the word ringing hollow in the air between them. "My God!"

Lord Rogersme stepped forward, laying a gentle hand on Morrich's shoulder while two large footmen stood waiting behind.

"Come, Your Grace, come," he said softly. "Leave poor Mrs. Bliss alone. There's a good fellow."

But the duke only shook him off, refusing to leave, or to look away from Marianna.

"What year, madam?" he demanded hoarsely. "How old are you now? How many years?"

She wrapped herself in the scarlet cloak, as if that scrap of silk could protect her from his ravings. "Eighteen, Your Grace."

"Eighteen," he said, his voice breaking. "Then it is so!"

"What is so, Your Grace?" Lord Rogersme asked cautiously. "What is it?"

"Yes, Your Grace, please," Marianna said. "Tell us, and explain your meaning."

The duke took a deep, gulping breath, and began, "When I was still in the nursery myself, a lad of tender years, my mother gave birth to my youngest sister, a most beautiful infant christened Frances. But to my family's torment, a maid-servant who had been dismissed from our house for drunkenness and theft took vengeance upon our happy family and, just as she had stolen plate from our sideboard, now stole this blessed child from her cradle. You can only imagine the suffering of my poor parents, the lamentations that rose from my sister's loss, and, too, the cry that rose throughout the countryside to find the lost babe."

"Was she found, Your Grace?" Lord Rogersme asked, the question that all in the room wished answered. "Was the maid ever captured, and duly punished?"

"Not by rightful means, no," he said, his sorrow still great. "The villainess's corpse was pulled from a millpond, where it was believed she had drowned herself to escape her sins of this life, only to find damnation in the next. The child she took was never found, and presumed dead. My poor mother's health was broken, and she died soon after, followed, alas, by my dear father. Yet now, at last, I believe the curse on my family may be lifted, and a dreadful wrong put to right, for my sister would have been eighteen years this summer past."

Marianna listened to this tragic tale, her thoughts spinning and her mouth turning dry as all around her gasped and murmured with amazement. She listened in silence, too awed to speak, yet still she looked at the duke's fair complexion and dark curling hair, and his unusual blue eyes that could have mirrored her own. Could they in fact share the same blood, the same parents? Could he truly be her brother, never known to her until this moment?

And more: could she truly have had such desirous thoughts for her own brother? She shuddered with horror to consider the possibilities. What if matters had progressed as they'd begun, and she had gone to the duke's bed that same night? What, if in the heat of passion and lust, they'd not observed their mutual birthmarks before it had been too late? What if she'd kissed him, and sucked his cock, and fucked him, and taken his seed, and generally done everything they'd both clearly been so longing to do?

"Forgive me, Your Grace," Rogersme said with cautious disbelief. "But there are sadly many discarded orphans in this world of ours, and without first contacting her benefactress and making other inquiries, you cannot presume that Mrs. Bliss is—"

"I do not presume, Lord Rogersme," the duke declared, his voice now ringing with confidence as he began to pull his arms from the sleeves of his coat. "I have the tangible proof."

Marianna's hopes plummeted, convinced now that His Grace's declarations were no more than the ravings of a madman. What other explanation could there be for him tearing away his coat and waistcoat, as if to join them in the tableau in the same state of nature?

"Please, Your Grace, please, please," Amoroso said, coming forward to try to stop the duke from shaming himself further. "This is no place for you, Your Grace, here among the goddesses, eh?"

"No, it is not," Morrich said, "nor is it a fit place for my sister."

With that he yanked his shirt free of his breeches, pulling it up over his left side. Marianna had an excellent view of his lean waist and flat belly, the handsome ridge of muscle that was most pleasing to the eye, and then a sight that shocked her beyond belief, and drove all other thoughts away.

For there, on the left side of his chest, was a heart-shaped birthmark, as perfect a match to her own in placement, shape, and size as if the same master artist had painted them. Once again those in the crowd gasped with marvel and amazement, but now the murmurs concentrated on the great likeness between Marianna and the duke, how much they resembled each other in so many ways that any observer must have seen the family link at once.

"Every one of my family has had this mark," he said, "from as far back as can be remembered. It is the unmistakable proof of Welborne blood."

Marianna stepped closer, her eyes filling with tears. "Oh, Your Grace," she said, overwhelmed, "I pray with all my heart that you are not teasing me in this cruel fashion, that you speak from your heart, and not from mischief!"

"My dear Lady Frances," he said, clearly disturbed that she'd suspect him, "if you knew me as sisters and brothers should, then you would realize how wounding such a suggestion is to me."

"Then let me be sure," she begged. "Please, let us compare our birthmarks side by side, so there can be no doubt."

She began to drop the cloak from her person and reveal herself once again, but Morrich caught her hand to stop her.

"That is not necessary, my dear," he said solemnly. "With all these others as my witness, I swear that you'll need never make such a tawdry show of yourself again."

He gathered up his coat from where he'd cast it aside, and draped it protectively over her shoulders to cover her more thoroughly than the cloak could.

"Come with me, Lady Frances," he said. "Let me take you from this loathsome, immoral place, and these people. Come with me, and come home."

* * *

It is a most beguiling notion. To be raised up in a single day from next to nothing to become the daughter of one duke and the sister to another: who can deny the allure of such a tale?

The great change that Marianna's life had taken when she left Worthy Hall and threw her lot in with Calliope Wiles was as nothing compared to her transformation now, under the watchful supervision of her newfound brother George Welborne, Duke of Morrich. She had been reborn, or rather, she had been born again, to live her life the way it should always have been. She was Lady Frances Welborne, and Madame Bliss (and Marianna Wren with her) had been swept away and forgotten as completely as if she'd never existed.

Lady Frances lived in a house (one of five her brother possessed, she was told) so grand that she'd call it a palace, excepting that it was larger than the palace His Majesty called his home. Her bedchamber alone was larger than the sum of her old lodgings had been, and that was but the beginning.

She was presented with attendants whose sole purpose was to educate her in the skills for being the lady she so suddenly was: a dancing master, a singing instructor, a tutor in French, and another to teach her manners and graces so she could, in time, be presented at court. She'd even acquired an elderly divine who was responsible for preparing her shopworn soul for redemption. The finest mantua makers and jewelers came to her, with her brother never questioning the bills. She'd the use of any of the duke's elegant carriages, all with the Welborne crest picked out in gold on the doors.

It did indeed seem a pretty enough place for a Heroine to

have landed, as sweet and soft as a feather bed strewn with rose petals. Yet for our particular Heroine, accustomed as she was to following her own pleasures and desires, this rich new life was little better than the harshest, most inhospitable prison.

She had always wanted a family, and now that she had one, they in turn did not want her. Her two older sisters— Caroline, Countess of Forthright, and Barbara, Marchioness of Covets—were distant and disapproving. None of the rest of the family had deigned to call on her, or invite her anywhere. Sadly she accepted that, for haughty, high ladies were always the same, and as jealous of their rights and territories as any nest of tabbies.

But the chilliness of her newfound brother was the greatest surprise, and the most hurtful as well. Oh, he was generous in the material advantages he granted to her, every last pearl necklace and silk garter that a duke's daughter should have. It was in less tangible matters that he was stingy as any miser.

He informed her that her former life was never to be mentioned. He forbade her seeing Calliope or any of her other previous acquaintances, and set footmen as guards to make it so. The charming regard that he'd shown her that one night had changed into icy, even disdainful, politeness that wounded her no end. She could understand if he were made uncomfortable by their former attraction, and how near they'd come to committing (however inadvertently) an unforgivable sin, for she shared that discomfort as well. But nothing *had* happened, and by her reckoning it was now time, even past time, to put that all aside, and determine instead how they were to be as sister and brother.

It was not the way any Heroine should be treated, and after one particularly unpleasant breakfast, wherein the duke had spoken no other words to her beyond "Good morning" before he'd disappeared into his papers, Marianna decided she'd had enough. With both hands, she picked up the French porcelain plate before her and slammed it hard upon the table so that the plate cracked and shattered, bits of porcelain and jam-covered toast flying over the cloth.

He flipped down the corner of the newspaper to look at her, and the mess she'd made on the white linen cloth. He sighed, but his expression didn't change one whit.

"Jamison," he said, calling to one of the footman hovering along the wall, "Lady Frances's plate has broken. Please bring her another."

"Is that all you can say, George?" she said with disbelief. "That my plate has *broken*?"

He blinked, all the maddening reaction he'd venture. "Do you deny that it has, Frances?"

"Don't call me that," she snapped. "My name is Marianna, and I won't have you try to do away with it as easily as you will that wretched plate!"

"I'm not trying to do away with you, Frances," he said testily. "I'm trying to follow our parents' wishes, and treat you as their daughter, with the rights and privileges to which you were born."

"Oh, yes, the *privileges*," she said darkly. "I'd rather you'd left me where I was. I might not have lived so grandly, but I would have been free to lie with whomever *I* pleased, and who pleased *me*."

He flushed and began refolding his paper, briskly pinching the folds crisp between his thumb and forefinger.

"You'll have a husband to satiate your baser needs soon enough," he said, concentrating on the folds so he needn't meet her gaze. "I hadn't meant to tell you until tonight, when we'd celebrate properly as a family at the announcement, but I have received an offer for your hand, and I have accepted it."

"A husband!" she exclaimed with undeniable surprise as the footman swept away the broken porcelain before her. John Lyon was the only one man in her life she'd ever considered as a husband, the only man she'd ever loved, and he—he was on the other side of the world. "Who is it, George? Have you bought some ancient, respectable relic who's so far in his dotage that he'll wed a harlot like me?"

"Not at all," George said, ignoring her bitterness along with quite everything else. "He is a youngish gentleman, and appears virile enough to satisfy a wife and produce an heir. He is also of such rank and standing that I'm surprised he's asked for you. It's an excellent match. As Marchioness of Blackwood, you'll outrank our sisters."

"Blackwood?" she repeated with genuine horror. More than two years had passed since she'd fled Blackwood Abbey with Colonel Goodleigh, but she'd never forgotten her perilous adventure with the marquess, nor would she now. "You would give me in marriage to Blackwood? Do you know what he tried to do to me?"

"I do," he said evenly. "And even if I didn't, Blackwood told me himself. He has changed his ways since then, Frances, and he now feels nothing but regret and remorse for how he mistreated you. I cannot imagine a better way for him to prove his penitence than by marrying the one woman who defied his wrongful intentions."

What Marianna could imagine was vastly different indeed. Clearly she'd seen more of the darker side of gentlemen, or perhaps as a duke her brother simply was above seeing wickedness such as the marquess possessed. For herself, she could not afford to be so trusting. She'd heard rumors of how Blackwood had spent his time in France, and none of them had included reflection and contrition.

"You do not know His Lordship as I do," she insisted. "If he wants to wed me, it's for vengeance, not penitence!"

"You wax dramatic, Frances." The duke sighed wearily. "You might do better to show a bit of repentance for your own past behavior and sins, you know. It's far more pleasing to see a woman as a Magdalene than the shrill harpy you are now."

"And once you liked me best as Aphrodite," she said, something she felt quite sure plagued his own conscience no end. "I've nothing in my life to feel guilty for, George, nor anything that shames me to look back and consider. I've done what I wish, with whom I wished, and I've no regrets for any of it."

"You will marry Blackwood," the duke said, more firmly this time. "I will not change my mind."

The footman set a new plate before Marianna so gently that it made not a sound on the cloth. She stared down at the circle of creamy porcelain, at the gold band along the rim and the two scarlet dragons that were painted in the center atop the Welborne crest. She could smash this one, too, and another would be brought to replace it, and another after that, and after that as well. To the duke, everything could be replaced and made right.

Even, it seemed, a sister.

"If you have any regard for me as your sister," she said slowly, "or for the memory of our parents, you will not do this to me, George. You cannot!"

"I can, and I have," he said, reaching for this tea. "I am your brother and your guardian, Frances, and by law I may make all decisions regarding your welfare. The solicitors are completing the settlement, and the archbishop has sent down a special dispensation to permit a swift wedding."

She stared at him, too devastated to weep. "How can you pretend to be my brother, yet do this to me?"

"Because I *am* your brother," he said, "and it is my duty to do what is best for you. You will marry Blackwood on Thursday, and that is an end to it."

For the next three days, the marquess came to call on Marianna, and three times she refused to come down to him in the drawing room. On the fourth day, the day before their wedding, the duke relented on what was proper, and let the marquess surprise her in her room, and she'd no place left to hide from him.

She was sitting at her dressing table, and she saw him enter behind her in the reflection of the looking glass before her. She caught her breath but didn't cry out, and turned on the bench to confront him. In a way, she'd been both dreading, and expecting, him.

"My dear Marianna," he said softly, bowing to her. "You are more beautiful than I could ever remember."

"My Lord," she said, her voice clipped, "you are likewise unchanged."

"You flatter me." He smiled, and motioned for her maid to leave them alone. He did look much the same as she'd remembered: lean, elegantly handsome in pearl gray silk and supremely dissipated. And if he'd attempted any sort of true reformation from his wickedness, it did not show upon his face. "But you will find me much changed, my dear bride."

"So my brother tells me," she said, on her guard. She would not have put it past him to throw her on her own bed and forcibly mount her. "I do not believe him, or you."

"You should," he said. "I learned many things during my sojourn in Paris. They are exquisitely adept at pleasure, the French. They understand how to intensify their satisfaction by making it a reward, not an expectation, and how the sweet torment of suffering, of pain, can only add to the joy. I've brought back many clever new amusements for play as well, most cunningly wrought devices. You will, I believe, be as entertained as I."

He needn't explain further. She knew what he meant. She'd heard of how those who'd a fancy for wringing pleasure from pain had claimed the torturer's tools for their wicked sport, delighting in breaking and blooding their partners. The marquess had already shown too fine a taste for demonstrating his power in this way; the thought of him intensifying his perversions only sickened her.

"There now," he said, coming closer to her, his eyes glittering with salacious delight. "I can see you're interested, excited, aroused. I know you, you see. If I were to lift your skirts and touch your notch, stroke you the way that made you purr for me, you'd be wet, wouldn't you? Wet for me?"

"No," she said, refusing everything to do with him, and everything he was offering. *"No."*

He turned his head slightly, cocking one dark brow in his singular fashion. "Yes, make a show of your denial. That's what fine ladies do, my lady Frances. I understand entirely. I won't have your maidenhead to take on our wedding night, but I'm certain we can find another virginity or two on that pretty body for me to steal away from you. We're much alike, you and I, and what enjoyment I'll have proving it to you!"

She regarded him evenly, without flinching or drawing away, and with the courage and resolution that a Heroine must display. Though the pious world might judge her otherwise, she knew they were different. She'd always found her pleasure in joy, and in love, not oppression or suffering. No matter what Lord Blackwood might claim, she was not like him, and she would never, ever become his wife.

She rose from the bench, the ruffled skirts of her dressing gown falling around her legs. "My answer remains the same, Lord Blackwood. I will not marry you. Now you may leave as you entered, like the villain you are."

"My bride." He smiled, and blew her his kiss of farewell on the tips of his fingers. "Until tomorrow."

"No," she said again, softly, as the door closed after him. She would find strength in that single, decisive word, and find hope in who she was, not what others tried to make her be. She would choose the joy and the passion that was in her soul, and the rest would follow.

She was Marianna Wren, Madame Bliss, and she'd not falter now.

With the duke clasping her firmly by the arm, Marianna stood outside the door of the chapel in Westminster, the chapel where all Welbornes came to be married. She was dressed in the palest of blue satins, shimmering silks fit for a fairy queen and a bride alike, and in her trembling hands she held a bouquet of white roses. Around her throat were the sapphires her brother had given her as a wedding present, and on her finger the enormous square diamond that was Blackwood's betrothal ring. She had never looked more lovely, nor felt less joy.

There had been crowds of well-wishers and the curious in the street, and there'd likely be more inside. Not even the

Welbornes could keep them away. The papers had been filled with nothing else. Truly, the scandal was too rich to resist: a young woman of the greatest beauty, the centerpiece of Black-wood Abbey notoriety, the model of countless titillating paintings, the long-lost daughter of a duke who'd been living in keeping to a much-decorated officer, now to wed the infa-mous Marquess of Blackwood by order of the Archbishop of Canterbury!

The music began in the chapel, and two attendants opened the doors. The pews were crowded, every face turned expec-tantly towards her, as so many other crowds had done before.

Her brother patted her on the arm with clumsy kindness.

"Be brave, Frances," he said. "I know it's hard for you, but you must trust me that what will happen soon is the best course possible for you."

She nodded, her heart racing as wildly as a horse that had thrown its traces. What happened would be for the best for her, because she meant to make it so.

They walked slowly down the aisle, as was fit for so mo-mentous an event. To the back, Marianna spotted Calliope beneath a broad-brimmed hat with extravagant plumage, a handkerchief ready to wipe her tears. She saw Signor Amo-roso, surrounded by his models, and Billy, his wicked-tongued apprentice. To the front, among the duke's friends, she saw Lord Rogersme, his plain, dull wife at his side, and others of the Welbornes, including her sisters and their husband peers.

The last person she saw was the one she wished least to see, standing before the altar as he waited for her. Lord Blackwood was smiling down at her, with more triumph than was proper, and when her brother passed her hand to him, he squeezed her fingers so hard she nearly yelped aloud. Move here, turn there, stand, kneel: it was all as if she were a well-dressed doll being moved about as part of someone else's game or masque, a play that she'd no real part in, even as it changed her life.

It would have been most easy, at this point in our story, for any Heroine to have resigned herself to her fate. She could have perceived hitherto hidden merit in Lord Blackwood that would have made him more palatable as a husband. She could have decided that to be a marchioness was not so very bad a lot, or that, once wed, she would be able to reform and tame His Lordship sufficiently to her tastes, in the manner of countless brides with recalcitrant grooms. Or she could have decided to embrace her new husband's libertine ways and wickedness, and become his partner in all things.

Yet as Marianna listened to the solemn words of the ceremony rolling over her, she knew she could do none of these, no matter how convenient. Such momentous and inspiring words should be used to consecrate a union based on love and trust, not this poisonous arrangement that had been thrust onto her, and tears welled up in her eyes at the very thought. It was wrongful, sinful, and she'd not do it.

She'd attended enough weddings to know when the moment would come. She knew the scandal would be worse than anything else she'd weathered, but she could not keep still, else answer to her conscience the rest of her life.

Soon, soon. Striving to still her tears, she tried to focus on the gold-thread embroidery on the minister's chasuble. She would throw herself on the mercy of God to save her from what she knew would be the ruin of her very soul. She took a deep breath, readying herself.

"If any of you can show just cause why they may not lawfully be married, speak now," the archbishop intoned, as if addressing her alone in that huge and holy place, "or else forever hold your peace."

She opened her mouth, the words already silver on her tongue, when another voice spoke for hers instead: another voice she'd feared she'd never hear again, yet never had sounded so sweet and dear as now.

"I have reason, and cause," John Lyon said, as loudly and clearly as Gabriel's golden trumpet. He stood in the center of the aisle, his golden hair washed in a beam of shining light through the clerestory, bathed in righteousness. "This marriage cannot take place."

The chapel roiled in uproar, with gasps and cries of disbelief, scorn, and wonder. The marquess swore, even there before the holy altar, and grasped her fingers more tightly in his own.

But Marianna could only stare, not daring to trust the proof of her eyes and ears. Could he truly have returned on this day of all days? Could John truly have come back to save her, now, when she needed him most? Could ever salvation and deliverance have come with such sweet Providence?

"Who are you, sir?" the duke demanded over the din and confusion of the others. "Who are you to interrupt us?"

"Yes, sir, if you please," the archbishop said with proper severity. "Explain yourself, and your reason for this interruption."

"Happily, and joyfully," John said, so full of manly grace

that every woman in the chapel sighed and envied Marianna her fortune in her champion. "I have loved this woman with all my heart for some years now, and though we have been most cruelly separated by fate and our enemies, I would believe that she has loved me with the same devotion and fervor, giving her heart to none other. With that love to guide me like the North Star in the night sky, I have come clear from the city of Calcutta, in the East Indies, to prove my love, and claim Miss Mary Wren as my rightful wife."

"Then claim me, my truest of loves!" Marianna cried, pulling free of Lord Blackwood to run down the aisle and into John Lyon's waiting embrace. "Claim me, and love me, and let nothing ever part us again."

There was much that could be told of John Lyon's adventures in the East Indies: of his perilous voyages, his encounters with wild beasts and savage brigands, his seduction by a raja's beauteous daughter, his perseverance to build a magnificent fortune in the trade of rubies and sapphires, and throughout his continued love and passion for the far-distant Mary Wren. All of this could be told, and is most deserving of the telling, too. Yet because these pages belong to our Heroine, and not her Hero, we must give leave to save his adventures for another telling, by another teller.

Suffice for us to say here that John Lyon returned to London a wealthy gentleman—very wealthy indeed—with sufficient resources and influence as to impress even the Duke of Morrich. With that assurance, as well as Marianna's heartfelt wish, the duke relented, and shifted his consent from the marquess to Mr. Lyon: for in truth, though he'd come lately into her life as her brother, he did wish for her to be happy.

Thus we will share one final scene with the Heroine on her wedding trip with Mr. Lyon, to offer one final assurance to the reader of her lasting joy and contentment.

They had taken the largest, finest rooms to be had at the largest and finest inn in Brighton. They'd left the windows open so they could see the water and the waves along the beach, and they'd kept the curtains on the bed (likewise the largest and finest to be had) open as well, so the breezes could play across their heated skin as they dallied away the afternoon. For three days now, they'd not left the room, nor let anyone else in beyond those who brought in trays of food and wine for sustenance, they were that content with each other's company.

Johnny nipped at the inside of Marianna's knee, which was raised high to rest on his shoulder. She laughed softly at the foolishness of it, his unshaven face and shaggy hair framed by her legs.

"Don't laugh," he chided, though he was laughing as well. "No man likes a woman to laugh whilst he does his best to pleasure her."

"I cannot help it," she said, wriggling beneath him as an enticement. "I'm too happy not to laugh."

"Then it's up to me to change that," he said. He slid her legs down his arms to hook over his elbows, spreading her wider. He bent to swipe his tongue along her notch, holding her open to reach and suckle her nub until she rocked against him in her urgency. He grasped her hips and raised her up like an offering, and drove his cock deep within her cunny. She gave a shuddering sigh as she felt him sinking so far within her, and she curled her legs over his waist, embracing him as completely as she could. She writhed beneath him, relishing their shared passion as her cunny began to tighten and tense with her coming spend. His prediction had been quite right: she'd no desire to laugh now, not when he was filling her so completely and so perfectly. She held him fast and cried out, bucking beneath him as she found her satisfaction, with his swiftly following.

Afterwards, when they were weary and pleased and slick with each other's sweat and spendings, Marianna lay on her back with her arms languidly over her head while John rested on one elbow beside her, tracing his fingertip over and over the little heart on her breast, the one that had caused her so much righteous mischief.

"I cannot fathom you as a Frances," he mused, "let alone a Lady Frances."

She laughed, her breast quivering beneath his touch. "But you can fathom me as Marianna."

"Oh, yes," he said. "Mary was too plain by half for you. You needed something more lush, more extravagant, and Marianna it is. Marianna Lyon has a pleasing ring to it."

She curled her hair behind her ear, and smiled up at him. Who would have guessed that passion and love would be so twined, that one would be so empty without the other, or so magically improved when combined?

"But what of Madame Bliss?" she asked teasingly, for as

she spoke she reached beneath them to coax another stand from his cock. "Has she been banished, too?"

"I'll always find a place for Madame Bliss," he said, rolling her beneath him. "Most especially here, I should think."

She laughed again, with happiness, with joy, and yes, with bliss. And truly, what better place can there be to bid our Heroine a happy and satisfied farewell?

Charlotte Lovejoy is the pseudonym of an award-winning novelist. She lives with her family in an old house outside of Boston, where she is currently writing her next erotic novel.